"I would not trust you any more than I would your master,"

Hester murmured as she paused to admire the horse.

"Which is to say, not at all, I warrant."

The duke walked slowly toward her. "Lady Hester, you are an intelligent woman, so I do not expect you to trust me."

"After yesterday, you can be certain of that," she snapped, her surprise making her sharp when she would have preferred to sound nonchalant. "Good day, Your Grace." She tried to walk boldly past him, but he stepped into her way.

"There is no need to run off. I promise you I will keep my distance."

"I am not afraid of you."

"My dear young woman, are you telling me I am losing my ability to inspire terror and awe in the female breast?"

Dear Reader,

Who would have thought that when we published Margaret Moore's first book, *A Warrior's Heart*, in 1992, we would be publishing her twelfth full novel, *The Dark Duke*, five short years later. This story is the next in the author's terrific new series of Victorian romances featuring a trio of "most unsuitable" heroes. This particular hero has a very nasty reputation, but that doesn't scare our brave heroine, who sees the lonely man behind the handsome facade. Don't miss this one. And come fall, be sure to keep an eye out for Margaret Moore's newest short story, "The Twelfth Day of Christmas," in our in-line THE KNIGHTS OF CHRISTMAS short-story collection.

Sweet Sarah Ross by Julie Tetel, which follows the next generation in the author's ongoing NORTHPOINT series, is a Western adventure story with enough perils to keep Pauline happy. *The Secrets of Catie Hazard*, by Miranda Jarrett, is a Sparhawk story, this time with a secret baby and lovers who must overcome not only a troubled past but a turbulent present in order to reunite. And *Enchanted* from Claire Delacroix is the magic-filled story of a valiant knight who can be rescued from a wicked curse only by the love of a beautiful noblewoman.

All four books this month are ones you won't want to miss. We hope you keep a lookout for them wherever Harlequin Historicals are sold.

Sincerely,

Tracy Farrell
Senior Editor

Please address questions and book requests to:
Harlequin Reader Service
U.S.: 3010 Walden Ave., P.O. Box 1325, Buffalo, NY 14269
Canadian: P.O. Box 609, Fort Erie, Ont. L2A 5X3

MARGARET MOORE

THE DARK DUKE

Harlequin Books

TORONTO • NEW YORK • LONDON
AMSTERDAM • PARIS • SYDNEY • HAMBURG
STOCKHOLM • ATHENS • TOKYO • MILAN
MADRID • WARSAW • BUDAPEST • AUCKLAND

ISBN 0-373-28964-2

THE DARK DUKE

Copyright © 1997 by Margaret Wilkins

This edition published by arrangement with Harlequin Books S.A.

® and TM are trademarks of the publisher. Trademarks indicated with ® are registered in the United States Patent and Trademark Office, the Canadian Trade Marks Office and in other countries.

Printed in U.S.A.

Books by Margaret Moore

Harlequin Historicals

A Warrior's Heart #118
China Blossom #149
A Warrior's Quest #175
†*The Viking* #200
A Warrior's Way #224
Vows #248
†*The Saxon* #268
The Welshman's Way #295
The Norman's Heart #311
The Baron's Quest #328
‡*The Wastrel* #344
‡*The Dark Duke* #364

Harlequin Books

Mistletoe Marriages
"Christmas in the Valley"

*Warrior Series
†The Viking Series
‡Most Unsuitable...

MARGARET MOORE

confesses that her first "crush" was Errol Flynn. The second was "Mr. Spock." She thinks that it explains why her heroes tend to be either charming rogues or lean, inscrutable tough guys.

Margaret lives in Scarborough, Ontario, with her husband, two children and two cats. She used to sew and read for reasons other than research.

For Ruth, Louise, Allison and Amy,
the other women in my husband's life.

Chapter One

Hampshire, 1863

Her Grace, the Duchess of Barroughby, was most seriously displeased.

Lady Hester Pimblett, who had been the duchess's companion for the past four months, recognized the symptoms at once in the older woman's compressed lips and furrowed brow.

"Have the goodness to bring the footstool with all speed!" the formidable woman snapped peevishly, her brown eyes full of anger, her white lace cap shaking with rage and her black bombazine dress suddenly looking like armor donned for battle. "And do close the drapes. I am getting a headache!"

At times such as these, Hester pondered the merits of being a companion to an older woman instead of living with her parents or one of her recently married sisters, for as she hurried to her ladyship's aid, she suspected her efforts to soothe the woman's perceived ills would be futile. The duchess crumpled a recently received letter in her long, thin fingers and Hester wondered what it contained to bring on this irate response.

The offending epistle appeared to be written in a masculine hand and, judging by the duchess's extreme reaction, was not from her treasured son. Therefore, Hester concluded, either the writer of the letter, or its subject, was her stepson, the notorious Duke of Barroughby.

Hester moved the footstool so that her ladyship could repose her rather large feet upon it. The duchess *was* upset if she would recline, for the duchess considered it the height of poor breeding to loll, as she had remarked to Lady Hester any time her young companion seemed to be displaying any predisposition to lean back against a chair.

Hester then closed the heavy damask draperies and prepared the vial of perfume with which the duchess would surely wish to anoint her temples.

"He *dares* to come to me!" the duchess suddenly exclaimed vehemently. "The scoundrel! The blackguard! His poor father would turn in his grave if he knew even half of what his son has done!"

So Lord Adrian Fitzwalter, the eldest son of the late duke, a man also known as the Dark Duke of Barroughby, was coming home.

He had not been at Barroughby Hall since Hester's arrival, and she had to admit to some curiosity to see this famous fellow up close. Once or twice the infamous rake had been pointed out to her at large assemblies, amid much whispering and speculation.

His powers of seduction were legendary, and Hes-

ter supposed if she were better looking she would
have cause to dread his arrival. However, she was not,
and so, surely safe from attracting such a rogue's notice, she was free to indulge in the harmless excitement of anticipating his arrival. For once, she thought
with a secretive smile, her family might actually pay
attention to something in her letters.

Jenkins, the butler, appeared in the doorway of the
drawing room. "Your Grace?" he inquired, leaning
toward the women, "is anything the matter?"

Hester smothered another smile. The aged retainer
was quite hard of hearing, yet he would have had to
be completely deaf not to hear the duchess's exclamations.

"Fetch the duchess some wine, please," Hester
said.

"Time? Time for what, my lady?" Jenkins inquired.

"*Wine!* Some *wine* for the duchess."

"Oh, very good, my lady." The butler tottered off,
and Hester once again regarded the indignant duchess.

"At least dear Elliot is abroad!" her ladyship exclaimed, choosing to ignore the fact that she had been
expecting her son to come to Barroughby Hall the
whole time Hester had been a resident there. "I
should refuse Adrian entrance to this house, the disgraceful creature! I shall send him from here at once.
The impertinence of the rascal!"

Hester remained silent and let the duchess ramble
on. She knew that her ladyship neither wanted nor
needed any response to continue to voice her opinion.

"Yes, I shall give him no greeting, or any mark of

attention. He may lodge at an inn in the town if he wishes, but he shall not stay here!'' She moaned softly and covered her eyes. ''Where is my perfume? Send for Dr. Woadly. I am most unwell. I feel quite dizzy!''

''I shall do so at once, Your Grace,'' Hester said, although she hastened not to summon a footman to fetch the doctor, but to dab some scent on the duchess's forehead. She wasn't sure calling out Dr. Woadly was necessary, and he spent an inordinate amount of time at Barroughby Hall for a variety of minor complaints as it was. ''When does the duke arrive?'' she ventured as she straightened and set the perfume on a side table.

The duchess lowered her hand and gave Hester a severe frown. ''Today, of course.'' Her hand returned to shielding her eyes. ''Oh, the audacity! He does not even wait for my reply!''

''Because I knew it must be all graciousness and felicity,'' a deep voice remarked from the vicinity of the door.

Hester turned at once and looked at the man standing on the threshold of the room, leaning against the frame in a casual pose, his arms crossed over his broad chest. He was tall and had a very fine figure displayed to perfection in a blue morning coat, brilliant white linen shirt, tan breeches and Wellington boots. His hair was black, as were his thick but shapely eyebrows, and he was so extremely handsome that Hester did not doubt she was beholding the Dark Duke himself.

If there was one thing surprising about his appearance, it was that his face was so pale, for the epithet "dark" also referred to a complexion browned by his time spent out of doors riding and hunting.

Hester made a slight curtsy and moved away from the duchess. The duke glanced briefly at her, then returned his attention to the duchess, who was regarding him with an expression that was a mixture of shock, anger and, Hester noted with some surprise, what might be fear. She had not supposed that there was a person in England who could intimidate the duchess even temporarily, but apparently here he was, in the flesh.

Or maybe the duchess's reaction was not so very surprising, for there was something about the man's overwhelming presence that seemed to inspire at least awe, if not more.

Her Grace, momentarily robbed of the powers of speech, watched as the duke sauntered into the room and took a seat without waiting to be invited. Hester made her way toward the door, for she felt her company was not wanted here. As she did so, she noted that the duke did not loll.

"Hester, where are you going?" the duchess suddenly demanded. She glanced uneasily at her stepson. "I have not told you to go."

"I believe, stepmother," the duke drawled, "that your charming companion feels it indelicate to remain. Is that not so, Miss...?" He turned to look at her with a slightly interrogative expression that Hester found quite unnerving. The least pretty of her sisters, she was not used to any kind of scrutiny, let alone the scrutiny of a man of the duke's reputation.

Before Hester could speak, the duchess intervened by making a proper, ungracious and overdue introduction. "This is Lady Hester Pimblett. Her father is Lord Pimblett."

"Charmed, Lady Hester," the duke said, rising slightly and giving her a sardonic, somewhat self-deprecating smile that made her realize how he came to have his reputation for seduction. With his looks, piercing gaze and that smile, he could win many a maiden's heart.

Although Hester felt herself equal to meet the duke, coming from a family at least as old as his if not of the same rank, she felt herself blushing at his steadfast regard.

"*I* wish her to remain. I am unwell," the duchess said, and Hester realized that after the initial shock of the duke's unexpected arrival, the duchess was returning to form.

The duke inclined his head in acceptance, or perhaps merely a reluctance to argue, and Hester resigned herself to the awkwardness of her situation.

"I demand to know what latest unsavory business has brought you here," the duchess said sternly. Apparently her triumph in the matter of Hester's continuing presence had emboldened her, or been enough to return her to her normal state.

"Is it not possible that I merely wish to visit my stepmother?"

The duchess's response was a sniff of contempt. "Was the woman married? Is that why you have to slink off into the countryside and disturb us here?"

"She was not married, but that is not why I have come."

"Why, then?"

Hester saw a flash of temper in the Dark Duke's eyes, yet he remained perfectly motionless, which was not what she would have expected from his passionate reputation. "I have every right to come home," he said evenly.

"I'm not surprised you had to leave London. I suppose there was another duel."

"Suppose what you like, Your Grace," he replied, using the most formal of addresses. "I am going to trouble you only a little while. Where is Elliot?"

"Mercifully, still in France."

"Ah. When do you expect him home?"

"Any day, Adrian, any day. I must say, I am *delighted* he is still abroad. He does not need to be tainted by another scandal involving you! Do you *never* think of us? Do you never think of your brother? No, don't trouble to answer! It is perfectly obvious! You only think of yourself!" The duchess glared at him and Hester shifted uncomfortably, wishing she was not present.

The duke rose slowly. "If you will excuse me, I shall retire to my room."

"I have not finished with you! I want to know what you have done now!"

The Dark Duke looked at the duchess, and Hester detected more than slight scorn in his black eyes. "As much as I am convinced your interest in knowing the details of the latest scandal is genuine, *I* am finished with *you*, Your Grace. My opponent was not the only one who was injured, and unless you wish me to get blood all over the carpet—'' both women gasped, but the duke remained coolly calm ''—you will not detain me. Lady Hester, I give you good day. Your Grace, my compliments.''

"Would you like me to call for a footman?" Hester asked, hurrying past him toward the door.

"Hester!" the duchess called out. "*I* need you."

Adrian watched with slight amusement as his stepmother's latest companion—or slave, as he always thought of these unfortunate creatures—hesitated. Then, to his very great surprise, Lady Hester did not immediately return to the duchess's side. Instead, with a determined expression manifested by a slight downturn of her full lips, she said, "If you will excuse me, Your Grace, I will be but a moment," and left the room without waiting for an answer.

Adrian would have smiled with satisfaction to see his stepmother disobeyed, except that he knew such a reaction from him would only inflame his stepmother's anger and make things more difficult for Lady Hester.

Why would a young woman of wealth and privilege waste her days tending to the duchess? he wondered. She must have more opportunities than that, even if she wasn't a beauty.

Pimblett. He knew that name, and recalled the daughters, although not a Hester. Helena Pimblett was reckoned a great beauty. He had seen her once at the theater, and thought her a vain, stuck-up creature. It was said by men of his acquaintance who could be expected to know such things that the younger sister was a beauty, too. However, he had never seen or heard of another sister, and it was fairly obvious why, for this young woman could never attract much notice in London.

Still, there was a certain wholesome prettiness to her. Her eyes were the friendly blue of cornflowers, fringed by lashes of soft brown that matched her chestnut hair drawn into a plain and rather severe knot of a bun. Her complexion was excellent and he had little doubt that she had been raised in the country, for her skin had the satiny texture of a country-bred lady. There was a delicacy to her features that he found interesting, and she had a nose that no woman need be ashamed of. She was simply and plainly gowned with good taste, and her figure was more than acceptable.

Judging by her response to the duchess, she must also be a rather uncommon young woman. He would not have said there was a young lady in all of England who would not be intimidated by his stepmother, yet apparently there was and, he realized with pleasure, she was in the duchess's company.

Lady Hester appeared in the doorway, followed by Jenkins and two footmen. By now Adrian's wound was aching badly and he could feel the blood seeping through the bandage. Nevertheless, he did not feel quite so decrepit as to need the assistance of three grown men.

"I took the liberty of sending for the surgeon to tend to the duke, as well as Dr. Woadly," Lady Hester said in a voice as friendly and pleasant as her countenance. She spoke to the duchess before looking at him, whereupon she regarded him steadily, as if he were a specimen in a bottle.

He returned the scrutiny, more out of curiosity than anything else, and then decided to conduct his own experiment upon this unusual woman. He smiled at her with all the charm he could muster. "Thank you, Lady Hester."

She did not blush or look away with false modesty or stare at him with impertinent curiosity. She simply resumed her seat.

Her reaction, or nonreaction, didn't mean anything, Adrian told himself. Why should it, when she was nothing to look at? And it could be that, sick and pale from the loss of blood, he was not at his best. Yes, that had to explain why a woman of her age would not respond to his charm.

He decided to ignore her, and limped toward the door. "Jenkins, if I may lean upon your arm, you may dismiss the footmen. Send the surgeon to my room as soon as he arrives."

"Lady Hester!" the duchess said. "Please fetch the smelling salts."

Without so much as a glance Adrian's way as he left the room, the young lady hurried to his stepmother's side.

"I must indeed look sick," Adrian muttered as he made his way toward the stairs, keeping most of his weight off the elderly butler, using Jenkins only for balance.

"Look at what, Your Grace?" Jenkins asked.

"I didn't say anything."

"Yes, you did, Your Grace," Jenkins corrected. "You said, 'Look at it.'"

"I meant my father's portrait. I think it needs to be cleaned."

They paused and surveyed the portrait of the late fifth Duke of Barroughby—in his full regalia for the House of Lords—which was hung on the landing. Beside it was a smaller portrait of Adrian's mother.

"Ah, those were good days," Jenkins said with a sigh. "I was younger then."

"So were we all," the sixth Duke of Barroughby noted as he passed them by.

"Don't look so glum, John," Adrian chastised the surgeon, who was applying a fresh bandage to the wound in his leg. "I've had worse."

"What caused it?" John Mapleton asked. The stout man puffed a little from the exertion of bending over Adrian's elevated leg. "Not a sword."

"Pistols at twenty paces."

"Ah!"

"It bled terribly, but no lasting damage, the London surgeon said."

"Lucky for you." Mapleton straightened with a grunt. "Lucky again. One of these days you're not going to be lucky. You're going to be dead."

"I didn't have very much to fear from my opponent. I was far more concerned that his shot not hit my second or some innocent bystander."

"Huh." Mapleton began repacking his black bag. "What was the cause? A woman?"

"Yes." Adrian lifted his foot and placed it gingerly

on the thick carpet. On the table beside the brocade chair was a basin full of bloodied water and a cloth the surgeon had used to clean the reopened wound, items that seemed distinctly out of place in the ornately decorated room with its expensive wallpaper, comfortable brocade chairs, delicate tables, large canopied bed, damask draperies on the tall, narrow windows and chinoiserie armoire.

Mapleton gave him a shrewd look. "Yours or Elliot's?"

Adrian didn't answer.

Mapleton frowned and went back to his task. "Elliot's, then. I should have known. The young fool ran off to hide in Europe and you took the blame. Again."

"All has been taken care of, so I would prefer to let the matter drop." Adrian winced as he stood and tried to put some weight on his leg.

"I would rest some more, Your Grace, if I were you. Tell me, did it never occur to you to take a coach here?"

"Drake needed the exercise, and after London, I wanted the air."

The deep, measured tones of Dr. Woadly were heard as he passed Adrian's door. "I fear my presence has sickened my stepmother," he noted sardonically.

"You could send her to the Dower House."

Adrian slowly resumed his seat. "And have her tell everyone I turned her out?"

"She has no *right* to Barroughby Hall," Mapleton said. "Your father left everything to you."

"So he did." Adrian reached into his vest for a cheroot. "I suppose, given my reputation, one more blemish shouldn't matter." He struck a match. "Don't imagine I haven't given it some thought. Still, my father wanted her to remain here. Along with Jenkins."

"Your father has been dead these ten years."

Adrian raised one dark eyebrow, well aware that Mapleton would never see eye-to-eye with him on certain things. "I was not aware there was a time limit on promises made to a dying parent."

"There should be!" Mapleton said forcefully.

"This is such an unpleasant topic, John," Adrian said as the smoke from his cheroot curled toward the high ceiling. "Sit down and have a drink with me."

Mapleton thought a moment, then nodded his head. "If you let me get it."

"Only too happy not to have to stir a hair," Adrian replied lightly.

Mapleton went to another small table that held a decanter and some crystal glasses. He poured two drinks and handed one to Adrian before sitting beside him. "I really think you should consider retiring Jenkins. Give him a cottage and a pension. He's getting too old for his duties, and his hearing…" Mapleton left off suggestively.

"I know. He's worse every time I come. I've made certain he has only the basics to attend to, for the one time I said something about his age, I thought he was going to cry." Adrian drew on his cheroot and let the smoke out gradually. "You can't imagine a more worrisome sight than old Jenkins with a tear in his eye.''

''Must you joke about everything, my lord?''

Adrian gazed at the surgeon with a thoughtful expression. ''It helps,'' he said truthfully.

''I'm surprised the duchess hasn't insisted he go,'' Mapleton said after a short silence. ''She doesn't strike me as having the patience to put up with his mistakes.''

''Ah, now *there* I can offer an explanation,'' Adrian replied, happy to be diverted from a serious subject like promises made on his father's deathbed. ''Jenkins was in his middle years when the duchess married my father. Now, if Jenkins is getting too old to do his job, well, how old is the duchess, then?''

Mapleton frowned. ''You mean, if she admits that Jenkins has to stop working, she's admitting she's getting old herself.''

''Exactly!''

''And I suppose I could extrapolate that she also feels by having a young woman who is not noticeably attractive for a companion, she maintains her position as the most beautiful woman in the household.''

''One could say that,'' Adrian agreed, for such an explanation might also illustrate why the duchess didn't get angry over Lady Hester's slight defiance. ''How long has Lady Hester been here?''

''About four months.''

''Helpful, I take it?''

''I believe Dr. Woadly would say so.''

''Ah. Fewer summonses from Barroughby Hall?''

''So I understand.''

"We've made a very good guess as to why she might suit my stepmother, but why do you think Lady Hester would stay here?"

"I'm sure I have no idea," Mapleton answered. "No alternatives, perhaps."

"What of her parents? Have they died?"

"Oh, they're alive. I understand they've gone to Europe for an extended period. Lord Pimblett apparently feels it would be better for his gout, or so Lady Hester said. She asked me some questions about the complaint. A most intelligent, compassionate young woman."

"Which again begs the question, why would she shut herself up here with my esteemed stepmother?"

"Why don't you ask her?"

"Perhaps I will."

Mapleton's brow furrowed and Adrian sighed with genuine dismay. "Oh, not *you,* too. I assure you, she will be quite safe from the clutches of the Dark Duke."

Mapleton chuckled, then finished his drink and rose. "I know it. Now I really must be on my way. Take care of that leg. No riding for the next few days."

Adrian nodded absently. "I wonder how long she'll stay," he mused aloud.

"Lady Hester?"

The duke nodded.

"Why should she leave, after putting up with the duchess for so long already?" Mapleton asked.

"Because while you and I both know she has nothing to fear from me, Lady Hester may feel otherwise."

Chapter Two

Later that evening Hester tried to pay attention to the card game she was playing with the duchess and not to let her eyes stray toward the drawing room door.

Indeed, there was no reason she should keep doing so. She couldn't expect anyone to walk into the room, except a servant, for the Duke of Barroughby had not come down to dinner. It was because of his injury, so Jenkins said, after also informing them that Mr. Mapleton did not think it a particularly serious one.

She also suspected, however, that the duke was reluctant to listen to his stepmother continue to denounce him to his face, a quite understandable reason.

"So, Lady Hester, you have never seen my stepson before?" the duchess asked. She was currently winning the game of piquet, which Hester thought explained her somewhat mollified tone, and the duchess's good humor was ample recompense for playing less than honestly.

"No, Your Grace."

"I daresay you moved in better circles in London society."

"I did not move much in any circle, Your Grace," Hester replied.

"Why not?" the duchess demanded. "Surely your father's rank made your welcome assured."

Hester tried not to squirm with discomfort, because the duchess would surely chastise her for wiggling. "I preferred to remain at home."

"With your mama? How sweet," the duchess murmured as she checked the number of tricks she had taken.

If that was what the duchess preferred to believe, Hester did not correct her. It was better than admitting she found it difficult to watch as her lovely sisters received all the attention, while she was treated as little more than a piece of furniture.

The duchess smiled with satisfaction. "I win again! You know, Elliot is quite a clever fellow at cards. He can even defeat *me* on occasion."

"Really, Your Grace?"

"Indeed. He is quite in demand at card parties, and when he can be persuaded to take a moment from dancing at balls. La, that is not often, I assure you."

Hester merely nodded.

"But you shall see his qualities for yourself when he arrives." The duchess opened her fan and frowned as she began to wave it. "Let us hope the duke is far away by then."

It was on the tip of Hester's tongue to ask the duchess why she didn't send the duke away, if she found his presence so odious, but she knew the woman would not enjoy being questioned. Therefore, she was forced to merely wonder about that, and about the duke himself.

In one way, he more than lived up to his reputation. She had had more than ample time to observe people at the social functions she did attend, and she had never seen a more handsome man.

On the other hand, she had found his patience with his waspish stepmother quite astonishing and completely unexpected. She would have thought a man who had done all the things he was said to have done would be rather hot tempered and quick to take offense. Maybe the fact that the duchess was a relation explained it.

Hester glanced at the door again, to see the duchess's maid waiting. "I believe it's time to retire, Your Grace," she said softly, nodding toward Maria.

"Ah, so it is." The duchess rose majestically, moving her beaded black skirt around the delicate chair with a graceful gesture before she glanced at Hester. "Aren't you coming?"

"In a moment. I believe I left my book in the library. I would like to read a little before I sleep."

The duchess frowned with disapproval. "You will ruin your eyesight," she admonished. "Or fall asleep with the candle lit and burn the house down."

"I shall be very careful, Your Grace," Hester said, trying to ignore being chided like a recalcitrant child. Again.

"Oh, all right," the duchess said ungraciously. "Mind you do not sleep too late." With that, she turned and left, preceded by the dark-haired Maria.

As if I ever do! Hester thought, taking a candle and heading for the library. She had never seen the duchess so much as pick up a book or newspaper, let alone read one, so it was no surprise the woman had no respect for reading.

It was a fair way along the corridor to the darkly paneled library, a room the duchess never ventured into, and where Hester went when she wanted a few moments alone. It was quiet and a little solemn, like an empty church, but Hester liked it all the more for its aura of benign neglect.

Barroughby Hall itself was an immense building, the work of several generations and several architects, each seemingly trying to outdo each other in the spending of the Fitzwalters' money. Fortunately, the estate was a large one, too, and more than one of the dukes had been a wise investor in art and sculpture, as well as business ventures, so there was little fear of putting the family into bankruptcy.

By this time the house and grounds were magnificent. Built in a square, with an open courtyard in the middle reached through the imposing main entrance, the hall boasted a corridor nearly a mile long around the inside, filled with paintings and statues purchased in Europe. The ceilings of the main rooms on the lower level were all painted by master artists; even the hearths of the fireplaces were works of art. The large dining room would easily seat one hundred at an immense mahogany table. There were over fifty bedrooms, not counting those in the attic used by the small army of servants.

Other rooms in the house included the large drawing room, the small drawing room, the library, the duke's study, two smoking rooms, a billiard room, the Tudor hall that formed the main entrance, the servants' hall and the kitchen, at an unfortunate distance from the large dining room. Outside, there were the formal gardens, a large shrubbery, the carriage house and the stables, as well as kennels for the duke's hunting dogs.

It was not a cozy place to live, yet it did have its compensations, not all of them architectural. Here Hester was not always being compared to her more attractive sisters, or made to wait upon her mother, who, believing herself sickly, was always in need of assistance and accepted Hester's help as her due. The duchess also pleaded a weak constitution, but not nearly as often, and she seemed to appreciate Hester's efforts a vast deal more.

In addition to that, Hester realized, there was now the exciting presence of the Dark Duke himself to make her stay here something out of the ordinary.

She reached the library, found her volume and headed toward the back stairs, which would be the fastest route up to her room. As she did so, she heard the servants still at work in the kitchen, talking and laughing among themselves as they completed their daily tasks.

Once upstairs, she paused in the corridor, realizing that one of the bedroom doors between where she was standing and her room, a door that had always been shut tight, was standing slightly open. Perhaps that was the duke's room, and she would have to pass it by.

This notion filled her with a curious mixture of excitement and dread, until Hester told herself she was being ridiculous. Surely she didn't expect the duke to lunge out of the room, grab her and drag her inside. The image was so...so romantically gothic that Hester had to stifle a laugh. As if she could ever be a heroine! Besides, with an injured leg, he could hardly be skulking about!

Emboldened, she confidently walked down the hall. Nevertheless, her steps slowed as she came even with the open door. A low moan caught her attention. No one else was near, so she cautiously stepped inside.

The room was dark, for no moonlight penetrated the drawn drapes. She lifted her candle a little higher, noting the fine proportions of the large room and splendid furnishings.

Including the canopied bed, with the curtains open and the duke slumbering upon it, lying on his side, and turned toward the door. He certainly wasn't a person to fear at the moment, she thought, smiling at her previous imaginings. At present he didn't look like the cold, sardonic man of this morning, or the villain rumor and gossip painted him. With his hair tousled and his eyes shut, he looked like nothing so much as a mischievous little boy—although there was a sensuality to his lips that had nothing of the child about it.

As she watched, he moved restlessly, rolling onto his back and throwing one muscular arm over his face. One naked, muscular arm. At the sudden realization that he might be nude beneath the bedclothes, Hester backed away, ready to depart.

The duke moaned again.

Perhaps he needed help. Maybe she should fetch someone—but then she would have to explain her presence in the duke's bedroom. She recalled hearing his valet's voice in the servants' hall downstairs. She could ring the bell for assistance and leave before the valet appeared. The servant might believe that the duke had summoned him.

Deciding that would be the best course, Hester moved farther inside the room, for the bell rope dangled near the head of the bed.

What if someone passed by? They would certainly see her light.

Hester blew out the candle, so that the room was in complete darkness. She waited for her eyes to get used to the change, then slowly began to make out the shape of the duke, and the bellpull.

She went slowly toward the bed and reached for the pull, hesitating for a moment as she looked down at the slumbering duke.

He shifted again, rolling toward her and exposing his powerful shoulder.

With a gulp, she yanked on the bellpull, then hurried from the room as quickly and quietly as she could.

When she was gone, Adrian Fitzwalter opened his eyes and smiled.

The next morning, Adrian sank onto the stone garden bench that was as cold and hard as his stepmother's heart and stretched out his left leg. His limb was very sore, and although he believed Mapleton when he said that the wound was not dangerous, Adrian couldn't help wondering when the devil he would be recovered enough to leave here, or at least go riding.

Still, he might as well take some time to enjoy the garden, seen far too little of late, and bask in the warmth of an unseasonably mild autumn day.

He slowly surveyed the flower beds, walks and shrubbery. His stepmother had been busy here, or busy giving orders at any rate. Very little of his mother's garden remained. All was now formal and, to his mind, lacking any sense of natural beauty. He wondered what his father would have made of the change, and then decided that thought was a foolish one. His father would have said nothing, no matter what he felt. He had always been reserved.

Far too reserved, except on that one memorable occasion.

As for the "improvements" Adrian did not like, his stepmother could not live forever. When she died, he would put it all as it had been before his mother had passed away when he was ten years old, and his life had changed forever.

Perhaps it had not been wise to come to Barroughby, with all its memories. He should have remained in London, at least until Christmas, and braved this latest scandal, too.

Adrian forced himself to concentrate on the scent of the roses, and tried not to remember Elizabeth Howell's tear-streaked face or the little body of her infant, robbed of life after a few short gasps, lying in the wooden cradle beside the narrow, filthy bed.

He leaned forward and rubbed his temples, as if he could rub out the memories. He had done all he could, knowing full well he could never make up for the loss of her honor, her happiness or her child.

"My dear duchess! How distressed you must be!"

Adrian turned his head so swiftly in the direction of the main drawing room that a pain shot through his neck.

It was the Reverend Canon Lyton Smeech, the vicar of the local church. He had held that living for several years at the discretion of the duchess, and apparently he still felt beholden enough to fawn over the woman.

Adrian heard another feminine voice murmur a greeting, and thought he recognized it as Hester Pimblett's.

A rare smile crossed his face. A most surprising young woman, Hester. Outwardly so timid and demure, obedient and pliable. But only outwardly, for it took no small inner strength to ignore his stepmother, and no small courage to enter the Dark Duke's bedchamber, even if he was ostensibly asleep, given his reputation as a lascivious libertine.

Well, perhaps not courage. Perhaps nothing more than feminine curiosity. Or a passionate nature beneath the self-effacing facade.

He rose slowly. He had met that type of woman before, the kind who used the trap of sweet modesty to get a jaded cad's attention. Once he got her alone, she would *say* they were acting most improperly, all the while pressing her lithe, shapely body against his. It was hypocrisy at its finest, and he knew hypocrisy very well indeed.

Another voice responded, that of a younger man. He wasn't aware of any visitors expected today, which was not surprising really, considering his hostile relationship with the duchess. Who could it be?

Maybe it was someone to be avoided, like the Reverend Canon Smeech. Or maybe it was a gentleman with some interest in the quiet Lady Hester. There was a fascinating course of speculation, and one worthy of further investigation, if for no other reason than to provide some necessary distraction.

Adrian smiled grimly as he limped into the house.

Chapter Three

"A, um, most trying surprise for you, I'm sure, Your Grace," the Reverend Canon Smeech intoned pityingly.

"Nobody knows how I suffer," the duchess responded plaintively. "Hester," she snapped in an aside to her companion, "I need my fan!"

Hester, seated in a small chair to the right and slightly behind the duchess's sofa, reached forward with the necessary article. The canon strolled to the windows, and Hester smiled at the curate who had arrived with the august clergyman, Reverend Hamish McKenna, who was looking decidedly uncomfortable. Whether it was because he was overwhelmed by the magnificence of his surroundings or not sure how to respond to the robust duchess's claims of illness, Hester wasn't sure. Nevertheless, he managed to smile briefly in response.

"Yes, nobody knows how I suffer!" the duchess continued. "Another scandal! The name of Fitzwalter—which my son also possesses!—dragged in the mud. What is a mother to do?"

"Perhaps if you spoke with the duke," Reverend McKenna offered gently, his Scots accent giving his words a slight burr.

The duchess looked startled, and Reverend Canon Smeech gave his curate a censorious look.

"It was merely a suggestion," the reverend said helplessly.

"An inappropriate one," the canon replied. "The duchess has no wish or need to sully herself by contact with the duke."

Hester couldn't help feeling sorry for Reverend McKenna. It wouldn't be easy working with Reverend Canon Smeech, who was the type of clergyman who clearly considered the few needs of the wealthy of his parish first and foremost, and left the bulk of the work to his assistant.

"Did I hear someone mention the duke?" the nobleman asked as he strolled into the room.

Reverend McKenna rose in greeting, the duchess frowned and the canon bowed. "Your Grace," he said with a smile. "We were not expecting you."

"So I gather," the duke noted as he continued toward the sofa and seated himself beside his stepmother. "We meet again, Canon Smeech."

The duchess inched away as if the duke had a disease, Hester noted.

She also noted that he looked quite rested, his leg apparently caused him no trouble, his hair was considerably more tidy than the last time she had seen him, his clothes fit to perfection, and he didn't seem to notice she was there.

Which should not be surprising or cause for dismay.

"My lord, allow me to present Reverend Hamish McKenna, my curate," the older clergyman said with an obsequious bow, and Hester had to stifle a smile. Obviously the poor canon didn't want to offend either the duke or the duchess. "Your stepmother was telling us of your, ah, wound."

"Was she?" he asked lightly. "Must have been a short discourse, since I have told her so little about it. Please sit down, Smeech. You, too, Reverend McKenna."

Reverend Canon Smeech blushed at the duke's lack of courtesy, and so did Hamish McKenna, from the roots of his red hair to the bottom of his freckled chin, as he sat on a chair opposite Hester, who gave him a warm and understanding smile. The duke's overpowering presence was enough to cast a pall over the most mundane of conversations, a fact brought forcefully home when he glanced at her. He made her feel as if she had suddenly been put on display at the Crystal Palace.

Adrian looked from Lady Hester, wearing the plainest of blue gowns and seated like some quiet little serving maid beside his stepmother, to the blushing young clergyman. Were they ordaining children these days? Surely this fellow was far too young to be in orders, Adrian thought, until Reverend McKenna smiled at Hester. Not so very young, after all. And what was he to make of *her*, so cool and composed? "I trust you slept well, Lady Hester?" Adrian asked.

"Quite well," she replied with equanimity. "Did you?"

"Yes," he replied, somewhat nonplussed. He began to wonder if he had imagined last night, when he thought she had come into his bedroom. Or maybe he had been dreaming, and he had pulled the bell rope to summon James, who had been dispatched to fetch his master a drink to soothe his restless sleep.

They all sat in awkward silence for several minutes, and Adrian did nothing to lessen the tension. He was well aware his stepmother was bursting to speak and complain about him. If his presence stopped her, he would sit here for the rest of the day, and they could all be silent. As for the others, including the confusing Lady Hester, he didn't care if they were uncomfortable or not.

Then Lady Hester addressed Canon Smeech. "I understand the harvest was particularly good this year."

"Ah, indeed, um, yes. Very fine, very fine."

The canon rambled on for some time about the crops and livestock of the village of Barroughby, needing no further prompting to indulge in the sound of his own deep, sonorous tones, and Adrian realized something had gone amiss. It was not for this mousy young woman to direct the conversation, nor was it fitting for her to look slyly at McKenna, as if sharing some kind of secret with him.

Not when the Duke of Barroughby was present.

"I suppose you've already collected the tithes?" Adrian demanded, not particularly caring if he sounded rude or not.

The Reverend Canon Smeech cleared his plump and pompous throat. "Yes, my lord."

"I did not think you would neglect that," Adrian noted dryly.

Lady Hester frowned slightly, a peevish little downturn of her full lips. So, she did not approve of his remarks. He didn't care. She had probably heard worse things about him than his lack of respect for a bombastic hypocrite like Smeech.

The duchess's companion rose gracefully and faced the duchess. "If you will excuse me, Your Grace, I promised Reverend McKenna that I would show him the garden the next time he visited on a sunny day. This one would seem to be perfect."

Hamish McKenna got to his feet awkwardly and flushed deep red. "Indeed, yes, I would be delighted," he said.

I'll wager you would, Adrian thought. "Apparently Lady Hester prefers not to be in my presence—today."

There! A flash of fire in her large blue eyes, just enough to tell him that she understood his reference, and that he had *not* imagined her in his room last night.

"Is it any wonder, when you are so abominably rude?" the duchess demanded.

"You wound me, Your Grace," Adrian said with a mockingly injured air as he put his hand over his heart, while at the same time resolving to be more courteous to Lady Hester. "I give them leave to go." Indeed, he was tempted to join them, but the idea that he would have to hide his limp or endure pitying remarks kept him in his chair.

Jenkins appeared in the doorway and bowed as far as his rheumatic back would permit. "Sir Douglas Sackcloth-and-Ashes and his daughter have arrived, Your Grace," he announced.

"He means Sir Douglas Sackville-Cooper and his daughter, Damaris," the duchess explained to the confused clergymen. "Poor Jenkins—his hearing is beginning to go."

Adrian made no effort to hide a smirk. Beginning to go? Jenkins's hearing had been going for fifteen years.

"Show them in," the duchess said brusquely, and Adrian was glad that he hadn't offered to walk in the garden, for this was surely going to be interesting.

He easily remembered Sir Douglas, a country squire with good manners, small intellect and vast ambition. As for Damaris, he had last seen her five years ago. She had been about twelve then, and a very pretty child, if rather dull.

Sir Douglas marched into the room, his bearing military and his fifty-year-old body remarkably well preserved. Obviously country life agreed with him, judging by his robust good health. "My dear duke!" he cried, taking Adrian's hand and shaking it vigorously. "I heard from Smythe at The George that you were come home." He faced the duchess and the risen canon. "Good afternoon, Your Grace. Canon Smeech." He bowed to Lady Hester, who made a small curtsy, and he nodded dismissively at Reverend McKenna.

Then Damaris Sackville-Cooper, no longer a little girl, entered the room. Adrian realized at once that she was a rare beauty, with dark hair topped by a pert dark green chapeau and veil, which hid limpid gray eyes that were quickly and demurely lowered, her dusky lashes fanning her satiny cheeks. Her figure was perfect in a very fashionable riding habit of dark green velvet, and her posture graceful and elegant.

If Damaris were to appear in London with him, Adrian thought, she would cause a sensation. However, he was quite used to causing a sensation, and somehow, the vision didn't excite him. He would just as soon appear with Lady Hester on his arm.

He smiled to himself. Now, *that* would cause a very different sensation. The Dark Duke in public with a homely woman—the gossips would have a high time.

He glanced at Hamish McKenna to see how the young man of the cloth reacted to the sight of such loveliness.

Reverend McKenna looked completely stunned.

And what of Lady Hester? Surely she would not welcome such a visitor.

Lady Hester smiled warmly at the young woman, apparently without envy. A rare woman indeed, to feel no jealousy in the presence of such pulchritude.

When Adrian rose to greet Damaris, he wondered why he felt absolutely nothing beyond mere curiosity as he regarded her. Could it be that he was getting old? Or had he simply seen too many beautiful women? He reached out to take her hand, and she drew back, shying like a terrified horse—not a completely unexpected reaction from a country lass, and not at all disturbing.

Her father cleared his throat, and Damaris held out her gloved hand, albeit as if she feared Adrian was going to bite it off.

"We were about to take a turn in the garden," Lady Hester said softly. "Perhaps Miss Sackville-Cooper would care to accompany us?"

"Charmed," the young lady replied, not looking in Adrian's direction.

"Delightful idea!" Sir Douglas said. "Delightful! I'm sure the duke knows many interesting things about the flora!"

"I regret my current indisposition forces me to remain behind," Adrian said. He had no great desire to stay here with his stepmother, yet he knew his leg couldn't bear the walk around the garden. He would wait until they were gone, then decamp to his room. Boredom was infinitely better than enduring the duchess and Canon Smeech.

Damaris Sackville-Cooper brightened considerably at his words. The other two young people turned away before he could catch their expressions, even though he didn't particularly care how they felt about his refusal.

"Nothing serious, I trust?" Sir Douglas inquired with grave concern.

"A mere flesh wound," Adrian replied lightly. "I have been advised to rest."

"Why don't you go, too, Sir Douglas?" the duchess suggested in her own, unsubtle way. "And you, too, Canon. You can explain to Sir Douglas about that new plant, the one you suggested I put in near the rose garden. I shall await your return here, for you all must stay to tea."

"Won't you join us, Your Grace?" Canon Smeech asked.

"I fear my heart couldn't take the strain of walking about in this unseasonable warmth."

The garden party departed, Lady Hester in the lead, followed by Reverend McKenna and Miss Sackville-Cooper, then the slower canon and a reluctant Sir Douglas.

They soon moved out of sight and presumably out of hearing. Adrian was about to rise and leave the room when the duchess turned to him. "You know what that man's trying to do, don't you?"

"Which man?"

"Sir Douglas, of course."

Adrian raised one eyebrow with sardonic speculation. "No, but I suspect you're going to tell me."

"Don't give me that look, Adrian. What I'm about to say is for your own good."

"Well, then, I must hear you out," he replied, wondering what the duchess considered "his own good."

The duchess frowned darkly. "He has *designs* on you."

"Carnal?" Adrian inquired nonchalantly.

The duchess gasped and reddened. "No! Of course not, you vile creature! He wants you to marry his daughter."

"I see."

"*She* is to be his bait."

"And I the prize?"

"Your *title*," the duchess replied, sneering as much as a well-bred woman could. "He wants her to become the next duchess. That little nobody!"

"She's a very beautiful young woman," Adrian noted.

"They have no family connections worth speaking of, and I will not see this estate in the hands of Sir Douglas Sackville-Cooper's daughter."

"Since you are likely to be deceased before I am likely to be wed, I do not see that you need to worry," Adrian remarked, beginning to stand.

"*Will* you take this matter seriously? Sir Douglas is going to be laying snares for you everywhere! We all know your reputation and, as you so flippantly point out, she is a beautiful creature. You must stay away from her! I will not allow you to pursue your own selfish pleasures!"

It was Adrian's turn to scowl, although he tried not to, for he could think of only one person on the entire earth who was more selfish than his stepmother, and that was her son. "Then I am not to deflower Damaris Sackville-Cooper?" he asked, regarding her steadily.

"*Must* you use such words in my presence?"

"Isn't that what you are trying to tell me? That Sir Douglas may not care how he manages to get his daughter married to me? That he might, in essence, throw her at my head?"

"Since you insist upon using such terms, yes."

"Obviously you were too preoccupied to notice that the young lady in question does not seem to regard me with a favorable eye."

"Don't try to talk smart to me, Adrian. You and I

both know that you could seduce a stone if you took it into your head. Heaven knows you have had enough practice!''

He made a mocking half bow. ''I thank you for the compliment, Your Grace. I believe it is the first one you have ever given me.''

''Just stay away from Damaris Sackville-Cooper!''

''But how am I to assuage my base desires, which you seem to think determine my every decision?'' he asked with deceptive calm. ''Surely you don't expect me to be as chaste as a monk.''

''I don't care, as long as you don't endanger the family honor.''

He knew she meant only the honor of herself and Elliot, her dear boy. ''I have no taste for servants,'' Adrian replied, wondering how far she was willing to take this subject. ''Perhaps Lady Hester?''

''You *are* a rogue to even *think* of corrupting Lord Pimblett's daughter!'' the duchess replied. Then she smiled coldly. ''Go ahead and try. Not even *you* would have much success with her.''

''Why not? If I can seduce a stone, surely I could succeed with her.''

The duchess fanned herself. ''She is no flighty, silly creature given to overwrought emotions. She is a good, quiet, dutiful young woman who will keep her virtue for her husband.''

''Does this mean I can expect a parade of eligible young men through Barroughby Hall?''

''Don't be impudent.''

''She seemed quite friendly to Reverend McKenna,'' he noted.

"Are you trying to be amusing?" the duchess demanded. "Lady Hester has more sense than to ally herself to a country curate, even if he does come from a well-to-do family. They made their money in *trade*."

"Oh, well, then, obviously he's out of consideration. What about Sir Douglas Sackville-Cooper? He's been a widower for years."

"Lord Edgar Pimblett's daughter and that man?"

"It would be a decent match for her."

His stepmother looked at him with something resembling respect. "You might be right, Adrian. She's rather old and certainly plain. She might be willing to settle for him."

Adrian reflected that he should have known that if his stepmother approved an idea, he would find it a bad one upon further consideration. The idea of Hester Pimblett and Sir Douglas now struck him as ludicrous, even if he couldn't say why. All he could be sure of was that he had had quite enough of this conversation, and more than enough of his stepmother for one day. "If you will excuse me, I'm going upstairs. My leg is aching like the devil." He bowed and strode toward the door.

"*Don't* use such vulgar terms in my presence, if you please, Adrian," the duchess replied tartly. "And I don't excuse you."

But the duke had already gone out the door.

Chapter Four

Hester led the way along the walk to the rose garden, feeling not unlike the Pied Piper as Reverend McKenna and Damaris, Sir Douglas and Canon Smeech followed. Reverend McKenna caught up to her quickly, matching her pace. Damaris soon joined them, walking on the other side of Hester.

"Well, isn't he just the most *wicked* man!" Damaris exclaimed quietly, with an anxious glance over her shoulder as if she expected to see the Dark Duke pursuing her like Hades after Persephone. "Papa says he's simply a spirited young man—spirited! I can believe everything I've heard, and more."

That Adrian Fitzwalter had a streak of devilment in him was all too obvious, Hester thought as she recalled his words this morning. He must have been awake when she entered his bedroom, a humiliating realization. And yet, if he was as evil as the duchess and everyone except Sir Douglas seemed to believe, he wouldn't have continued to feign sleep. He would have done something horrible, like leap from the bed and kiss her.

Moving his full lips, which curled with such secretive, knowing smiles, over hers. Slowly. Seductively. Pressing his hard, muscular body against hers. Embracing her with a fierce and wild passion, perhaps even picking her up and carrying her to the bed—

"Oh, dear, have we been walking too fast?" Damaris asked. "You seem all out of breath, Lady Hester."

"No, no, I'm fine," she replied, trying to compose herself. She had never known she possessed such a vivid imagination!

"We should be charitable," Reverend McKenna offered meekly, although his tone seemed to imply this would not be an easy task. He gave the lovely Damaris a sidelong glance and Hester was sure she heard him sigh.

"He is very handsome," Hester said.

"Handsome in a sly, nasty way!" Damaris said. "And, my dear, I have it on the very best authority that he doesn't confine his unsavory activities to London. The butcher's girl told my maid that she actually saw him leaving that house on Stamford Street when he visited here once before."

Hester knew to which house Damaris was referring with that knowing, condemning tone. Even Barroughby had a brothel. "She was quite sure it was the duke?" Hester inquired, finding it hard to believe that a man of the duke's attributes would have to pay for services of that sort.

"Well," Damaris equivocated, "she did see only his back—but the man was the right height, and very well dressed, and when he said good-night she recognized his voice."

Hester didn't respond, and Reverend McKenna only stared at the ground.

"Why has he come here again?" Damaris demanded. "He and the duchess have no liking for each other."

"He was hurt," Hester replied.

"How?"

"A duel, or so I understand," she said.

"Oh, dear!" Damaris responded, her eyes widening. "No wonder the duchess dislikes him! And to think Papa—" She paused and colored, then continued. "It's *illegal* to duel!"

"I daresay many things the duke is alleged to have done are illegal," Hester noted.

"Are you going to stay here?"

Hester paused and looked at Damaris. "Why should I not?"

"Because of his reputation, my dear!" Damaris said. "No woman is said to be safe around him!"

Hester began walking again. "No *beautiful* woman, perhaps," she replied, hoping Damaris would take the hint. "I think I shall not tempt him."

"Nevertheless, it might be wise to advise the duchess to suggest he leave," Reverend McKenna said with unusual boldness.

Hester could easily envision what the duchess's reaction would be to Hamish McKenna's advice, clergyman or not, so she said, "I believe he shall soon grow bored and go back to London, so let us not cause more dissention in the family."

"But still—!" Reverend McKenna began.

"Oh, let's not talk about such a disagreeable subject!" Damaris ordered with a very pretty pout.

Reverend McKenna fell silent.

The young people turned down the footpath to the rose garden, leaving the older men to follow some distance behind. From the snatches of conversation Hester could overhear, they were discussing the duke's financial situation, as best as people could who had no real knowledge.

If only Sir Douglas could be a little more aware of the danger! He was naive if he thought the duke would see Damaris only as an object of matrimony, not seduction, yet it was obvious listening to him speak of the estate with Canon Smeech that the knight considered only the title and wealth that would belong to the wife of the Duke of Barroughby. The taint of scandals and gossip clearly meant nothing.

Hester thought Damaris's denunciation sincere enough, yet she didn't doubt that Adrian Fitzwalter possessed enough persuasive abilities to make the most virtuous woman's honor falter, if he cared to exert himself, which he might very well do for the beautiful Damaris. Add to that his good looks and muscular body—well, a woman might be tempted to overlook many things in the face of such attributes.

This did not bode well for Damaris, or Reverend McKenna, either, Hester thought, as she saw the young man glance at the beauty again. It didn't take a lot of perception to see that he was completely smitten with her, and extremely worried about the presence of the duke.

Poor man! Hester feared his romance was doomed to failure, for even supposing Damaris's father did not succeed in his plans concerning the Duke of Barroughby, Hester was sure Sir Douglas would set about searching for an equally advantageous marriage for her.

Hester repressed a sigh of her own. Her parents had no such ambitions for *her*. After Helena had made a match with a rich manufacturer's son, and Henrietta with a clergyman who had a wealthy lord for a patron, they seemed to feel they had reached the end of their responsibilities. After all, Hester was no prize—or so their attitude seemed to suggest.

The reflection stung her as it always did, for she knew it did not have to be so. She had a lively and intelligent mind; if she could but have been taught more, she would at least have been able to find solace in learning. Instead, she was reduced to being little more than an elite companion for a difficult old woman, who complained about everything except her dear son, Elliot.

Could it be possible for one son to be such a paragon of virtue and the other apparently the very devil in human form?

If Adrian Fitzwalter was a devil, Hester thought him a perceptive one. No one else seemed to feel as she did about Canon Smeech, whom she had disliked from the moment she had met him, when he had looked at her with such condescending pity. She had listened to him condemn the duke with nearly as much venom as the duchess, only to see him smile at the duke as much as he dared while the duchess was present. Still, the duke shouldn't have been so rude to the man's face. The canon did represent the Church of England, after all.

Perhaps the duke's animosity to a clergyman wasn't so surprising, if one considered that the duke seemed to sin with such regularity and relish.

"Isn't the scent delightful?" Damaris said, holding up a rose for Hester's inspection and catching her quite off guard. "Don't you think so, Reverend McKenna?"

"Beautiful," the young man murmured, blushing, as Damaris bent her head toward another bloom. She colored very slightly, and Hester couldn't be sure if it was because of her action, or because she, too, realized the remark was not strictly intended to refer to the flower.

Hester hoped Damaris would fall in love with Hamish McKenna. Damaris could do much worse for a husband, and she wanted the young woman safe from her father's machinations.

And those of the Dark Duke, if she was being absolutely truthful.

Adrian spent the next few days closeted in his bedroom, where he did not have to put up with his stepmother, or make pleasant conversation with Sir Douglas and his daughter, who visited every day, or listen to the canon attempt to lecture him on the errors of his ways while trying not to offend him.

He saw nothing of Lady Hester, but he could guess that she was spending her time attending to his stepmother, whose various and sundry ailments would all have been made worse by the arrival of her prodigal stepson.

If Adrian regretted anything about his self-imposed confinement, it was missing the opportunity to study that interesting miss a little more. She certainly did not seem to begrudge Damaris Sackville-Cooper her beauty. Perhaps that could be explained by Lady Hester's lovely sisters. She was probably used to being the plain woman in any gathering. However, he had been rather more surprised by her apparent lack of jealousy where the attentive young reverend was concerned. Adrian was quite sure of his ability to gauge reactions, and he was certain that Reverend McKenna was smitten with Miss Sackville-Cooper. Did Lady Hester see this, too, or did she simply not care?

That Sir Douglas was making grandiose plans for his daughter was also painfully obvious, and completely useless, for Adrian did not intend to marry for a very long time. He had enough responsibilities without adding those of a wife and subsequent children.

Nevertheless, by this time Adrian was heartily sick of his own company. To make matters worse, it began to rain, making his bedroom unremittingly gloomy. If the weather brought any comfort, it was that no unwelcome visitors would come to Barroughby Hall on such a day. Therefore, Adrian reasoned, he could venture to the library, a room his stepmother never entered. Jenkins could be counted on to have a fire there, for he lived in perpetual fear of the late duke's library falling prey to mildew. It would be warm and cozy and he could find himself something new to read.

As he had hoped, a fire burned merrily in the library's grate, making the dark-paneled room seem like a book-lined cavern. Adrian felt like Robinson Crusoe, marooned with only books for company. This did not particularly trouble him, for he had spent many such hours in this comfortable room, which had been his father's favorite. His mother's, too.

The peace of the room enfolded him. How much better it was to be here, instead of clubs and theaters with the men people liked to call the Dark Duke's Dandies. Not a one of his London cronies was what a man could call a good friend. They simply amused him, and helped him pass the time.

He chose a book at random, something silly by Mrs. Radcliffe, and settled into a wing chair. He propped the foot of his sore leg on the grate as he prepared to read about the terrible dangers faced by the virtuous heroine in *The Mysteries of Udolpho.*

Soon Adrian was lulled into sleep by the warmth of the fire and the dull pit-pat of the rain on the window.

He drifted down into a dream, a memory. Of finding Elizabeth in that hot, filthy, dingy room. The efforts of her labor. The way she wailed and sobbed. The long, terrifying wait for the doctor and the dismissive look on the man's face when he entered the room. Then the doctor's fear when Adrian grabbed him by the throat and identified himself.

Too late. He was too late. The doctor was too late.

But there was someone else in the room. A woman. Quietly and competently swaddling the dying baby, cooing softly. Then, with infinite tenderness and patience, she turned to Elizabeth and wiped her feverish brow before looking up at him, with calm forgiveness and understanding.

It was Lady Hester, her smile like a balm on his tortured soul.

"Your Grace!"

Adrian awoke at once, to find Lady Hester shaking him gently, her face close to his, looking at him with worry and concern. Without thinking, he took her face between his two hands and pulled her toward him, kissing her deeply as if he could drink her in, like a dying man who finds water in the desert. For the briefest of moments she yielded, her lips soft and pliable against his.

How much he wanted her, he realized, the strength of his desire shocking him.

But only for a moment. She pulled back, staring at him with what could have been surprise or horror, her hand wiping her lips of his unclean touch—so different from his dream.

He cursed himself for a fool. Why, she wasn't even pretty! It had to be because of the lingering effects of his dream that he had kissed her. "What do you want?" he demanded, wearily leaning back in his chair and waiting for her to slap him, or denounce him, to start crying, or run from the room.

She did none of those things. Instead, she took a step back, watching him, the expression in her large and shining blue eyes changing from shocked surprise to puzzlement. "Why did you do that?" she asked softly.

"Why not?"

"Because it was not a gentlemanly thing to do."

"Given my reputation, this surprises you?"

"Yes, Your Grace," she answered calmly.

What a strange woman! Does she never react like other females of her age and rank? he thought. He smiled cynically. "My stepmother would tell you I am no gentleman."

Lady Hester nodded her head slowly, although not with agreement, he didn't think. It was more a pondering of his words with a gravity he found extremely disconcerting, considering what they were discussing. "You were very rude to Reverend Canon Smeech."

"He's a greedy hypocrite."

She didn't look at all shocked. "That is no excuse. He is a representative of the church."

"That excuses him, I suppose."

This plain woman in her simple, unadorned gown of gray regarded him so steadily that despite his efforts to assure himself that her opinion could not be important, he was quite nonplussed. "No, it does not," she said, "although I agree with your estimation. However, you can't expect him to change because you are discourteous to him. You would do better to use your influence to get him appointed to a position where he will have less opportunity to *be* a greedy hypocrite."

"Well, well, well," Adrian said, rising slowly. "You seem very confident of my influence." He went to the fireplace and leaned against the mantel.

"Your rank alone assures it."

"If not my personal attributes?"

"I'm sorry to have disturbed you, Your Grace. If you will excuse me—"

"I don't excuse you." Surprisingly, despite moments of discomfort, he was enjoying himself, perhaps because it had been years since anyone had responded to him with something other than blatant animosity or fawning flattery. "What are you doing here?" he repeated.

"I came for a book."

"And instead you found me. Why didn't you creep away?"

"You were...dreaming. I thought..."

"I take it I did not appear to be enjoying my dream?"

"No, Your Grace."

"As it happens, I was not. Grateful to be awakened, I kissed you. A moment of weakness."

"I gather you have many such moments," she noted dispassionately.

Adrian frowned slightly. "Where is my stepmother? Doesn't she require your constant attendance?"

"She fell asleep. That's why I came for a book. I'm sorry to have disturbed you, Your Grace."

Quite unexpectedly, he realized he didn't want her to go. "There is no need for you to rush off. I haven't had a decent conversation in three days. Sit here beside the fire and tell me how you come to be living in my house."

Hester hesitated, torn between the desire to flee and the desire to stay. She knew she should leave, especially after the duke's impetuous and impertinent kiss, which would seem to lend credence to the popular opinion of the duke as a notable lecher.

However, she felt more confident in his presence now, because of the look on his face when she had awakened him. He had not been the handsome, sardonic, provocative nobleman then. He had been as vulnerable as anyone she had ever seen, and his eyes had been full of anguish, as had the soft moans that had escaped his lips as she had entered the library, sounds that had compelled her to approach him.

As for the kiss, she had never known anything more unexpected and exciting in her entire existence. She had never been kissed by a young man, and the sensation had been every bit as wonderful as she had ever imagined. Nor had she ever felt so flattered. To think that the Dark Duke, known for his taste in women, had bestowed that mark of favor upon her, even if she had been returned to prosaic reality by his admission that he had kissed her because of "a moment of weakness."

Propriety demanded that she leave, but her own lonely heart told her to stay, and for once, Hester decided she would follow her heart. Surely they would be safe from discovery, for the duchess was a sound sleeper, and she had only just nodded off in the drawing room. They were in the usually empty library, and nobody even knew they were there.

She sat in a chair near the one upon which he had been sitting. "So, Lady Hester," he said in a low tone that set her heart beating rapidly, "what are you doing at Barroughby Hall?"

"Your stepmother corresponds with my mother, and when she heard the duchess was looking for a companion, she thought I would do," Hester replied matter-of-factly, trying to regard him with composure, reminding herself that he was a flirtatious man by nature, and his attention had nothing to do with her personally.

"What did *you* think?" He strolled behind her chair, and she wished she could see his face.

He sounded as if he truly cared, which created a sense of intimacy far more dangerous than his kiss had been. Nevertheless, she would remember who and what he was, and who or what she was. "Since I had no better prospects, I agreed."

"No better prospects?"

She didn't answer. He knew very well what she meant.

"But you cannot like it here," he said, as if she could not possibly disagree.

"This is a lovely estate. I enjoy the garden very much, and—" she smiled and gestured at the walls "—the library."

"My stepmother is not an easy woman."

"Perhaps she has mellowed during your absence."

The duke's response was a sniff of disdain.

"The duchess provided a change of scene," she replied honestly.

"I daresay," he said, continuing his stroll around the room. "I have seen your sisters in London, but not you, I don't believe."

"No doubt you didn't notice me."

"Are you often overlooked?"

"Yes, Your Grace."

"You don't sound very bitter," he remarked with a wry smile.

She shrugged her shoulders. "My sisters are beautiful. I am not. There is nothing I can do about that."

"I see."

She didn't think he did. No man as handsome as he would ever understand what it was like to be the ugly duckling in the family.

He moved back to the fireplace and continued to regard her with a scrutiny that grew increasingly unnerving. "I wonder what you really want, Lady Hester," he murmured.

"I told you, Your Grace. A book."

He smiled, a more genuine smile, she thought, than she had yet seen him bestow upon anyone, including Damaris Sackville-Cooper. "I meant from life."

"I hardly think, Your Grace—" she began to protest.

"Oh, I suspect you do a great deal of thinking," he interrupted. "Let me guess at the deepest desires of Lady Hester Pimblett."

She started to stand. "My lord, I—"

"First, attention."

She straightened her shoulders and frowned deeply. "Your Grace, I really must protest—"

"Second, excitement."

"If by that you mean the type of excitement you seem to crave, Your Grace, I assure you I can well do without!" Hester said sternly. "Since you are apparently only interested in making sport of me, I will take my leave of you, whether you excuse me or not!"

"I promise I shall stick to only the most mundane of subjects," he pleaded unexpectedly, and with a most beguiling smile. "The weather. My injury. The fungus on my horse's hooves. Whatever you wish, as long as you will stay a little longer."

Hester suddenly realized there was nothing about this man that was *not* seductive, whether it was his looks or his voice or the way he could make every word an invitation, every gesture intimate. "I believe I have stayed far too long as it is. Good afternoon, Your Grace."

She hurried to the door, then turned on the threshold and faced him with a mocking little smile of her own. "I shall tell your stepmother you are feeling better, as you most obviously are, and that you will surely join us for dinner."

When she was gone, Adrian stared at the fire and tried to tell himself that Hester Pimblett was nothing so very special. They were both unappreciated children—they had that one little thing in common.

Well, that and a kiss. And he would *not* come down to dinner, even if he was finding the thought of speaking with Lady Hester again very tempting indeed.

Chapter Five

"Hester, where on earth have you been?" the duchess demanded when Hester returned to the drawing room.

Hester, having never felt so frazzled before, dearly hoped her absence would not be remarked upon further. Her wish was granted as the older woman rose from the sofa with more alacrity than Hester had ever seen her demonstrate before and waved a letter as if it was a call to battle.

"I have just received the most exciting news!" the duchess declared unnecessarily.

Hester thought she had had quite enough excitement for one day; nevertheless, she put a happy smile on her face as she tried to calm down.

"Elliot is coming home tomorrow!" the older woman cried triumphantly. "My darling boy, here, tomorrow!" She paused in her exclamations, and a small frown creased her alabaster brow. "If Adrian will send the barouche to Barroughby. Oh, but he must. Just think of it, my own dear boy home at last!"

The duchess paused in her raptures. "You seem very dull this afternoon."

Hester was still considering the part of the duchess's declaration that had seemed rather odd. Why should the duke have to approve the order of a carriage? Was the duchess not in command of the estate? Had it not been left to her upon the fifth duke's death? She always acted as if it had, and spent money frequently and lavishly.

The present duke had referred to Barroughby Hall as "my house," but she had assumed he meant his family's house.

If this were not so, and he was in sole possession of the estate, why did he endure the company of a woman he so obviously disliked, and whom he could send away whenever he chose? *That* would be the response one would expect of a scoundrel.

"I am so happy for you," Hester said, attempting to sound delighted, and reflecting that if she wasn't careful, she would become as hypocritical as Canon Smeech. Nevertheless, she couldn't help mentally contrasting the reception of the news of this son's return with the way the duchess had received word that the duke was coming home. Still, one was a stepson, the other her own child. The duchess would not be alone in preferring the child of her body over that of a son by marriage.

"He writes from Dover to say he can hardly wait to get here!" the duchess exclaimed. She walked to the windows and gazed out at the drive, as if she expected to see Lord Elliot's carriage at that very moment. "He *was* ill, and only now recovered. I shall have to be a little cross with him for not telling his mama.''

"What is all the excitement?" the duke asked nonchalantly as he strolled into the drawing room. "Have we been robbed?"

Hester eyed the door with a view to escaping, but knew she was trapped as surely as any fly in amber. She would just have to forget about his kiss and try to maintain her composure.

"Of course not!" the duchess replied. "Elliot is coming home.''

"Is he, indeed?" the duke said, regarding his stepmother with a steely gaze such as Hester had never seen, at once cold and pleased. Thankfully, no one had ever directed a look like that at her, and she was reminded that the duke was also said to be a violent man. She had forgotten that, thinking of his other reputed qualities, but anyone witnessing him now could well believe the other, too, even if the expression was gone nearly as rapidly as it had appeared.

His initial response seemed to penetrate the duchess's unbridled happiness. "I hope you won't make things difficult, Adrian," she said anxiously.

"Not I," he said, sauntering toward the sofa and sitting. "I'm quite looking forward to seeing Elliot again."

The duchess visibly relaxed. "Good. Unlike *some* people, he tries not to fret his family."

The duke ignored her pointed remark. "What else does dear Elliot say?"

"He will be here tomorrow, if you will send the barouche to Barroughby."

The duke smiled. "Heaven forbid I should do anything to delay Elliot even more. Of course he may have the barouche."

"We must have an especially fine tea tomorrow, too," the duchess continued, and Hester noted that she did not thank her stepson for his acquiescence.

"Ah. So we should kill the fatted calf?" The duke glanced at Hester, a mocking expression on his face.

It was a peculiar comparison. Was *he* not the prodigal son, wasting his inheritance in indulgence and indolence?

"We really should have a party or a ball to welcome him back from Europe," the duchess said.

Hester could not suppress her displeasure at that thought. She had spent too many boring and disturbing hours sitting against the wall, watching other couples dance, to think of balls or other such entertainments with any pleasure.

She realized the duke was looking at her again, and she quickly smiled. "A ball will be quite delightful," she lied.

"It will be too much work," the duke said firmly. "And too expensive."

"I might have known you would begrudge us the pleasure," the duchess replied peevishly. "You seem to have no trouble finding money to fritter away on your own vile pursuits, but when I suggest a ball—something we should have done long ago, as befits our place in society!—you are suddenly lacking in funds!"

"Expense aside, if I were to agree, who would

make all the arrangements?'' the duke inquired calmly.

"Why, I would, of course!'' the duchess exclaimed.

"I'm sure,'' the duke muttered. He glanced at Hester with a knowing smile that seemed to suggest he knew who would do most of the work if such an event were approved. Further, as the blood rushed to her face, she felt he sympathized with her. "That a ball will require much effort I do not doubt,'' the duke commented to his stepmother. "However, if you are willing to take it on, I suppose I could find the funds.''

Hester addressed the duchess. "Your Grace, considering that the duke will surely be unable to dance, perhaps we should postpone consideration of a ball until a later date.''

The duchess looked at Hester as if she had proposed a beheading. "I understand my stepson is said to go hunting after drinking all night. Surely he will be able to manage a few short dances, for propriety's sake.''

"Why, stepmother!'' the duke said, placing his hand upon his heart. "I am so touched to think that you want me to attend. By all means, then, Lady Hester, we must and shall have a ball.''

The duchess shot Hester a black look, as if she had been the one to suggest the ball in the first place.

"I'm sure all the county will want to see Lord Elliot again,'' Hester said placatingly.

Which, she realized when the duchess smiled, was the best thing she could have said. "Indeed they will!'' the duchess exclaimed. "Everyone adores him!"

Not everyone, Hester thought. Not the duke.

"Hester, you must help with the invitations. Now, what day would be best?"

"Should we not consult with your son, Your Grace?" Hester asked softly. "He may be too fatigued from his journey to attend such a function for a few days."

"Lady Hester is forever concerned about other people's welfare, I see," the duke remarked.

Hester felt herself blushing again and told herself to stop at once.

"I didn't think of that," the duchess said. "Of course, you are quite right. And we should have him to ourselves for a little while." She laughed as gaily as a women twenty years younger. "He is so popular, he is sure to be invited riding and hunting every day, and he is so accommodating, he will never refuse."

"Elliot never says no," the duke confirmed before standing. "I believe I shall retire to my room. I find all this talk of balls fatiguing."

"As you wish," the duchess replied.

The duke bowed politely. "Your Grace. Lady Hester." He turned on his heel and strolled out of the room.

"Did anyone ever have such an infuriating relation?" the duchess demanded when he had closed the door. "Really!"

"It seems a pity you need his permission to hold a ball," Hester said nonchalantly.

"It is! Let this be a warning to you, Lady Hester,

to make sure that your husband leaves you your own money, and not in the control of his heir. It is most aggravating, I assure you."

Hester dutifully nodded as she digested the import of the duchess's words. The duke apparently had complete control of the estate and the money. Complain as the duchess might, it was undeniable that the duke was generous, for only last week the duchess had ordered several jewels reset, three new gowns, several hats and five pairs of shoes. The meals at Barroughby Hall were inevitably bountiful and excellent, the wine the finest and the servants well attired.

"Now, whom should we invite?" the duchess said happily, resuming her usual seat on the sofa. "I suppose we'll have to have Sir Douglas and his daughter."

"Yes, Your Grace," Hester replied, fetching some paper, pen and ink, ready to write down her orders. Then she realized that the duchess was giving her a rather peculiar look. "Is something the matter, Your Grace?"

"You seem a little flushed, Hester."

"The excitement of your son's return and the ball, Your Grace," Hester answered, hoping that would do for an explanation.

"Sir Douglas is not a very old man to have a grown-up daughter, is he?"

"No, Your Grace." Hester gazed at the duchess, wondering what the woman was getting at. She usually spoke of Sir Douglas with undisguised loathing; this morning she seemed disposed to be gracious. Perhaps the news of Elliot's return ensured good spirits. Hester certainly hoped they would last!

"He seems in good health, too."

"Yes, Your Grace."

The duchess said nothing further about Sir Douglas, except to put his name on the list, which soon grew to fifty families. By the time they were finished, it was the hour to dress for dinner.

The duke did not join them at the meal, and Hester told herself she was glad to be spared the anxiety his presence would no doubt have engendered.

"He is three hours late," the duke said, nodding at the antique German clock on the lacquered table in the drawing room. Hester followed his gesture and tried not to sigh. The barouche had been dispatched, and the weather was fine. Although it was difficult to know the exact hour Lord Elliot might arrive, she, too, was wearying of sitting in disappointed expectation in the drawing room. "We should have our tea," the duke continued.

Hester regarded him silently as he stood near the mantel, for he was not looking in her direction, but only at his stepmother. His attitude was one of graceful negligence, yet he was not fooling her. She could see the tension in his well-dressed body, the anger in his shoulders and the frustration in his frown.

"Nonsense!" the duchess exclaimed. "Elliot is only slightly delayed. Perhaps he had to rest awhile on the journey."

"No doubt," the duke remarked, and Hester knew by the tone of his deep, rich voice that he was still not impressed. "Nevertheless, we do not want Lady Hester to perish from hunger."

"I am quite all right," replied the lady in question, wishing she could retire from the room. She had absolutely no desire to be drawn into a family dispute.

"But I would be remiss as a host if I did not do my best to see to your needs."

There was something in his tone that commanded her attention, and when she looked at him, she wished she had not, for he was once more giving her a slight smile that seemed to promise that he could, and would, fulfill any and every wish she might make of a handsome man.

How many times had she sat at a ball and overheard this type of remark, and how many times had she silently replied, always mentally responding much more cleverly than the actual participants. But now she seemed to have been rendered incredibly stupid, for she could think of nothing at all to say except, "I assure you, I am in no hurry for tea."

The duchess stalked to the window, her body visibly shaking with what seemed a combination of agitation and excitement, setting the several blue silk flounces of her dress to dancing. "I see no harm in waiting a few more minutes."

"You must be sure to tell me if there is anything else I can provide, Lady Hester," the duke said with a decorous bow and twinkle of knowing laughter in his eye.

"As long as it's not too *expensive*," the duchess said snidely without turning around from her vantage point.

"I appreciate your generosity, Your Grace, but I am content," Hester said to the duke.

"You are a rare human being, then, to be content."

"You make contentment sound boring, Your Grace."

"Isn't it?"

"To one of your temperament, perhaps, but it suits me well enough."

The duke raised his black brows. "I think you do not approve of my temperament."

"Since I hardly know you, I am not in a position to judge."

"Then you *are* a rare woman, for most people have no compunction about judging me, whether they know me or not."

"What are you two prattling on about?" the duchess demanded, glancing at them over her shoulder and reminding Hester that there was another set of ears in the room, and another mind to interpret their banter.

Which was very unfortunate, for Hester was just beginning to enjoy herself. She felt as if she was being offered a glimpse into the duke's character, and she wanted to know more.

"You did send the best horses, did you not, Adrian?" the duchess demanded.

"My finest pair," the duke replied. "I fear I am responsible for his tardiness," he continued sorrowfully, "for I sent my finest carriage, best horses and a large sum of money to cover any expenses he might have incurred at the inn."

"There's the coach! I see it!" the duchess cried suddenly, excitement and relief in her voice as she stared down the long, winding drive leading to Barroughby Hall. "I can see Elliot! Come, Hester, look!"

Hester did as she was bid, and watched the black barouche with the ducal arms on the door, drawn by equally black horses, sweep up the drive. Inside was a tall young man wearing a hat; more than that, only a mother's eye could discern.

The duchess watched until the carriage disappeared behind the stable wall, then turned triumphantly to her companions. "There, Adrian. I *told* you we should wait tea for him. He is sure to be hungry, the poor boy, after his tiring journey." The duchess lifted her bounteous silk skirt and hurried from the room, no doubt intending to meet her darling boy at the front door.

Hester realized she was alone again with the duke, just as she noticed that the duchess had left her shawl. Mindful of the crisp autumn air and her own racing heart, she quickly decided to take it to her. She hurried to the sofa and picked up the soft wool shawl.

The duke raised one eyebrow inquiringly as he watched her. "You seem in a very great rush to meet the epitome of virtue," he remarked, drawing a cheroot from the breast pocket of his jacket.

"I have never met a paragon before," she retorted.

"If you do not take care, Lady Hester, I could be jealous."

His mocking smile told her that he was merely teasing her, so she met his gaze boldly. "If he is virtuous, so you should be."

Adrian's eyes widened. It seemed there was no end to the surprises Lady Hester could provide.

She faced him now as one equal to another, again a trait that set her apart from every other woman he had ever known. Some, the vain ones, had believed themselves superior to him; others, the hopeful ones, had an almost pathetically needy manner. "Should you not take that to the duchess?" he said at last. "We wouldn't want her to catch a chill, would we?"

"No, Your Grace, *we* wouldn't."

He watched her go, wondering at the emphasis in her final words to him. We. We, as in you and I together here? We against the others?

Not alone anymore.

Tempting thought. Tempting, foolish thought.

He lit his cheroot and sauntered after her, deciding his stomach could bear witnessing the tender reunion of mother and son, if only to see how the surprising Lady Hester would react to his half brother, the fair and charming Lord Elliot Fitzwalter.

Chapter Six

By the time Adrian reached the foyer, a pair of footmen were already carrying in a trunk, maneuvering the bulky piece of baggage up the wide stairs. Outside, three more servants stood ready to receive smaller pieces of luggage at the direction of Elliot's Italian valet.

Elliot, all five foot nine of him, looking healthy as a horse, his hair lighter from the sun of southern Italy, his eyes bluer in his tanned face, and sporting the latest in European fashion, met his mother at the door, smiling blandly as she embraced him.

"Elliot, my dear boy, how are you?" the duchess cried.

"I am much better, Mama, now that I am here with you."

The duchess hugged him again, but his attention had already wandered toward his half brother. "I see you have other company, Mama."

The duchess drew back. "Yes."

"Elliot, how good of you to arrive at last," the duke said in greeting.

Lord Elliot made a crooked little smile, one side of his mouth rising slightly higher than the other, and continued to survey the foyer. His gaze came to rest on Hester, who stood silently at the bottom of the stairs, the shawl draped over her slender arm, waiting patiently, more like a good servant than a woman of rank.

The duchess had some right to be vain of her son, Hester thought. He was tall, attractive, fair and blue eyed, his manner pleasing, his posture erect and his movements athletic. His lopsided smile added to his charm and was not nearly so sardonic as his brother's. They were nearly the same height, and their voices remarkably similar in their smooth, deep tones. She also realized that for a man who had been too ill to travel, he looked extremely healthy. Indeed, it was interesting to contrast the appearance of Lord Elliot with that of the duke upon his arrival.

"And who is this delightful creature?" Lord Elliot asked, moving toward her.

When he took Hester's hand in his, she was acutely aware of two things. The first was that the duke was watching, the second was that despite Lord Elliot's manner and good looks, she was not pleased by his touch, although there was nothing obvious to make her feel that way.

Except, perhaps, a certain speculation in his expression. The type of speculation she could imagine a man giving the inmates of a house of ill repute before selecting one. The comparison leapt into her mind so swiftly and so strongly, she could think of nothing to say.

Then she chided herself for a fool. Perhaps her mind had been unduly influenced by the presence and reputation of the Dark Duke. "Good afternoon, my lord," she said as she curtsied.

The duchess hurried forward and clasped her son's arm in her long, clawlike fingers. "This is Lady Hester Pimblett. Hester, my son, Lord Elliot Fitzwalter."

"I am charmed, Lady Hester," Lord Elliot said. He glanced at his mother. "You did not tell me she was so lovely." He pressed his lips to the back of Hester's hand and smiled at her.

Hester fought to keep her displeasure from her face. What kind of foolish girl did he think she was not to realize that his overt flattery was completely outrageous? It was better to have a man explain his kiss as a moment of weakness than to be subjected to such empty praise.

She gently pulled her hand from his grasp and moved to give the shawl to the duchess.

"We were beginning to give you up," the duke said, walking closer.

"I was unavoidably detained," Lord Elliot said, facing his sibling.

"I thought so," the duke replied sarcastically.

How could any man's voice be so warm one moment, and then so chillingly frigid another? Hester wondered as she looked at him. And how was it that a smile could look so much like a threat?

Surprisingly, Lord Elliot Fitzwalter seemed quite immune to the hostility in his brother's eyes. "When I stopped in London, I heard you got hurt in a fight."

"Yes."

"Too bad."

"I'll tell you all about it later." The duke took one step toward his sibling. "When we are alone."

Lord Elliot's gaze faltered for the briefest of moments before the duchess took her son's arm and drew him toward the drawing room. "Come, Elliot, we've been waiting tea for you."

He smiled at her. "I knew I could count on you, Mama. I'm famished."

"Come along, Lady Hester," the duchess commanded.

Hester took a few steps after the retreating pair, then regarded the duke, who had not moved. "Your Grace?"

"I have lost my appetite," he muttered before striding out the front door, pushing past the footmen.

His brusque discourtesy was quite a contrast to the charming manner of his brother, Hester thought as she followed Lord Elliot and his mother into the drawing room, and her curiosity as to the cause of the animosity in the family grew, for it was surely based upon more than a difference in their treatment by the duchess.

"I must say, Mama, that I am surprised to find Adrian here," Elliot said as he guided his mother to her customary seat on the sofa.

"He came to recuperate," she said. "Another nasty episode in his vice-ridden life, I fear. But let us not ruin our talk with tales of Adrian's doings. How was Italy?"

"Sunny, hot, delightful," Elliot replied with a smile as warm as the Italian sun. "I am only sorry I wasn't here to be with you through another trying time. When I heard about Adrian, I was in London on my way home. I thought he was quite badly hurt.''

"Not at all,'' the duchess sneered, ''as you could see for yourself.''

"I am glad of that,'' Lord Elliot said, smiling at Hester, who hovered uncertainly in the doorway. ''Do take a seat, Lady Hester. Ah, the tea!''

Hester made way for the housekeeper and a maid-servant as they set out the tea things on the large round table before the fireplace. There was a host of delicacies and small sandwiches, the light meal far more elaborate than any tea Hester had partaken of at Barroughby Hall before.

Hester sat on the farthest chair, nearest the window. When she glanced outside, she caught sight of the duke walking down the garden path, his dark head bowed in thought, and he was limping. Not badly hurt, perhaps, but more so than he let on, she suspected.

Why hide the true extent of his injuries? To seem impervious to the duchess's slights and angry words? Could it be that he was affected by his stepmother's opinions more than he let on, just as he affected *her* more than she dared to show?

Hester turned her attention back to the duchess and her favored son as the servants finished their work and left the room.

"We are planning a ball for you, Elliot,'' the duchess announced as she poured the tea gracefully.

A bored and peevish look that had more of the mother than the brother in it crossed Lord Elliot's face. "That's delightful, Mama," he said. His words were filled with an enthusiasm that was a distinct contrast to his expression moments before. "Lady Hester, you must be sure to save at least two dances for me," he continued.

"I shall be happy to," Hester said, not entirely lying. It would be a new experience for her to stand up with so handsome a young man, and although she felt something was amiss with him, she was willing to dismiss her first impression as faulty, influenced by the tension in the household.

Then she reminded herself that Lord Elliot hadn't seen Damaris Sackville-Cooper yet. It would be better not to expect to be asked to dance except out of duty.

"I suppose Adrian will be gone by then," Lord Elliot said lightly.

It had not occurred to Hester that the duke would *not* be at the ball, and she found this idea rather distressing. Why should she be upset, she chastised herself, for surely he would not dance with her anyway. Indeed, with his leg injured, he probably wouldn't dance at all.

"I have no idea how long Adrian intends to stay," the duchess said with an aggrieved sniff. "You know he never deigns to inform me of his comings and goings." The duchess picked up a sandwich, then turned her stony gaze onto Hester. "If you have finished your tea, Lady Hester, you may leave us."

Hester had barely touched her beverage, but she knew a dismissal when she heard it.

"We shall see you at dinner, Lady Hester," the duchess said.

Lord Elliot rose and bowed, and gave her the merest hint of a smile and an apologetic shrug. "At dinner, Lady Hester."

Hester tied her bonnet firmly on her head and wrapped her thick woolen shawl about her shoulders. The day was fine, although cool, and she needed some fresh air. The atmosphere inside Barroughby Hall had grown stifling, with the increase of tension Lord Elliot's arrival had occasioned.

She hurried down the back stairs and headed for the stables. She chose that destination for two reasons: the first was that she liked to go to the stables, which were always warm, and the smell of the straw reminded her of the barn at home where she used to seek refuge when her sisters were quarreling. The second was that they were in the opposite direction to the way the duke had taken.

The grooms, heading for the servants' hall after a day's work, nodded silently at her as she entered the dimly lit brick building, leaving her in blissful solitude. This was not her first visit here, and she knew most of the animals. As she walked slowly down the center aisle she took note of the duke's fine carriage horses and his saddle horse, which stamped impatiently. He was not getting enough exercise, she suspected. "But I would not trust you any more than I would your master," she murmured as she paused to admire the animal.

"Which is to say, not at all, I warrant."

Hester whirled around to see the duke standing in the middle of the aisle, his weight leaning on his uninjured leg, his arms crossed against his broad chest, his face barely illuminated in the weak light so that she could not clearly see the expression in his eyes.

He walked slowly toward her. "Come now, Lady Hester, don't be demure. You are an intelligent woman, so I do not expect you to trust me."

"After yesterday, you can be certain of that," she snapped, her surprise making her sharp when she would have preferred to sound nonchalant. "Good day, Your Grace." She tried to walk boldly past him, but he stepped into her way.

"There is no need to run off. I promise you I will keep my distance."

"I am not afraid of you."

"My dear young woman, are you telling me I am losing my ability to inspire terror and awe in the female breast?"

She eyed him warily, wishing she could see more of his face in the dimness. "It would be better if you tried to inspire admiration and respect."

He put his hand on his chest in a gesture of surprise. "Do you tell me I do *not* inspire admiration and respect? Alas, fair maiden, say it is not so, or else I have to drown my sorrows in yonder trough."

"A good dunking might help," Hester observed coolly, trying her best not to smile at his melodramatic words.

"But then my hair would cling damply to my fevered brow, and I assure you, Lady Hester, that will certainly not inspire admiration."

"I meant admiration for your character, not your looks."

He staggered back a few steps, one hand over his eyes. "Woe is me! She wants me to be known for my character—a hopeless business." He put down his hand. "I fear it is far too late to inspire any such sentiments," he said, and this time she thought she detected a serious note in his tone.

"It is never too late," she said.

"What can you know about such things?" he asked softly, his voice suddenly intimate. "You are a blameless, respectable young woman."

Hester's face flushed and her heart started to beat quickly. "I...I must go, Your Grace."

He did not get out of her way. "I suppose dear Elliot inspires admiration and respect. Most women seem to think so."

Hester wasn't sure how to respond. She didn't want to be dragged into the family conflict. "I haven't known him long enough to say," she finally replied.

"But which way tend your thoughts?" he pressed.

"I cannot say, at this particular moment."

"So, you are telling me that you are not swift to cast your judgment?"

"I should hope that I would never judge in haste, in case I was led astray by first impressions."

He came a little closer. "So, it is possible that although my reputation is well-known, you were not predisposed to dislike me?"

She nodded slowly.

He chuckled quietly. "A most rare woman who gives no credence to gossip. Pray tell, Lady Hester, what was your first impression of me?"

"I thought you held your temper remarkably well."

"What, no remarks on my good looks or sardonic wit?"

"If you ask me questions only to receive compliments, I believe you are wasting my time, and yours."

"Stay a moment!" he said as she once again prepared to walk past him. "You don't trust me, do you?" he challenged.

"While I do not believe unreservedly in gossip, I do hear it, Your Grace, and I do not think it would be wise to trust you, given what I have heard."

"Ah!"

"You asked me, so I told you, Your Grace."

"Oh, I am not offended. Indeed, I applaud your rational wisdom, Lady Hester. There is just one thing I wish to say, and then you may go, as seems to be your heart's desire. I hope you do not trust my dear brother, either."

"Why should I not?" She regarded the duke steadily, trying to read the inscrutable expression on his face.

"He is a man, after all, and a damned attractive one. You might forget yourself."

"If I do not *forget myself* in the presence of the infamously handsome and seductive Dark Duke, why would I do so for your brother?"

"Half brother," he specified.

"Very well. Half brother."

"So perhaps only half as dangerous—but dangerous still."

"Do you mean to keep me here until it is time to dress for dinner?" she demanded, quite fed up with his banter and, deep down, truly confused. He sounded so sincere, she could believe he was truly concerned for her well-being, something that touched her heart.

He laughed softly. "Very well, run away, my dear. As long as you promise me you will not trust either one of us."

She forced herself to meet his bold gaze steadfastly. "*He* has not kissed me upon the lips, Your Grace, or made any improper advances," she said, as much to remind herself of that fact as him. "If I do not make my decisions based on gossip, I will not make them based on what you tell me, either."

"I see." He stepped back, out of her way, and she finally saw his face completely.

She wished she hadn't, for there was a hard and cold expression upon it that chilled her. "If anything happens, don't say you were not warned," he said.

"Such as?" she inquired.

"I am not the only Fitzwalter guilty of breaking hearts," Adrian replied lightly, retreating from his serious manner. He had given her fair warning, and now it was up to her to heed it, or not.

"I do not believe myself to be in any great danger," she replied just as lightly. "Now I really must beg to be excused," she said. Then she hurried past him without so much as a backward glance.

Which was just as well, Adrian told himself. He was beginning to enjoy being alone with her far too much. She was better off avoiding him, as long as she avoided Elliot, too.

He softly and eloquently cursed as he walked toward his stallion. "I tried, Drake," he murmured, stroking the beast's muscular neck. "I tried."

Lady Hester had no conception of her danger. A woman like her, lonely, plain, past the first blush of youth—she would be easy prey for Elliot's elegant allure. Unfortunately, Adrian feared his warning had fallen on deaf ears, for despite her words about not making judgments, surely she would never believe anything the Duke of Barroughby had to say, and Elliot's fatal charm could sway the most virtuous of women.

The narrow door at the other end of the stable opened, and Jenkins came tottering in as fast as his ancient legs could carry him. The sound of his wheezing breath was too loud in the silence, and Adrian faced the old retainer with concern. Perhaps it was time he pensioned Jenkins off, whether the duchess agreed or not, or whether Jenkins agreed or not.

"Your Grace!" the elderly man panted.

"What is it?" Adrian asked loudly. "What is the matter?"

"Young Bolby's come by, all in a state, Your Grace. It's his father. He's not expected to last the night."

Adrian swallowed hard, then hurried to grab a saddle.

"Should I fetch the groom?"

"No. I shall do this myself."

"You're not dressed for riding, Your Grace."

"I don't give a damn. Where is young Bolby?"

"Already left for home, Your Grace. He said he wouldn't stay to see you, but he hoped you'd come."

"Convey my regrets to the duchess and the others," he said as he tightened the cinch. "I will not be dining at home tonight."

Chapter Seven

Elliot whistled a tuneless air as he watched the stable doors from his bedroom. Interesting what unexpected things one could see from this vantage point, he mused, such as Lady Hester entering the stables, and Adrian going there a short time later.

While his valet continued to unpack his baggage in the adjoining dressing room, Elliot drew out his watch and checked the time. He made it fifteen minutes since Adrian had entered the stables.

Before he could close his watch, Lady Hester came hurrying out as if she were being chased.

What to make of this?

The first and most obvious conclusion was that Adrian had gone to the stables for a private meeting of some kind with Lady Hester. For what purpose?

It could hardly be business, for Adrian jealously oversaw the estate and the family purse. He would not need or want any input from his stepmother's companion.

They could be discussing the duchess, but that seemed far from likely. What was there to talk about, after all? Adrian had no liking for the woman who had supplanted his own, apparently saintly, mother, especially after she provided his father with someone else to love.

There then remained but one reason Adrian would wish a private conference with a young woman. He was either in the process of, or had already succeeded in, seducing her—an astonishing concept, given Lady Hester's lack of attractive features.

Perhaps it was simply that there were no other suitable females at hand. Indeed, his mother seemed to have picked the servants with an eye to the least attractive.

Or maybe it was that Lady Hester possessed no *obvious* charms. The fact that Adrian apparently found her attractive enough to pursue at all was not something to be dismissed lightly.

Elliot recalled the other Pimblett girls, for Helena had been the belle of her debut season. But she was a coldhearted wench, and the youngest sister a fool. This Hester he recalled not at all. She would have made her debut when he was involved with the Spanish dancer, so it was no wonder he didn't remember such a lackluster creature. Consuela had been exciting and volatile and completely time-consuming.

Right now she was surely duping some young fool into thinking he was madly in love with her, wherever she was. He had been wise to get rid of her when he did, before she took him for even more money.

Adrian always had interesting taste in women. He had been the one to discover Elizabeth Howell, who had not been particularly striking until Elliot had provided her with finer clothes and a hairdresser.

Such ruminations were fruitless and a waste of time. Far better to think about the situation developing here.

He recalled that Lady Hester did have lovely hands, delicate and long fingered. He liked women with such hands, so much better for stroking.

Perhaps Adrian had discovered some untapped passion in the seemingly reserved young woman. And if Lady Hester was already a soiled dove, it would take considerably less effort for *him* to woo his way into her bed.

All in all, this visit with his doting mama might prove far more interesting than he had anticipated.

"Guiseppe, I believe I shall have a little chat with Lady Hester," Elliot said, and as he exited his bedroom, his whistle became very jaunty indeed.

"Oh, Lord Elliot!" Hester gasped, halting abruptly on the staircase at the sight of the duke's sibling coming toward her, his crooked smile on his handsome face. "Isn't it time to dress for dinner?" she asked, trying not to sound too anxious to be on her way, for that might call for an explanation on her part, or speculation on his.

"I thought I had time for a turn about the garden," he said. "Perhaps you would do me the honor of accompanying me?"

The duke's reminder not to trust his half brother came to her mind, and yet, as she regarded Lord Elliot, smiling so charmingly, his expression gently inquiring, she thought it no great danger to agree. Besides, she reasoned, Lord Elliot might cast some additional and welcome light onto his brother's mysterious personality. "I would be delighted," she replied.

He held out his arm for her, and she placed her hand lightly upon it. He covered it with his other one, and she was surprised at how distasteful this innocuous gesture was. It was too intimate, considering their brief acquaintance, and too possessive, as well.

"Mama seems most delighted with your company," Lord Elliot said, leading her toward the large front door.

"I am pleased to be of service to the duchess."

"I hope you will be able to remain here at Barroughby Hall for quite some time," he remarked. "Mama is more pleasant when she has a patient companion."

"She cares for you a good deal," Lady Hester noted, realizing he was headed toward the tall shrubbery. "There are some beautiful flowers this way," she said, nodding toward the formal flower beds.

The nobleman immediately began to walk in the direction she had indicated. "I'm surprised your family can spare you."

"My parents are traveling in Europe at present, and my two sisters are recently wed. They would not care to have me underfoot."

"Their loss is our gain," he remarked, "especially when Adrian is here. Mama gets so agitated."

"She is happy now that you have come. It is a pity you were delayed."

He glanced at her sharply, and Hester thought he must have understood that she thought him remiss, for he immediately said, in a low and rueful voice, "I should have written more about my affliction. Unfortunately, I did not think Mama would care to hear that while in Europe, her dear boy had developed a hopeless passion for a young Frenchwoman of great rank and fortune. The woman in question was quite plain in her renunciation of my attention, and I was too upset to present a cheerful countenance to Mama."

"How thoughtful of you, my lord," Hester replied, wondering if this was true. Somehow, she couldn't reconcile this man beside her with a broken heart. Even as he spoke of this excuse, there was a levity in his tone that belied his words.

"You know Mama by now. She would never believe that any woman would reject me, so I made up the story about being ill."

"You lied to spare her feelings?"

"Please do not be censorious, Lady Hester. I do confess I wanted to spare myself having to listen to her response, but surely that is not a crime!" He stopped and turned toward her, smiling with all the sly sweetness of a youngster cajoling an adult. "Is it?"

He was not a youngster, and Hester couldn't help feeling it was wrong to lie to his mother. The duchess had been worried about him, thinking him sick and far from home. "I think it was inconsiderate of you to frighten the duchess by saying you were ill."

"You are a hard-hearted creature!" her companion

exclaimed with a chuckle. "Quite impervious to my appeals, merciless lady."

Hester did not appreciate hearing herself so described, even in jest. "I believe you'll find the roses grew very well this year," she said, turning back to walk farther down the path.

Lord Elliot stopped again, and this time he raised her hand to his lips. "You are a sweet young woman, and I am sorry for my sins," he said softly, looking at her with a pleading expression in his shining blue eyes.

Which would have been most effective if Hester had detected any sincerity there. However, she did not, even as she blushed at his action. "I believe we should return to the house, my lord."

"As you wish, Lady Hester." They walked some way in silence, until he halted and faced her abruptly. "What do you know about the duke?"

Has he been reading my mind? she thought wildly. "I never met him before he arrived here," she answered.

"Have you not heard of him?"

"Yes, a few times."

"You know what people say about him, and his disgraceful conduct?"

"I have heard the gossip, Lord Elliot."

"Sadly, he does not act any different here than he does in Town. The good citizens of Barroughby could tell you many tales of his dissolute ways."

Hester recalled Damaris Sackville-Cooper's comment about Stamford Street, and remained silent.

"What knowledge have you of his latest disgrace?" he asked intently.

"Very little. All I know for certain is that he dueled, and was wounded. I believe a young woman was involved."

"That should be enough to warn you to beware of him."

Hester looked at the warm, masculine hand still covering her own. Strange how everyone wanted to warn her. So much apparent protectiveness—and from people she barely knew.

The fact that the brothers apparently disliked each other could be enough to account for their cautions.

Who to believe?

If she were to listen to rumor and gossip, it was the Dark Duke she should beware of, and didn't that surprising kiss in the library provide evidence of his lustful proclivities? In contrast, Lord Elliot Fitzwalter had so far behaved as a gentleman should, if in a somewhat overly friendly manner.

Her heart told her to trust neither of them. Yet. "Shall we go inside, my lord?" she said. "I am getting cold."

"Pa! Pa!" the elderly Mrs. Bolby said, gently shaking her slumbering husband. "Pa, look here! It's the young duke himself, come to see you!"

Adrian walked farther inside the two-room cottage, smiling at the man who had taught him to hunt, taken him on long rambles about the estate and listened to him complain, always silently sympathetic. "How are you, Bolby?" he asked softly.

"Sit here, Your Grace, please," Mrs. Bolby said, offering him her stool, which had been drawn up beside the bed that had been moved into the main room close to the hearth.

"Oh, no—"

"Please!"

With a nod of agreement, Adrian took the proffered stool and reached out to take Bolby's gnarled hand.

The old man opened his eyes. "It's you, is it?" he demanded in a whisper, but with a mischievous twinkle in his eye that made Adrian believe it would take more than death to subdue Bolby. "It's me," he responded, in their customary greeting.

"I'm a-dyin', young master," Bolby remarked.

His wife began sobbing from her place in the corner, and Bolby rolled his eyes. "Poor old girl, she can't get used to the notion. But when the time's come, the time's come."

Adrian nodded. "So you always said. I daresay the foxes are having a party."

Bolby chuckled silently, until he had to stop to catch his breath. "I taught young Tom here all I know, but he's a slow study, Your Grace." He winked at his son, standing in the other corner, tall and thin and silent, but Adrian saw the young man's dry-eyed anguish. "Not like you, Your Grace."

"I daresay he's too kindhearted."

"Who was it bawled like a baby when he found he'd killed a fawn?"

Adrian shrugged, but his grip on the old man's hand tightened.

"Ah, those were good days, young master. Do you

remember the time you got caught in the leg hold and I said you'd have to stay there until you chewed your leg off?''

''I shouldn't have ignored your warning.''

''God, yes, I was some mad! You took it with good humor, though.''

''I knew if I waited long enough, you'd forgive me and come back.''

''Still, not many boys would sit and wait in the dark, and be humming a merry tune to hisself.''

''Probably other boys would have cut the line.''

''And ruin a perfectly good snare!''

The old man's breathing was growing labored, and Adrian began to think he had stayed long enough. He started to rise, but Mrs. Bolby moved from her place and gestured for him to sit again. ''You've cheered us all up considerable, Your Grace,'' she said between sobs. ''Stop a bit yet.''

Bolby regarded him steadily, a serious expression on his wrinkled face. ''I've got something to ask of you, Your Grace,'' he said slowly.

''I'll be happy to oblige,'' Adrian replied. What was one more deathbed promise? Surely Bolby's request, whatever it was, would not cause him more trouble or money than the first.

Bolby struggled to sit up, and leaned closer to Adrian. ''The wife's a worryin' about where she'll go,'' he whispered. ''Tom's a good son. He's gettin' married in the spring, and he says she can come live with them, but I say two women in the house are trouble.''

''I'll see to it that your wife will not want,'' Adrian

said, understanding what Bolby was asking. "You have my promise."

"Ah!" Bolby sank back onto the pillow. "I knew I could count on you," he murmured.

John Mapleton, walking home after being called to attend to a man who had fallen from his horse and cut his head, turned down a narrow, cobblestoned street. Along one side of the way was the stone wall of a warehouse; on the other, doors led into run-down row houses that had small windows and shabby curtains. He quickened his pace, for this was not the place for a lone man to be after midnight.

Another figure entered the street from the other end, a tall man walking toward him, if walking was the proper term. The man wasn't quite staggering, but moving in a way that was somehow in between a walk and a lurch. However it could be described, Mapleton recognized the effects of too many drinks, just as he regretfully thought he recognized the man, who should not have been wandering about in such a condition and in a public place. "Your Grace?" he called softly.

The man stopped. "Who the devil wants to know?" he demanded.

Although the man's voice was very like the duke's, Mapleton knew Adrian Fitzwalter well enough to realize that it was not Adrian, but his half brother standing drunk in the middle of the street. Mapleton hurried toward him. "You should go home, Lord Elliot," he whispered sternly.

"Ah, is that you, Mr. Mapleton?" Lord Elliot replied. "How kind of you to take such an interest in my welfare."

"You are making a spectacle of yourself."

"I am? Who can see?" Lord Fitzwalter's broad gesture encompassed the narrow way. "Besides, they'll just assume it's the duke, up to his old tricks."

"I know. That's all the more reason for you to return to Barroughby Hall."

"That boring old pile of stone," Lord Elliot muttered. He turned toward the stone wall and opened his trousers. "God, that feels better."

Mapleton frowned in disgust. "How vulgar!"

"You shouldn't stand downhill," Lord Elliot remarked sarcastically. He chortled nastily when Mapleton jumped away from the trickle moving down the gutter. "You don't look so pleased to see me," the young man observed. "Sorry I'm not dead, no doubt."

"To say I am surprised you are not would be more accurate," the surgeon replied quietly. "I see you continue to drink to excess. Have you listened to my advice and given up opium, at least?"

"It gave up on me," Lord Fitzwalter remarked calmly and with absolutely no contrition as he buttoned his trousers. "Too expensive."

Mapleton made no attempt to hide his dislike of the young man. He knew full well what had happened as the fifth duke lay dying, so he understood more than any other person what the situation was between Adrian and his half brother. He would gladly have told the whole world, had Adrian not made him promise to be silent.

"What are you waiting for?" Lord Elliot asked, sauntering toward him. "You'll get no business from me."

"That also surprises me, given your predilection for whores."

"Trying to insult me, Mapleton?" Lord Elliot halted in front of him, a sneering smile on his handsome face, a lock of fair hair hanging over one bloodshot blue eye. "You'll have to come up with something better than that. And you'll be happy to know, for the martyr Adrian's sake, that while I may like my fun, I'm not stupid."

"For Adrian's sake, I am glad to hear it," Mapleton replied.

"I'm not the only one you should be warning about certain maladies, either," Lord Elliot continued. "It is not *I* who is on such friendly terms with Sally Newcombe and her girls. If you're so concerned about Adrian, maybe you should ask to examine him. I know how you enjoy such things."

The implication of his statement was so apparent, so rude and so shocking, the doctor was rendered speechless as Lord Elliot Fitzwalter, swaying slightly, continued on his way.

Chapter Eight

Being an earlier riser than the duchess, Hester usually ate breakfast alone. This morning appeared to be no different, for there was no one else in the small dining room when she arrived.

She paused for a moment to admire the effect of the early-morning sunlight shining through the lace curtains, making shadows dance on the delicately flowered wallpaper. The cherrywood furnishings were polished to a high gloss, and several prints of flowers and fruit adorned the walls. The woodwork had been painted white, and the draperies were of a soft white muslin over lace panels.

Hester liked this room very much. It was much cozier than the large dining room, although not so well situated in terms of view. When she had expressed her admiration, Jenkins had told her it had been one of the late duchess's favorite rooms, too, and he had remarked that the new duchess had not troubled herself to redecorate it since she had arrived, something he seemed rather pleased about.

Now, as she enjoyed the sunlight and the fine

breakfast, Hester turned her thoughts to the rest of the inhabitants of Barroughby Hall.

The duchess was not hard to comprehend. She was a vain, selfish woman who doted excessively on her son, and who didn't approve of her stepson. All Hester had to do to keep from upsetting her was to do as she was told, and keep quiet—nothing particularly difficult.

It was in considering the duke and his half brother that the confusion arose.

Lord Elliot Fitzwalter had been charming and attentive last night during dinner. He had talked to her often, whenever the duchess could spare his attention, in a way that almost made Hester forget her discomfort in his presence while they were in the garden together.

Afterward, when a somewhat flushed Lord Elliot had finally joined them in the drawing room, he had claimed that the brandy had been stronger than he was used to, and had proceeded to amuse them with stories of his travels.

As for the Dark Duke, Hester was as puzzled by him as ever. Their meeting in the stable had been disturbing, because of what he had said and because of the excitement that being alone with him inspired, try as she might to deny it.

The stories she had heard painted him as a debauched Lothario, a man given solely to his own pleasures.

Yet if that were so, why would he generously support a woman who made no secret of her dislike for

him? No doubt he paid Lord Elliot's way, too—
hardly the actions of a selfish cad.

He had kissed her, and come upon her when she
was alone in the stable, but she had never felt in any
peril. Surprised, embarrassed, excited—not endan-
gered or entrapped. In fact, in the stable she had enjoyed his melodramatic antics very much.

The duke intrigued her, too, by his shifts from
drollery to intensity with unexpected speed. And if
she took his warning seriously, she could easily be
influenced by the notion that such a man cared about
her.

But no matter how she felt at present, she had heard
the gossip about the Dark Duke's deeds, and she
couldn't forget it.

When he had not appeared at dinner, his relatives
had not seemed surprised, until Jenkins had announced that the duke had gone to see someone
named "Old Bolby." This knowledge had not
pleased the duchess, and Hester had decided that by
asking who Old Bolby was, she would only make
matters worse. Nevertheless, she had spent several
minutes in bed last night racking her brain for any
reference to "Old Bolby" she might have heard before, to no avail.

"What are you doing here?"

The duke's harsh words interrupted her reverie and
she stared at him as he limped into the room, his face
even more ashen than it had been when he had first
arrived. He wore what he'd had on in the stables,
there was mud on his boots and his hair was so disheveled, he looked quite wild.

"Is that coffee hot?" he demanded, reaching for her cup and downing the contents in a gulp before she could respond. He pulled out a chair and winced as he sat down.

"Are you ill, Your Grace?" she inquired gently.

"I am not ill."

"Is your leg troubling you?"

He regarded her with a tired and cynical expression. "While I appreciate your concern, Lady Hester, I would prefer some peace and quiet."

Hester turned her gaze back onto her plate. If he was going to be rude, she would remain silent. As for his state, no doubt he had been drinking too much. Maybe he had even fallen off his horse. Given his incivility, she didn't pity him.

"Jenkins!" the duke bellowed.

"I want some eggs and bacon," he ordered when Jenkins appeared. "And more coffee, for me and Lady Hester, if you please."

"Oatmeal at once, Your Grace."

"I said eggs and bacon," the duke repeated impatiently.

"That's not as filling as oatmeal, Your Grace," Jenkins murmured, not meeting his lordship's petulant gaze.

"*I want eggs and bacon!*" the duke repeated, and this time Jenkins nodded.

When the door closed behind the butler, the duke sighed heavily, leaned back in his chair and closed his eyes. "I'm going to have to speak to that man," he muttered. "Oatmeal indeed! I'd rather eat mud."

He opened one eye and regarded Hester. "Do you think oatmeal more wholesome?" he demanded.

"I believe it does not matter a whit what I think, Your Grace," Hester replied. "You will eat what you want."

The duke barked a laugh. "You read my character aright in that, anyway," he acknowledged. "You might also have realized by now that sometimes Jenkins hears only what he wants to hear." He sat up straighter and looked at her. "No doubt you suppose I have been out all night carousing?"

"I have no idea where you have been, or what you have been doing. It is none of my concern."

"Very prettily said, my lady. Noncommittal to perfection—but the effect is somewhat weakened by the frown of your lips and the censure in your eyes." The butler returned with a tray bearing a covered plate and another silver coffeepot. "Jenkins, about time!" the duke said wearily. "I have been forced to converse to fill the time of waiting. Please refill Lady Hester's cup."

"May I inquire how Bolby is this morning, Your Grace?" the butler asked quietly as he poured the hot, dark liquid into Hester's cup.

"He's dead," the duke said flatly. He didn't look at Jenkins, or her, all his attention apparently riveted on the table.

"I'm sorry to hear that, Your Grace."

"Yes, Jenkins."

"Will you be attending the funeral, Your Grace?"

The duke nodded, still without raising his eyes. "Tomorrow morning."

The butler nodded, then silently withdrew.

"Mr. Bolby was a friend?" Hester asked after a moment.

"Yes."

"I'm sorry that he has died."

The duke regarded her coldly. "You never knew him. Why should you care if he is alive or dead?"

Hester could think of no response to that, other than to say that she was sorry because he had been the duke's friend, but she could easily guess how scornfully he would react to that remark. Therefore, she said nothing.

Adrian started to eat, trying all the while to ignore the quiet presence of Lady Hester as she drank her coffee.

Instead, he recalled the things he and Bolby had spoken of, the hunts and the sport, the tricks and the jests, until Bolby had grown so weak, Adrian had insisted that his wife take his place on the stool. She had cried until she could cry no more, and at the end, when Bolby had breathed his last, her wail had been a sound Adrian hoped he never heard the like of again. Then young Bolby, who had been silent all night, began to cry, great choking sobs racking his slender frame.

Adrian had realized that it was better to leave them alone with their dead, and so had quietly slipped out to ride home. By the time he reached Barroughby Hall, his leg was aching terribly. All he wanted now was to eat and go to bed. He didn't want to sit here with a young woman whose eyes held such tender sympathy, as if she understood what he was feeling.

"Your Grace, are you quite all right?"

He glared at her, wishing she would leave him alone. "I'm fine."

"You're crying." She said the words very, very quietly and regarded him with calm compassion.

He angrily swiped his cheek. "I have something in my eye."

She rose and came around the table, standing beside him and drawing a handkerchief out of her narrow sleeve. "Let me see."

"It's nothing," he replied, not looking at her. "Just a piece of soot or dirt."

"Your Grace, it would not be wise to leave anything irritating in your eye."

Adrian told himself he was too tired to argue, and too weary to explain away the lie, so he half turned and raised his face to her. With a wrinkled brow and pursed lips, Lady Hester took hold of his chin and peered into his eyes.

Her touch was gentle, but firm, like the very best of nurses. "It is a pity you come from a titled family," he remarked, trying not to notice that her eyes were a very bewitching shade of blue, or that her lips were half-parted.

"Why do you say that, Your Grace?" she answered absently, her gaze still scanning his eyes. "Look toward the window, please."

"With that tone of command, you would have been a remarkable governess."

She let go of his chin. "I do not see anything here," she said, stepping back.

He tried not to be troubled by the loss of her touch.

It didn't take a great deal of perception to realize that he had upset her. He had not meant to, but then, being compared to a governess was probably not much of a compliment, and he regretted distressing her.

What was he doing, having such feelings? He was the Dark Duke, and no decent woman should come near him.

"You look very tired, Your Grace. I think you should go to bed."

"I shall. Care to join me?"

She stared at him, aghast. "No, I do not!" she declared before hurrying from the room as if he had started to disrobe in front of her.

He would feel no remorse over his coarse request. It was better that she think the worst of him.

Hester paused outside the library and tried to catch her breath. She wrung her hands together anxiously, mindful still of the feel of the stubble on the duke's chin when she had held him there, and the look in his dark, intense eyes. As if he was asking her something. What? What could he ask of her?

To share his bed was the obvious, most disturbing answer. She, with her lack of beauty, had never expected any man to make such a proposal, and certainly not the Duke of Barroughby, especially after what she had seen when she examined his eyes. There had been no lascivious speculation, or even his usual sardonic cynicism.

She saw a yearning that touched her heart.

Maybe she *should* have been a governess, if she

could see the Dark Duke as more like a man asking for her regard than the rogue he was reputed to be.

Oh, she was being ridiculous and far too sentimental. A man like that—what would he know or need of tenderness? He wanted only one kind of love, or so it seemed, and she was not prepared to give him that. Not now, and not ever.

"I tell you, I ain't a-goin'! Not till I see the duke himself!" a male voice said loudly from the direction of the side entrance.

There was a small room there that Jenkins had told her was used as an office when the duke was in residence, for meeting the tenants of the estate. Obviously, a disgruntled tenant wanted to speak with him now.

Another man's murmuring voice seemed to deny this request, and Hester realized that the hushed tones sounded suspiciously like Reverend Canon Smeech. Surely it was not his place to interfere in the business of the estate, unless it touched upon the welfare of the people of the parish.

At that moment Lord Elliot came trotting down the stairs. He smiled when he saw Hester, and despite her reservations as to his character, she couldn't help but feel warmed by his friendliness, which was blessedly different from the coolness his sibling exhibited most of the time. "Something sounds amiss," he noted jovially.

"I believe a tenant wishes to see the duke."

There was another loud, confirming demand from the same direction as the previous one. "So I hear," Lord Elliot noted. "I suppose he isn't back yet," his lordship continued with a condemning frown. "He was out all night."

"He is. I left him in the small dining room just now."

"Did you?" Lord Elliot ran his gaze over her in a most unexpected, measuring way she did not at all appreciate. It struck her as much more impertinent than even the duke's impromptu kiss, which could at least be excused on the grounds that she had awakened him unexpectedly.

"He is eating his breakfast. I understand he was visiting a family friend, who died."

Lord Elliot's face expressed surprise. "Who, pray tell, was that?"

"His name was Bolby."

"Ah, Old Bolby, of course." Lord Elliot did not seem particularly affected by the news of the man's death. "I suppose Adrian started at the Bolby cottage and ended up...somewhere else."

With a pang of disappointment Hester realized Lord Elliot might be correct in his assumption. She had no idea when Bolby had passed away, or how long the duke had stayed with him. She did not doubt that Bolby's death had truly grieved the duke; however, taking himself to a local tavern to drown his sorrows in drink would, unfortunately, be in keeping with the duke's reported habits.

The duchess appeared at the top of the staircase, surveying the foyer imperiously. "Where is Adrian?" she demanded angrily. "The scoundrel! Not home a week, and he's already acting as if this house were no more than a hotel!"

"Eating his breakfast, Mama—or so I was given to understand," Lord Elliot replied, with a significant look at Hester, and she couldn't help feeling as if he was somehow attaching blame to her. It was not *her* fault the duke was eating his breakfast after being away all night.

"I believe he spent the night at the bedside of a dying man, Your Grace," Hester said, hoping this was the truth.

The duchess proceeded down the steps in awful majesty. "Adrian visiting the dying? I'd as soon believe Queen Victoria was sleeping in the stable!" She paused as she reached the bottom steps, and the sounds of conflict grew slightly louder. "What is that abominable racket?"

"It appears someone wishes to speak to Adrian, Mama."

"Why does he not go to the office, then? Surely he can hear all the noise. Selfish creature, he only thinks of his stomach. Hester, fetch him at once."

Hester bristled slightly. She was not a servant, and it was not her place to "fetch" anybody.

Thankfully, Jenkins tottered around the corner of the staircase. "May I be of assistance, Your Grace?"

"Yes. The duke is in the small dining room."

Jenkins's face was all astonishment. "There is a duck in the dining room? I shall get young Bolby to remove it at once, Your Grace. Fortunately, he is awaiting the duke's convenience in the office."

Bearing in mind what the duke had said about Jenkins sometimes hearing only what he wished to hear, Hester wondered if Jenkins was purposely confusing the situation. She glanced at Lord Elliot, who had half turned to hide a delighted smile.

"No, no!" the duchess cried impatiently. "The *duke!* The *duke* is in the small dining room. Fetch him at once! I cannot bear all this noise so early in the morning!"

"Neither can I, Your Grace," the duke noted dryly.

They all turned in the direction of the corridor leading to the small dining room, to see the duke strolling casually toward them. To Hester's surprise, he didn't look nearly as weary as when she had left him.

Perhaps the food had had a restorative effect. Whatever it was, his eyes were bright and challenging, his manner brisk. "Good morning, everyone," he said jovially.

The duchess frowned darkly at the butler, then her stepson, but the duke ignored her.

"Your Grace," Jenkins said. "Young Bolby and the Reverend Canon Smeech wish to speak with you regarding the Bolby cottage."

"I shall see to them at once. Since this is estate business, I shall leave you all to your various pleasures," he said, heading toward the office, which was on the other side of the house.

"Come to breakfast, Elliot," the duchess ordered, grabbing her son's arm. "I shall expect you to be in the drawing room when I am finished, Lady Hester," she continued. "We have to complete the invitations to the ball."

"Yes, Your Grace," Hester replied.

The duchess and her son walked away, Elliot with

a rueful glance over his shoulder, the duchess in outraged dignity.

Hester decided she would get her book from her bedroom and read for a little while. It was likely to be some time before the duchess finished eating, considering that she would probably stop several times to criticize her stepson.

Instead of proceeding upstairs immediately, however, Hester waited until Lord Elliot and his mother had turned the corner toward the small dining room. Once they were likely to be inside, she hurried along the corridor, tiptoed past the closed door of the dining room where she could discern the angry muttering of the duchess, and made her way toward the far side of the house. This was a rather roundabout way to the servants' stairs, but this route took her very near the duke's office.

Chapter Nine

"Do you think this is the proper time to discuss this?" Hester heard the duke say in a reasonable tone of voice.

"He didn't give me no choice, Your Grace," a young man said in angry response. "Me dad's barely washed, and he's at the door sayin' we got to get out."

"Is this true, Canon?" the duke asked, his voice so quietly lethal that Hester was very glad she had never heard anything like it before. Drawn by the prospect of seeing the pompous canon in such a situation, she cautiously crept near the door and peeked inside.

The room used as an office for the estate was small and painted plainly in white. An undraped window let in natural light, and some small shelves on the walls held what looked like ledgers. The duke sat behind a desk that fit neatly into the available space, leaving room for a wooden chair across from it, upon which an obviously uncomfortable Reverend Canon Smeech sat. A tall, slender young man with a thick thatch of sandy hair and many freckles stood awkwardly in the corner, his eyes puffy either from lack of sleep or crying or both, and with his hat in his work-worn hands. His glances toward the duke were pleading, and to the reverend gentleman, vicious.

"Your Grace," the canon began, "the Bolbys have been in that cottage by your leave these past five years, although the rent is always late, and they rarely attend services. The duchess and I have discussed this matter many times, and I know she agrees with me that this is the time that cottage is given to a more deserving family, one who will appreciate the bounty of the duch—yourself, Your Grace. I have the perfect family in mind. The parents are decent, respectable people with several small children. I have tried to be merciful—"

The young man snorted derisively and his fist clenched as if he were sorely tempted to hit the plump clergyman on the head.

"*Merciful,* Your Grace," the canon continued after casting a severe look at the youth, "but young Bolby threw me *bodily* from the doorstep. Therefore, I have no recourse but to appeal to Your Grace."

"Could this not have waited until Bolby was decently buried?" the duke asked, and again Hester was glad she was not the one he was questioning.

The canon was not immune to the displeasure in the duke's tone, for beads of sweat appeared on his forehead as he ran a finger around his clerical collar. "Your Grace, I—"

"Just because me mam wouldn't sell him her hen!" young Bolby blurted out.

"What are you talking about?" the duke inquired, looking from one man to the other as he leaned back and straightened his injured leg.

"My mam had a fine hen. A right beauty. And he wanted to buy it from her, but she wouldn't sell. He's been out to get us ever since!"

The duke turned an even more malevolent glare onto Reverend Canon Smeech. And then he smiled. "I'm sure you must be mistaken, Tom. Surely this gentleman wouldn't be so petty. Not over a chicken."

"The Smiths need the cottage, Your Grace."

"And you should have waited," the duke said harshly. "Who are these Smiths? I don't recall any family named Smith on the tenant rolls."

The sweating clergyman cleared his throat. "They are new to the estate, Your Grace. The duchess approved of them, and indeed, Your Grace, they are a most trustworthy, reliable, decent, hardworking family."

"How kind of you to assist the duchess, and by extension, myself, in the running of the estate, Canon."

"Your Grace, I—that is, we—take great care to ensure that deserving people are employed on your property."

"Hah!" young Bolby ejaculated. "They're related to him!"

The duke raised his eyebrows quizzically. "Is this true, Canon?"

The canon cleared his throat and gave young Bolby a very murderous look for a man of the cloth. "*Distant* relations, Your Grace."

"Well, Canon, if they are related to you, I am sure they are worthy of *something*."

And not anything good, Hester completed in her thoughts, for she could hear the slight scorn in the duke's voice. So, obviously, did the other men, for young Bolby looked pleased, and the expression on the canon's face as he struggled not to give an equally murderous look to the mocking duke was enough to make her cover her mouth to suppress a pleased chuckle.

"Is there no other cottage for them?"

"None large enough, Your Grace."

"Your Grace," young Bolby said, apparently somewhat mollified by the duke's reaction to the controversy, "we know we got to move, although it'll break Mam's heart to leave where she come as a bride. He just should have waited, and he ought to give us some time to get ready."

The duke regarded the two men steadily. "I quite agree. However, if the Smiths are such virtuous tenants, I would be foolish not to let them stay, even if they are related to you, Smeech. Therefore, this is what I shall do."

The duke opened a drawer in the desk and took out paper, a pen and a bottle of ink. "Tom, I am giving your family the cottage and the acre of land upon which it sits."

"What?" the two men cried in unison, the one in happy disbelief, the other in dismay.

"I will provide the Smiths with a new cottage. Beside the rectory, I think. And since you are their champion, Canon, you will be pleased to hear that I will charge them only a slightly higher rent than the Bolbys have been paying.''

The canon looked annoyed as he reached for a large handkerchief and wiped his face, but he said nothing. Indeed, Hester thought with a devilish grin, what *could* he say? The duke had finessed him completely.

She realized, as she noticed the secretive smile on the duke's face as he bent over his paper, that he thought so, too. Suddenly he raised his eyes and glanced at the door. With horror, Hester realized she had leaned so far forward to hear, her skirt was surely visible. She grabbed it and pulled it back.

Too late. ''Ah, Lady Hester!'' the duke called out, and she silently cursed herself for lingering so long.

Nevertheless, she put a smile on her face and went to the threshold of the office. ''Good morning, Your Grace, Canon,'' Hester said. ''I was on my way to the back stairs.''

The duke smiled, and Hester had the strange feeling that he knew *exactly* why she had gone that way, just as he had discerned that the canon's concern for the Smiths was not entirely disinterested.

A dangerous man, indeed. She began to back out of the room, hoping he wouldn't notice her as he returned to his writing. ''Lady Hester, allow me to introduce young Tom Bolby,'' the duke said without raising his eyes. ''I trust he will be as fine a game-keeper as his father was.''

As Hester dipped a small curtsy, young Bolby's eyes lit up excitedly. She suspected this was the first he had heard of being made the gamekeeper for the estate of the Duke of Barroughby. "I will, Your Grace. That is, I'll try. Thank you!"

The duke waved his pen in a gesture of dismissal before returning it to sit in the ink bottle. He looked again at Reverend Canon Smeech. "You didn't bring your curate with you?"

The question was an odd one, Hester thought—and so, obviously, did the canon. "No, Your Grace. He is visiting the sick this morning."

"While you discuss tenants' cottages? Well, no matter. You are a very busy man, I'm sure. He must be a fine curate, to allow you to accomplish your many tasks."

"Yes, Your Grace, he is."

"Scots, is he not?"

"Yes, Your Grace, from Edinburgh."

"My stepmother is planning a ball, Canon, and we shall need all the young men we can find. I trust you don't have any scruples about allowing clergymen to dance?"

"No, not at all, Your Grace. We shall be delighted to attend."

Hester had managed to maneuver nearly to the door when once again the duke affixed a steely gaze upon her. "I believe we are all impatient to be on our way," he said, and Hester blushed at being found out. "Bolby, here is the deed." He handed the paper to the young man, who handled it with reverence. "I'm sure you're anxious to get home to your mother."

"Yes, Your Grace. Thank you, Your Grace! Good morning, Your Grace!" The young man bowed and backed his way past Hester and out the door. In moments they could hear the clatter of his running feet.

The duke sighed, but his eyes twinkled with devilment. "There is nothing quite like charity, is there, Canon?"

"No, Your Grace," the canon replied wearily.

"The duchess will soon be in the drawing room. No doubt you'd care to stay and speak with her? I know she enjoys your little chats."

"Thank you, Your Grace. I would be delighted to."

The duke rose. "Good morning, Canon."

"Good morning, Your Grace," the clergyman said, bowing before leaving the room.

"I believe I have upset that esteemed gentleman," the duke reflected as he resumed his seat, just as Hester was reflecting that she had absolutely no cause to stay there. Nevertheless, she couldn't quite bring herself to depart. "I'm certain you have, Your Grace, and what's more, I think you're happy to have done so."

He regarded her with apparent astonishment. "You seem to be able to read my mind with astonishing accuracy, Lady Hester. Are you part Gypsy?"

"No, Your Grace. You were not very circumspect."

"Ah. Another area in which my character is seriously flawed." He frowned, but she didn't think he was truly dismayed. "You, I believe, are more than capable of hiding your true feelings," he noted.

"When necessary, Your Grace."

He frowned again, and this time she believed he

was almost angry. "Must you keep calling me 'Your Grace'?" he demanded.

"It is the appropriate title in conversation," Hester replied, secretly delighted that he found the formal address annoying when she used it. "Your Grace," she added mischievously.

"The Archbishop of Canterbury is also to be addressed as 'Your Grace,' and I'm sure you'll agree that I am not one to share such an honorific with him."

"It is my understanding that the form of address belongs to the holder of the title 'duke,' whether he personally deserves it or not."

"Nevertheless, I am going to insist that you call me..."

Hester held her breath as she waited for him to continue, anxious to hear what improper thing he was going to suggest, perhaps even to the highly inappropriate use of his Christian name.

"'My lord.' Only when we are alone, of course, so we don't upset society."

"Considering those moments are sure to be rare, I have no compunction about doing so, my lord," Hester answered. "Now I really must be going."

With that, she left the room, contemplating that if she were not careful, she could come to enjoy conversing with the duke very much.

As Adrian closed the door to the office and limped back to his chair, he smiled to himself. He had enjoyed his conversation with Lady Hester. The look on her face when she waited for him to reveal how he wished to be addressed! He had never met a woman who made anticipation so fascinating. How her eyes had sparkled, and as for her delightful, half-parted lips—he had been sorely tempted to kiss her again, and if his leg had not been so sore that moving was agony, he might have.

Especially when his mention of Reverend Mc-Kenna seemed to produce no change in her. Either she was indeed the most inscrutable woman in England, or the young clergyman was nothing but a clergyman to her.

Which should mean nothing to him. Nor should he have been so absurdly pleased to think that she knew of his gift of the cottage to the Bolby family. He didn't need or want her praise or approval.

Indeed, if he began to seriously care what she thought about anything he might do, that would not be good. He already had enough to concern him.

He would do better to recall that the surprising Lady Hester had apparently been spying on him. Try as he might to condemn her for her curiosity, though, he had an almost irrepressible desire to laugh at the image of Lady Hester creeping about listening at keyholes.

She was indeed a most fascinating female. He would almost be sorry to leave.

"It is unfortunately true, Mama," Elliot said to his mother as she sat to take tea later that day and well after Canon Smeech had taken his leave. "Adrian refused to speak to me about it—just growled like an angry bear and told me to go away." If

Elliot were being truthful, he would have said that Adrian swore at him like an uncouth dockhand and told him to leave him the hell alone. "The canon was probably also correct when he said the deed would be legal."

"I knew it was foolish to hope that Canon Smeech was mistaken, or that Adrian was simply playing some kind of terrible joke." The duchess set her Wedgwood cup and saucer down so hard, they rattled. "Adrian is a fool to give away a fine cottage and acre of good land to a family like the Bolbys, no matter how tender a sentiment he appeared to harbor in his breast for the old reprobate. *I* never liked Bolby, and I'm convinced he was poaching the whole time he was employed here."

"I wouldn't be surprised if Adrian did it just to irritate Canon Smeech," Elliot replied. He regarded his angry parent thoughtfully. "It might not be amiss to contact our solicitor in London."

"Oh, that's useless," his mother complained, pressing one hand to her temple. "Adrian will get another opinion, then so will we, and on and on. The papers might even get hold of this. No, it isn't to be thought of," she finished with a heavy sigh as she reached for a pastry. "We shall just have to endure."

"Nevertheless, it's disturbing to think of the estate disappearing piece by piece. I suppose we should be relieved he hasn't sold any of it."

"He wouldn't *dare!*" the duchess exclaimed.

"I believe Adrian would dare almost anything," Elliot remarked.

"Oh, what is taking Lady Hester?" the duchess

demanded querulously. "I told her exactly where to find my shawl. I shall have a sore back tomorrow if she is not here soon."

Hester appeared at the door of the drawing room and hurried inside, shawl in hand. She curtsied to the gentleman, then gave the required item to the duchess and sat beside the tea table on a slender rosewood chair across from Lord Elliot. "Would you like me to pour, Your Grace?" she asked softly.

The duchess frowned and shook her head. "I have already done so," she said peevishly. "Have you heard of the duke's latest folly?"

"Folly, Your Grace?" Hester asked, feigning ignorance. She didn't want anyone to know she had eavesdropped. She also wanted to hear what the duchess would make of her stepson's generosity, although she had made an excellent guess, which the duchess was already confirming by her choice of words.

"He has given away land and a cottage to the family of a man who was once the *gamekeeper!*" she replied.

"It was kind of him, of course," Lord Elliot remarked, "but a bit foolhardy, perhaps. Now he has the expense of another cottage to build."

"I should think the duke could afford to pay for the construction of several cottages," Hester noted while she refilled Lord Elliot's teacup.

"That's not the point," the duchess declared. "The man Bolby was lazy and most profane, too. By giving the cottage and land to his family, Adrian appears to be *rewarding* the fellow."

Hester had not considered the gift of the cottage in

that light, and she could not disagree, if the duchess was right about old Bolby.

"Your Grace, Sir Douglas Saxon-Cowper and Miss Saxon-Cowper," Jenkins declared from the doorway.

"Who?" Lord Elliot asked his mother.

"Oh, how tiresome!" the duchess exclaimed. "It's Sir Douglas Sackville-Cooper and his daughter. I might have known they would come. I should tell them I'm not at home."

"But Mama, you are," Lord Elliot observed. "I should like to see the Sackville-Coopers. Please show them in, Jenkins."

Chapter Ten

Jenkins ushered in Sir Douglas, who bounded into the room like a dog loosed at a hunt. He made a bow toward the duchess, who inclined her head slightly in acknowledgment, and then dutifully and absentmindedly bowed toward Lady Hester, all the while smiling broadly at Lord Elliot. By this time Damaris had glided gracefully into the room. She wore a lovely confection of a gown, with miles of delicate blue skirt and lace and ribbons, and a very pretty straw bonnet decorated with sprigs of flowers that matched the small bouquets embroidered on her gown.

She looked, Hester thought with a pang of envy, like a young goddess, beautiful and worthy of worship. The sunlight caught the glints of Damaris's dark hair, and the merest hint of a blush bloomed on her lovely cheeks as she smiled at Lord Elliot.

Lord Elliot rose with alacrity and hurried toward her, pausing for a moment to greet her father with easy grace, and not for the first time in Hester's life, or the hundredth, she felt herself grow invisible.

"Don't tell me this is little Damaris!" he cried as if awestruck.

The young woman blushed even more as he led her to a chair near the window, well away from the duchess, who was eyeing them with something that was not approval.

Sir Douglas was also eyeing them, and not with outright approval, either. "Where is the duke this morning?" he asked, demonstrating again his lack of perception when it came to the duchess's opinion of her stepson. Obviously, Hester thought, he still had his hopes pinned to the main prize.

"I have no idea where he is," the duchess replied stonily. "Won't you have a seat, Sir Douglas?"

He complied by sitting on the sofa beside the duchess, who suddenly seemed to be on the verge of fainting in a way that was quite new to Hester and that no doubt had much to do with the presence of Sir Douglas so close to her.

The atmosphere grew even more strained when the duke entered the room. "Jenkins told me we had company, but he failed to mention that one of the Graces themselves had deigned to visit mere mortals," he remarked.

It was the most outrageous flattery, yet Damaris seemed pleased by it, for she turned her head away from Lord Elliot and smiled benignly at the previously feared duke. Perhaps she felt safer with Lord Elliot beside her, Hester thought grimly.

As the duke nodded briefly to his stepmother and Sir Douglas before moving toward Damaris, Hester realized she might have been in another country for all the notice either of the Fitzwalter men were paying to her.

This was just what she had left home to avoid—this feeling of being not merely superfluous, but not even worthy of the most basic attention from others.

From men, she meant, if she were being completely honest. That notion hit home now more than it ever had in the past.

Worse, she was being treated as little more than a servant. The duchess was putting all the planning for the ball onto Hester's shoulders, something Hester had also wished to avoid by leaving home. Her mother had entertained lavishly and often, and in the past few years Hester had been forced to take on more and more of the organization. Although her experience was standing her in good stead at present, for she could almost arrange the duchess's ball in her sleep, she would rather have done without the work.

Apparently there was to be no escape, from balls or from men who acted as if she wasn't there.

"Don't you agree, Lady Hester?" Sir Douglas said loudly.

She turned to the man with a polite smile. "I beg your pardon, Sir Douglas?"

"I said this ball will be an absolute delight and I was rather hoping Damaris could be of assistance to you, Lady Hester, for the duchess tells me you are being most helpful in taking care of the many small yet necessary details." Sir Douglas leaned a little closer and glanced at Damaris, one handsome nobleman on either side. "She needs to learn about such things, for when she has her own household."

"Lady Hester is a marvel of organization," the duchess remarked placidly.

This compliment—indeed, any outright sign of approval—was so rare that Hester scarcely knew what to do or say. She glanced at the other three people in the room, and was nearly as startled to find the duke regarding her speculatively, while his half brother's attention was still claimed by Damaris, who stared modestly at the floor.

Hester colored at once and murmured something completely meaningless in response.

"I don't know how my stepmother would manage the ball without her," the duke remarked languidly. "At the duchess's time of life, one begins to need assistance."

Hester frowned at the duke. She had no wish to be used to bait the duchess, and she resented the duke doing so, and in company, too. It did not help that Lord Elliot was obviously stifling a smile.

The duchess shot her stepson a venomous glance, then smiled at Sir Douglas. "The duke is always so droll," she said. "However, he is quite right about Lady Hester's value to me. I shall be sorry to lose her. Still, she will make some lucky man a fine wife."

What on earth was the duchess talking about? Hester thought, blushing. This was the most awkward conversation she had heard or been witness to in her life, and she began to consider ways she could excuse herself.

"We hope you and your charming daughter will be able to attend the ball," the duke said to the knight, his deep voice penetrating the sudden heavy silence.

"Oh, of course," Sir Douglas said eagerly. "I only regret that I must leave to visit London tomorrow. Business, you know. However, I shall certainly be able to return in time for the ball."

"We have already heard from the Duke of Chesterton, who shall attend. And the Earl of Wopping-Hedgehorn, and dear Viscount Albany with his charming wife."

Hester watched Damaris listen to the duchess's recital of the guests who had already written of their attendance at the ball, her eyes growing larger and more fearful. She realized better than Sir Douglas that they really were out of their sphere in such company, which was precisely what Hester supposed the duchess wanted her to realize. Sir Douglas, on the other hand, seemed to swell with pride.

"The guest list appears to have grown considerably," the duke observed. "Are we to have the entire House of Lords in attendance?"

"Of course not!" the duchess replied. "All the guests are friends of the family."

"I haven't seen the Duke of Chesterton since my father's funeral. In fact, I had thought he was dead."

Lord Elliot laughed. "Oh, he's very much alive, I assure you. He has found a very interesting way of keeping his youth."

"What is that, my lord?" Sir Douglas asked studiously.

"He picks his fruit younger on the vine all the time."

Hester flushed, for she had heard things about the

Duke of Chesterton, too, and knew that Lord Elliot was referring to the man's appetite in mistresses.

The duke's face darkened with a frown, and even the duchess looked slightly pained, for she would know to what her son referred, given her large circle of correspondence. Damaris looked puzzled, and Sir Douglas appeared worried. "He'll get indigestion if he eats fruit before it's ripe," he said gravely.

"Indeed he will," the duke agreed. "I believe we should have a fine harvest from our orchard this year, Sir Douglas," he continued, deftly changing the subject.

"I am glad to hear it, Your Grace," Sir Douglas responded heartily. "I must tell you about a new strain of apple we have been growing in our south orchard. Really, a most remarkable fruit…"

The talk turned to agricultural matters, at least between Sir Douglas and the duke. Hester had no idea what Lord Elliot and Damaris were whispering about, nor was she the only one who noticed their hushed conversation. Several times the duchess addressed her son, and each time he gave her a short, polite response before turning back to Damaris.

Hester said nothing at all, and nobody seemed to notice.

Finally Sir Douglas rose and gave his daughter a significant look. "Regretfully, Your Grace, we should be on our way."

The duchess graciously—and Hester thought, quite sincerely—nodded her goodbye while Damaris rose.

A pleased look crossed the young woman's face

when Lord Elliot took hold of her hand. "Farewell for the moment," he said quietly.

The duke waited until Lord Elliot had released her hand, and then he very slowly repeated the gesture. Bending low, he brushed his lips across the back of her hand in a kiss that was more of an intimate caress, glancing up at Damaris with what Hester knew was the overwhelming intensity he was so capable of. "Adieu, Miss Sackville-Cooper."

Hester swallowed hard, and Damaris seemed powerless to move, which was a perfectly understandable reaction.

"Good day, Miss Sackville-Cooper," the duchess said sharply, and suddenly Damaris found the ability to walk.

The two young men watched her graceful exit, and Hester thought she had rarely seen two such similarly speculative and approving expressions.

The type of expressions that never had been, and never would be, directed at her.

The next few days passed in agonizing slowness for Adrian, as he was forced to keep to the house again while his leg recovered from the strain he had put upon it.

This time the waiting was much worse than when he had first returned to Barroughby Hall, because Elliot had come home. Mapleton had already reported meeting Elliot drunk and careening down a public street, and repeated the rude remarks his drunken half brother had made.

That was not the worst of it, though. Because of

Elliot, Adrian had been forced to ignore Hester and pretend an interest in Damaris, when he wished very much to do otherwise. Unfortunately, it was the only way to ensure Hester's safety. If Elliot thought Adrian the slightest bit interested in a woman, he would do everything he could to seduce her, just to spite his brother, usually—and unfortunately—with success. He had done so with others, most recently Elizabeth Howell. Hester had no family to guard her, and she was under the same roof.

Damaris, on the other hand, had a father to protect her, and she lived in another house.

Therefore, Adrian had had no choice but to feign indifference to Hester, no matter how contrary that was to the wishes of his heart.

Once his leg was somewhat better, Adrian attended to other matters pertaining to Elliot's presence in Barroughby. He had already gone to speak to several publicans and told them, in no uncertain terms, that he would pay Elliot's current debts, and no more. The tavern keepers had not been pleased to hear that. Nevertheless, they agreed when Adrian suggested rather pointedly that they should limit the volume of ale and wine they sold to his sibling.

At present, Adrian was at a different establishment, for a different purpose. He knew that sooner or later Elliot would probably find his way to Sally Newcombe's, too.

As Adrian sat upon the red-velvet-and-gilt sofa, he gazed at the equally garish red brocade wallpaper, the crystal lamps and the heavy, blood red velvet curtains. This room had been the drawing room when the house had been a family's home; now it could more properly be described as a combination waiting room and display area.

Sally was taking her own sweet time coming downstairs, he thought grimly, not wishing to spend any longer here than strictly necessary in case another "patron" should appear. That would cause a spate of gossip he could well do without.

A petite, black-haired sprite of a woman, with snapping black eyes and wearing nothing but a smile, a corset and drawers, came sauntering provocatively into the room. *"Bonjour, monsieur le duc,"* she said huskily when he rose politely. "Please, sit."

She lounged in a sofa opposite him, in a pose reminiscent of classical paintings of nymphs or goddesses, and incidentally giving him quite a view of her voluptuous breasts.

The woman had no sooner arranged herself when another young woman entered the room, a willowy brunette with long legs and green eyes, wearing a silk peignoir. By the time he had resumed his seat again, a third woman had joined them. She was a rather plump young lady with dark brown hair, brown eyes and excellent skin.

Then another came, and at her Adrian looked the longest. He gave her a warm smile, too, for he remembered the slender blonde with blue eyes.

"Good afternoon, Your Grace," Maisie said, returning his smile as she sat near the windows.

Adrian recalled another pair of blue eyes that would never, ever witness a life such as these women led. He was glad for Hester's sake, and once again cursed the path that gave him such easy familiarity with Sally and several of her counterparts in London.

After Maisie came a redhead with freckles and a most shapely figure, and another brown-haired beauty.

Adrian noted with quiet satisfaction that not one of Sally's "employees" was a child, or ill fed, or bruised. Theirs was not an easy life, but at least with Sally they were as safe as women in that profession ever could be. Without her they would be beggars or streetwalkers, and several of them would already be dead.

Finally Sally deigned to arrive, clad in a pink negligee that revealed far more than it concealed. She was a voluptuous woman of middle years, but she hid her age well with the clever use of cosmetics. A cloud of floral perfume attended her. "Out you go, girls," she ordered, and the cavalcade of women departed in an atmosphere of speculation and disappointment.

In Adrian's youth Sally had been lover, friend and teacher, and he regarded her fondly as she slid onto the sofa beside him. "What a pleasure to see you again, Adrian."

"And you, Sally."

"Maisie's looking well, isn't she?" Sally asked archly.

"Very well," Adrian replied noncommittally. "I notice Angela wasn't among the parade."

"Oh, she's got herself a little shop in Liverpool. Doing very well, so I hear." She moved a little closer. "Maisie's glad to see you, too."

"I didn't come here on business of that sort, Sally," Adrian replied.

Sally gave him a puzzled look. "Why, then? For old times' sake?"

"I came to let you know that Elliot is home."

Sally's lip curled with undisguised disgust. "So I heard. I won't have him here," she said firmly. "Not after last time. Daphne was scared half to death. She ran off the next week. Probably to London, poor dear. You know what sort of thing'll happen to a girl there. Relation or no, you can tell him he's damn well not welcome here."

"I understand," Adrian said, "and I'm sorry about Daphne. But no matter what I say to Elliot to try to prevent him from coming here, he will probably arrive at your door eventually."

Sally wrapped her skimpy garment about herself and shook her head. "I'll bar it."

Adrian took her hand, gazing into her world-weary eyes. "Sally, if he's not allowed in here, I don't know what he might do."

Still Sally shook her head. "That's not my lookout, is it? He's a selfish beast. I've got the girls to think of."

"I know. Believe me, Sally, I know." He gripped Sally's hand more tightly and thought of a certain young woman who was residing in his house, and another equally innocent young woman who would surely tempt Elliot. "I don't like to ask this, yet I feel I must. Isn't there someone…?"

Sally gazed at him, aghast. "I see what you're getting at! I said, relation or no, he's not welcome."

"I'll pay whatever you like."

"It'll cost you plenty!"

"Then I will pay plenty. Won't you please do me this favor, Sally?"

At first Adrian thought she meant to refuse, but then she sighed and looked him straight in the eye. "Well...I do have someone who might do," she said. "The new girl. Desiree."

"The dark-haired French girl who came in first?"

"I thought you might take a fancy to her, even if she didn't have blue eyes."

"Not a bad choice—but I've given up such expensive luxuries."

Sally's eyes widened with surprise, then she grinned. "Why pay when those rich, bored ladies will give it away, eh?"

Adrian thought it better to return to the business at hand. "This Desiree, she's not new at...?"

"The job? Good lord, no. Comes from Paris. Born into it, I gather. They take a different attitude, those French. More civilized, if you ask me."

"I suppose that depends upon what you mean by 'civilized.'"

Sally chuckled, a deep, throaty sound that partly accounted for her success. "More practical, then." Sally grew serious again. "She knows how to defend herself, that one. Keeps a knife under the pillow. Her mother and her aunts taught her how to use it, too. If anybody can be safe with that scum, it'll be Desiree. I remember he was plenty fussy, but he seemed to like the small ones. All the easier to frighten, I daresay."

"Couldn't you have a watch, or a signal, or something?"

"Oh, I'll have that, never you fear."

Adrian drew out his wallet and waited.

"It'll cost you twenty pounds a visit. I keep what *he* pays, too."

Adrian nodded. It was money well spent if it prevented Elliot from trying to seduce young women less able to defend themselves. "A fair sum. I brought that much, knowing that we could surely arrive at an understanding," he said, handing her the money.

Sally eyed the rest of the cash in his wallet, and Adrian suspected she was wishing she had named a higher sum. However, he knew she wouldn't ask for more. Once she made a bargain, she kept it.

Sally tucked the money into the bodice of her negligee, then smiled seductively. "Not having to rush off, are you, Adrian?" she said in a soft and sultry voice as her hand reached out and stroked his thigh. "I'm not busy."

Adrian was very tempted. Sally was here, she was willing, she was doing him a vast favor and she was the only type of woman he deserved, one who made him pay for his pleasure.

He felt her breath hot on his cheek, the weight of her breast against his arm, smelled the cheap perfume on her flesh—and suddenly hated himself anew. He was sullied enough; he didn't need to add to his condemnation.

He gave Sally a brief and regretful smile as he rose. "Sorry, but I have many things to do. Perhaps you've heard that the duchess is giving a ball?"

"Yes, I heard," Sally said, her eyes once again as hard and sharp as the dangling crystals on her lamps.

"Then I must be off." He bowed. "Thank you, Sally, and Desiree, if necessary. I won't forget this."

Sally nodded and watched the Duke of Barroughby walk out. Then she went to the window and saw him mount his fine black stallion. "No, you won't forget, Your Grace, not after paying twenty pounds," she murmured, and then she sighed.

Meanwhile, Elliot sat on a very comfortable sofa in the drawing room of the large and newly built manor house of the Sackville-Coopers and watched Damaris as she played the pianoforte. The autumn sunlight fell across her ornately dressed hair and lit her beautiful face. She wore a very pretty gown of light green muslin, with a costly necklace and lace mitts. He would have admired the gown more if it had revealed more of its wearer, and he would have admired her playing, if she'd had any talent at all.

However, he was not the least interested in her musical abilities, although he had discovered that women with an appreciation of musical rhythm carried that appreciation to their other passionate activities. He was far more interested in watching the movements of her breasts while she played.

She finished her tune and turned to look at him. So eager, so innocent, so very beautiful. "Would you care for something else, Lord Elliot?" she asked brightly.

Elliot smiled slowly, thinking of the many "something elses" he would care to do with her. "I would be very happy if we could dispense with the formalities," he replied softly and with his most seductive manner as he stood and approached the instrument. "Please, won't you call me Elliot?"

Damaris's cowlike eyes widened. "Oh, but I couldn't! It wouldn't be proper!"

"I know," he said, smiling down at her. "But then I would be able to call you by your beautiful first name, instead of that awkwardly long last one."

She blushed and stared down at her slender fingers as they lay on the keys, as if she were about to caress them. "I suppose if we didn't do so in public, it would be all right, my lord," she whispered, glancing up at him with a shyness he found most alluring.

"Elliot."

She nodded. "Elliot."

"Good. Now I think I would enjoy something lively, Damaris."

She chewed her delectable bottom lip as she searched through the sheets of music on the piano.

Elliot shifted, feeling that familiar, pleasant tumescence, and wished there wasn't a footman stationed outside the drawing room door.

Still, even with the hovering presence of the footmen in the hall, seducing her would not be impossible. Not for him. He would just have to be careful. As for any potential aftermath, he wouldn't have to worry. Sir Douglas would be far too concerned about his family's name to want his daughter's shame made public knowledge.

In the meantime, there was always Sally Newcombe's. He fingered his wallet in his breast pocket.

If he was low on the actual cash, he was certain Sally would give credit to Adrian's half brother.

"Shall I turn the pages for you, Damaris?" he offered graciously when he realized she had finally selected a piece and was preparing to play.

She smiled at him. "Oh, indeed, yes...Elliot."

He gestured at the sheet. "And you start...?"

"Here." She reached out and touched the place on the sheet music.

"Here?" he repeated, placing his hand beside hers so that they touched.

She yanked her hand away, blushing and giggling self-consciously.

Elliot hated women who giggled, but he was pleased by the blush and the sensation of her warm flesh against his. "Forgive me," he murmured.

She glanced up at him, and his gaze held hers for a long moment—long enough for him to experience a surge of triumph.

She would be his, and it wouldn't take long.

Out of the corner of his eye he saw the butler enter the room. "The Reverend McKenna," the man announced, stepping aside to make way for the young clergyman, who took one look at Elliot and Damaris and colored as much as the young lady had.

"I'm sorry to intrude," he stammered, glancing about like a man seeking a way out of a burning building.

He wants her, too, Elliot realized, and the thought increased his desire, as any competition in such matters always did. To beat Adrian and this young fool into Damaris's bed—it would be a double victory.

"How may I help you?" Damaris asked Reverend McKenna with a hint of annoyance, and Elliot noticed she did not rise from her seat at the piano.

"I just thought...that is, I wondered, since your father is away, if you needed... If I could be of any assistance?"

"Thank you, Reverend McKenna, but I can't think of anything," Damaris answered.

"Oh, well, then, I'll wish you a good day. Both of you." He made a funny, awkward little bow and left.

Damaris sat motionless for a moment, a small crease of worry in her brow as she regarded the door, until Elliot moved beside her. "Shall we resume?" he asked softly.

She smiled at him and said, "Whatever you wish, Elliot."

Chapter Eleven

That same afternoon, the duchess took to her bed with a mild stomach complaint, and Hester sought permission to indulge in the harmless, selfish pleasure of a walk to the town of Barroughby, a distance of nearly five miles.

The day was cold, and the sky held portents of rain, the duchess pointed out.

However, Hester wasn't about to let the weather get the better of her, for she felt as if she had been imprisoned the past few days, so with quiet determination she showed the duchess that she was prepared, with her stout shoes—which the duchess kindly pronounced "hideous"—to keep her feet dry and warm. Her plain woolen gown and cloak would be ample protection against the chill air, and her bonnet, while unflattering, was a suitable barrier against the breeze.

At last the duchess condescended to let Hester go, provided she made a preliminary selection of fabric and ribbons for the duchess's new ball gown. The seamstress would, of course, have to come to the hall with samples for her to make the final choice, but

Hester had been deputized to "sort through the unsuitable." The duchess had so many restrictions and opinions on fabrics and colors, Hester hoped she had managed to get everything right when she visited the dressmaker's shop.

That duty now discharged, Hester was free to amuse herself a little while, or begin the journey home. As she lingered for a moment to look into the milliner's window, she reflected that apparently she was not the only person who wished to be away from Barroughby Hall today. Jenkins had mentioned, with a worried frown, that the duke had ridden off "somewhere" shortly after breakfast. Lord Elliot had likewise departed for Oakwood, the home of the Sackville-Coopers.

Not that their comings and goings should mean anything to her.

She focused her attention on the bright bolts of fabric she could see through the glass, then smiled at her own silliness. She had been hard-pressed not to order a new ball gown for herself, which would have been a completely wasteful and unjustifiable expense. She had worn her blue velvet gown only once, at a party. To order another gown so soon was pure vanity and extravagance. Besides, even so attired, she would never be able to detract from the attention sure to be paid to Damaris. A new gown wouldn't make a new Hester.

A glance at the cloudy sky made her decide to go back to Barroughby Hall before it rained. She walked along briskly until she spied Reverend McKenna moving slowly along the street bordering the market square, his head bent and shoulders slumped, which was quite different from his usual purposeful stride.

Perhaps something had happened to upset him. She knew he was much more involved with the welfare of the parishioners than the canon, who mainly concerned himself with the duchess and his tithes.

"Reverend McKenna!" she called, and he halted and turned toward her.

"Ah, Lady Hester!" he exclaimed softly when she reached him. "How do you do?"

"Quite well, Reverend. Would you care to join me for some tea and cakes?"

"Oh, thank you, no. I should be going. Mrs. Nandy isn't very well today." His brow suddenly wrinkled with concern. "You came to town all by yourself?"

"Yes. I enjoy walking. I shall be quite safe in the daytime."

"Of course," he replied with an absent air.

"How are *you?*" she asked, noting that he was once again despondent. "You seem very tired. I know you are working too hard." *Or are you thinking about Damaris?*

Reverend McKenna regarded her thoughtfully for such a long time that she thought he indeed might be ill. "Thank you," he said at last. "I am quite well."

Despite his effort to smile, she thought she had never seen a man less happy. "What has happened?" she asked, putting her hand gently on his arm, and noticing that it wasn't nearly as muscular as that of the duke, a thought she dismissed as quickly as it had arrived. "Is anything the matter?"

"Not at all," he replied at once.

"How is Miss Sackville-Cooper managing without her father?" Hester asked, knowing that it was wrong to pry, but assuaging her doubts by telling herself she was trying to help.

This time he made no effort to look cheerful. "Well enough, I gather."

Hester was quite sure she had ascertained the reason for Reverend McKenna's despondency, but she had no idea how to proceed. It was a delicate subject, especially with one as shy as Hamish McKenna, and she had already overstepped the bounds of delicacy.

"She is not lacking for company," Reverend McKenna muttered in a barely audible voice before glancing at Hester. "Come, I will walk with you as far as the road to Barroughby Hall."

He must be upset to say even that much about Damaris, Hester thought as they went on their way. "Miss Sackville-Cooper has many visitors?"

"Yes," Reverend McKenna said, then he raised his head and looked at her, with a smile on his lips that did nothing to assuage the pain burning in his eyes. "It was very kind and generous of the duke to give the Bolbys the cottage," he said, startling her with his abrupt change of subject. "Do you suppose Lord Elliot would have done the same?"

It was on Hester's lips to say "Of course he would," but she did not. She could not be sure that Elliot Fitzwalter would be so generous even under duress, epitome of virtue though his mother thought him. "I would like to think so," she answered at last.

"He seems a fine young man," Reverend Mc-

Kenna continued, and now Hester was sure she grasped the clergyman's trouble.

"Miss Sackville-Cooper is like a lovely picture that draws many admirers," Hester said gently. "Yet she is not a lifeless object. She has a mind and opinions. She might be momentarily swayed by flattery or the words of another, but that doesn't mean she will make her decisions based on such things. And the admirers may be flighty creatures who will soon be gone."

Words she would do well to heed herself, Hester thought glumly, her brief lapse of foolishness over. The duke would surely move on to greener pastures soon enough, and if he would not choose the untitled daughter of a knight, beautiful and rich though she may be, he would not want the homely daughter of an earl, titled though she may be. He would want beauty, wealth *and* title, and surely there would be plenty of families willing to dismiss the scandalous stories told about him for such a rich prize as the Duke of Barroughby.

"Do you really think so?" Reverend McKenna asked.

"Yes, I really do," she affirmed.

"I wish they were both gone!" her companion said with some venom. He saw Hester's startled face and smiled ruefully, something she was glad to see. It was better than the utter hopelessness that had darkened his countenance before. "Lord Elliot is too handsome. He makes the rest of us look like haggis. And although the duke was generous to the Bolbys, I don't like having such a man in the neighborhood."

"He owns the neighborhood," Hester noted.

"He does that," Reverend McKenna acknowledged. "But to have a man of his reputation for a landlord!"

It suddenly occurred to Hester that if she wanted answers to some questions about the duke's past, this might be the time, and Reverend McKenna might be the very man to answer them. "Then the stories about the Duke of Barroughby are true?" she ventured.

"I think some of them are exaggerated. I *hope* some of them are exaggerated."

"What, for instance?" Hester asked.

"Oh, I couldn't speak of such things with you, my lady," Reverend McKenna demurred with a modesty that would have done credit to many a young lady.

"I've heard a few of the more recent ones, anyway," she countered, "from my sisters and their friends. Besides, if I'm staying in his house, I should know with whom I'm dealing, don't you think?"

Reverend McKenna nodded slowly. "Very well, my lady. I hope I won't offend you."

"I don't think you will," she replied, certain he would omit several of the more salacious details, an unnecessary chivalry, since her sisters and her friends spared no detail in their gossip. "Tell me what happened at Oxford."

"Ah, that. The start of his infamous career, or so Canon Smeech says. The duke got into an argument in a tavern about a woman, which turned into a brawl. A fire broke out. The place burned to the ground. Several people were injured, including the duke's friend, the Earl of Ravensbrook, who was quite badly burned. The duke has never even gone to visit the poor man, they say.

"The worst part of it was, the duke's father, who wasn't a well man when this happened, took to his bed after hearing about it. He died a short time later."

"How terrible," Hester said weakly.

"There were other things at Oxford, too. Gambling debts, and..."

"And...?" Hester prompted, noting the clergyman's blushing face. "And more women?"

Reverend McKenna nodded. "Several. Most of them soiled doves, or so I understand. Even here—" The young man stopped talking and halted abruptly. "I really don't think this is a fit subject for us to be discussing."

Hester silently agreed, for she had suddenly discovered that she did not enjoy hearing about the duke's women.

"It's most puzzling," Reverend McKenna continued thoughtfully as they resumed walking. "For a man like that to spend all night with a dying man..."

"I beg your pardon?"

"The duke sat with poor old Bolby all night, until he died."

"Really?"

"Young Bolby told me so himself."

This evidence of a depth of devotion previously unknown in the duke pleased Hester more than she could have anticipated.

Until she remembered the other women in the duke's life.

"Well, this is where I must leave you," Reverend

McKenna announced, and Hester saw that they were
at the far end of the town, near the river. The road
split, one way leading to the poorer homes of some
of the townsfolk, the other toward Barroughby Hall.
"Good day, Lady Hester."

"Good day, Reverend," she said warmly. "Please
remember what I said about Miss Sackville-Cooper.
She does like you, you know."

Reverend McKenna smiled wistfully. "Liking is
not what I want," he said softly before tipping his
hat and going on his way.

After he left her, Hester quickened her pace, for
another glance at the sky had shown her more gathering clouds. They were not yet as dark as they might
be, though, and she judged that there would be time
to get back to Barroughby Hall before it began to rain,
a decision made easier by the knowledge that the only
place she might conceivably seek shelter would be
the rectory, the home of Reverend Canon Smeech.

She decided to take a shorter route directly through
the part of the town near the river, for the main road
to Barroughby Hall skirted this rather run-down por-
tion of the town. She could rejoin it on the other side.
This area was not the best of places, but staying on
the main road would add several minutes to her journey.

The buildings here, made of stone and wood and
combinations thereof, were used as warehouses by the
several sheep farmers and wool merchants of the area.
On the river, barges were being loaded and unloaded.
At riverside taverns, polemen drank pints of ale until

they were needed, beggars plied their trade and, she was sure, so did some pickpockets.

Soon she came near the street she had heard whispered of by the servants when they thought she couldn't hear—Stamford Street, where Sally Newcombe lived, despite the efforts of Reverend Canon Smeech. The canon made it very clear *how* Sally Newcombe earned her living, along with her "jezebels," for it seemed she employed, if that was the right term, a bevy of other young women, too.

Hester walked more quickly, anxious to get away from the place, and the remembrance of Reverend McKenna saying "even here" in reference to certain of the duke's activities.

What would it be like to be a prostitute? she wondered as she hurried along. To belong to a man like the Duke of Barroughby, for him to possess her body for an hour or a night? To feel his hands upon her, touching her, caressing her? His lips on hers, so strong and yet gentle, too.

But then to be passed along like used goods to another man, one she might dislike on sight. One who might beat her, or even kill her.

Hester suppressed a shudder, and hoped that the stories of the duke and Sally Newcombe were not true. After all, why would a man like him ever have to pay for a woman's feigned affection?

Besides, what was she doing even contemplating being in the duke's arms for a moment, let alone a night?

A few feet away was the start of Stamford Street. With renewed resolve to get back to Barroughby Hall,

Hester continued on her way, albeit at a slightly more decorous pace, until the clatter of hooves on the cobblestones and a shout made her halt in her tracks.

Chapter Twelve

With a curse, Adrian reined in so sharply, Drake almost sat on his haunches. "Get out of my way, you fool!" he snapped at the stupid woman who had walked into the middle of the road as if trying to get herself killed deliberately.

When he saw Hester Pimblett's startled blue eyes in a very pale face looking up at him, he wished he had stayed at Sally's. She gazed at him only a moment, then she lowered her eyes and blushed as if she had been the one leaving a house of ill repute, and he wondered if she had somehow guessed where he was coming from.

Which was completely ludicrous. How could she?

"What the devil are you doing in the middle of the street?" he demanded as he dismounted. "And in this part of the town, too."

"I might ask you the same thing, my lord, if I didn't believe I already knew the answer," she replied, darting a sidelong glance in his general direction and wrinkling her nose.

It was only then he realized that he smelled of Sally's perfume. He might just as well wear a sign that declared that he had been in the company of women, and with his reputation, she would probably make an assumption as to the kind of women. Unfortunately, she would be right, although he had not been a customer. "You might have been attacked, or robbed," he declared defensively.

"By an errant seller of perfumes, perhaps?" she inquired calmly. "I was on my way back to Barroughby Hall, and since the weather looked chancy, I took the shorter route."

"This is no place for a woman."

"It is no place for a duke, either," she countered, and he was momentarily struck speechless by her impertinence.

"If you will excuse me, my lord, I had better be on my way."

"You are always running away from me," he noted.

"Am I not supposed to?" she replied, pausing. "I thought you wanted me to beware of you."

Touché, my lady, Adrian thought ruefully. "Nevertheless, my lady," he said firmly, "I must insist that I be allowed to escort you home." He took hold of Drake's reins and held out his arm.

"I don't think—"

"I did not ask for your opinion. I will see you home. It is not safe for a lone woman to be on the road, not even to Barroughby Hall."

With obvious reluctance she laid her hand lightly on his arm.

"Perhaps you would prefer me to walk some dis-

tance behind, like a eunuch following a potentate?''
he asked, a small measure of annoyance creeping into
his voice.

She gave him a sidelong glance. ''Oh, I do not
think anyone would ever mistake *you* for a eunuch,
my lord.''

Was she serious, or not? If she was, then she must
be condemning his apparent activity today. If she was
joking, she must forgive him. She had called him by
the less formal title, and he took that for a hopeful
sign. Suddenly, and uncharacteristically, he found he
didn't know what to say next.

It was for Lady Hester to break the silence, and
when she spoke, she didn't look at him. ''Why is the
road not safe these days, my lord? Is it because *you*
are here?''

Heaven help me! he thought with despair, *I said
too much in the stable. She must think me the worst
blackguard in the world—and with this stench about
me, how can she not?* ''Because it is,'' he finally said.
''Why did you come to the village on foot? Would
the duchess not permit you to use a carriage?''

He saw that she was genuinely startled. ''No, my
lord. I wanted to walk.''

''Next time you shall have the barouche, if you
like.''

''I prefer to walk.''

As they continued some way in silence, Adrian
found himself desperate to know what she was thinking, but afraid to ask. What if she was considering
her escort the worst sort of man in the world? ''Your
family,'' he said at last. ''They are well?''

"Yes, my lord."

He was so disgusted with this feeble attempt, he decided he would stay quiet.

"Giving the Bolbys the cottage was most generous, my lord," Hester said after several minutes.

He looked at her, but couldn't see her face because of her cursed bonnet. "It was nothing. They have been employed on the estate for years."

"Others would not have been so generous. I also heard…" She hesitated, and just as his curiosity was becoming nearly unbearable, she continued. "I also heard that you sat up all night with Bolby before he died."

He nodded his head, and wondered who had told her. Whoever it was, he was in that person's debt for letting her know that however much she condemned him, he wasn't completely evil.

Hester paused and he halted, puzzled, as she turned toward him, an expression of earnest concern on her face. She took her hand from his arm. "My lord, why do you go to such places?"

He made no attempt to hide his surprise. "What places?"

"Sally Newcombe's."

"Who said I have been there?"

"Are you saying you have not?"

"You have no right to ask such a question."

"I know." She colored, but regarded him stead-fastly, again with that studious expression, as if he were some kind of strange animal.

Maybe to her, he was. "I am surprised a woman of your background could even bring herself to speak of such things," he remarked, trying to sound cool and unconcerned.

"You do not have to answer, my lord. I merely wanted to understand."

"I don't think you know what you're asking."

She frowned in frustration. "My lord, I'm not a child. Granted, I don't know about the world the way you or most men do, because my father didn't think young women should. But I want to know why men patronize such establishments, when..."

"When?"

"When there are lonely women in the world who would enjoy their companionship."

"Like you?" He surveyed her with mock astonishment. "Lady Hester, are you telling me you would offer yourself for such *intimate* companionship as Sally provides?"

He was genuinely astonished when her eyes began to glisten with angry tears. "Please do not make fun of me, my lord." She swallowed hard, and he upbraided himself for being so derisive. "I thought you might tell me, that's all. I know it's none of my business, but it cannot be...good for you, either."

However he felt about hurting her feelings, and although he was truly touched by her apparent concern for his health, he had no desire to discuss Sally Newcombe and her ilk with this young lady. "As you say, it is none of your business, and Sally's business is her own, too."

"Sally's business is sinful."

"You sound just like Smeech," he replied. "What could he, or you, know about Sally's life? Do you

know she was abandoned by her mother and sent to
an orphanage when she was five? Do you know that
by the time you were leaving the tender care of your
governess she had already been attacked more than
once?''

"I know that I am fortunate. I understand something of the fates many women suffer," Hester responded. "But not many of them have the acquaintance of a duke. Couldn't you do something to help
her?''

"I tried. She refused. She has her pride, too,
strange as that may sound to you. As for the women
in her house, they don't have many alternatives, either.''

"You do," she retorted, still determined to understand him. "You can have any woman and yet you
still..."

"Visit Sally?''

She nodded.

"Today when I went to see Sally," he said quietly,
gazing at her intently, "I went as a friend, and only
a friend.''

"I am glad to hear it, my lord," she said, truly
relieved. "Those places aren't safe.''

He grinned sardonically, and she felt their relationship, such as it was, had returned to its normal course.
"This from a girl who's walking alone and unchaperoned through the warehouses!''

She gave him an accusing look. "My lord, you
know as well as I that the warehouses aren't dangerous during the day.''

"Are you not afraid of the scandal of being seen

alone and unchaperoned in such a location?'' he asked in mock dismay.

"This from a man who has been involved in more scandals than days of the week!'' she replied with similar sarcasm.

"My God, you *are* an impertinent miss!'' he said with something approaching a laugh. "My stepmother couldn't have picked a better companion if she'd searched a hundred years!''

"I am rarely impertinent to my elders,'' Hester observed somewhat primly, for she prided herself on keeping her temper.

"That's the beauty of it, my sly young lady. To think of you sitting so silent and demure, knowing that inside that clever head of yours, you are contemplating such snide opinions!''

Hester flushed, but more from pleasure and his warm regard than shame that he had discovered one of her secrets. "Alas,'' she said, imitating his melodramatics she well remembered from the stable, "the secret is out! I fear I must disappear into yon misty moors. Oh, for shame!''

She looked at the duke, expecting to see him smile. Instead, he was regarding her with a most peculiar and serious expression. "Why aren't you married?''

"Because...because no one has ever asked me,'' she stammered. "Nor have I ever been in love.''

"Not ever?''

She shook her head. "Have you?'' she asked softly. "Been in love?''

He slowly shook his head, too. "Not ever.''

Suddenly he cleared his throat, and Hester found

she could breathe again. "I haven't married because I have yet to find a suitable woman," he continued nonchalantly. "Given my reputation with the ladies, surely you realize I am not particularly troubled by this lack."

"A brief liaison satisfies you?"

"Yes."

"I don't believe you."

"I beg your pardon?" he demanded incredulously.

"I don't believe you are satisfied, or content."

He moved away from her, his expression wary and annoyed. "You don't know me, Lady Hester. You don't *want* to know me. Nor can you possibly understand me."

"I can try," she said staunchly, seeing beyond his wariness and annoyance to the loneliness that had appeared in his dark eyes. "I've been lonely, too. Many times."

"You have your family."

"So do you."

He sniffed dismissively.

"I have two beautiful sisters, and I am homely. I have a father who wanted sons, a mother who thinks only of entertaining. I wanted an education—it was not considered fitting." She tried to smile. "Sometimes I think I must have been a foundling left on the doorstep."

"I don't think you are homely," the duke said quietly.

Hester stared at him in disbelief, telling herself his compliment had to be meaningless, a polite pleasantry and nothing more. "You can't mean that."

He took her hands and stared into her eyes. "Shall I tell you what I see when I look at you?"

She could only nod.

"I see a kind and patient young woman who makes my home more bearable than it has been for years. I see beautiful, honest blue eyes. I see strength of purpose, intelligence, true modesty, thoughtfulness and diplomacy." His fingers stroked her hand, and she could feel the blood throbbing through her body. "I see—" He stopped and drew back, letting her hands drop.

"Yes?" she said breathlessly.

"I see my barouche and four coming toward us."

She stepped away from him quickly, acutely aware of how close together they had been standing seconds before, and what construction might be put on such intimacy.

A construction *she* was putting on it.

"It's Elliot," the duke said. Suddenly he turned to her with a fierce and determined air. "Hester, don't listen to Elliot. Don't believe a single word he says. And don't *ever* be alone with him."

"But why—!"

"Because I tell you not to." He lowered his voice and stared at her with that intensity she found so intimate and compelling. "Because you *must* trust me in this."

Before Hester could even begin to formulate an answer to his impassioned request, the barouche rolled to a stop in front of them.

"Hullo, Adrian. Afternoon, Lady Hester," Lord Elliot called out as the coachman climbed down from his seat and opened the door for Lord Elliot to disembark. "I came to find you, Lady Hester," he said, "because I noticed a change of weather upon my return to Barroughby Hall. When Mama told me where you had gone, I thought it wise to meet you."

Hester suddenly realized the sky was much darker than it had been; she had been too involved in the conversation to notice before.

"How thoughtful," the duke remarked flatly.

With an equally nonchalant manner, Lord Elliot regarded his half brother. "You smell like a whore."

While the observation was not without merit, Hester was shocked that any gentleman would use such language in a lady's presence. It demonstrated a lack of respect for her as well as the duke. "I must beg your pardon," she said, affecting a repentant air. "I spilled a bottle of scent in a shop. Most careless of me, wasn't it?"

She dared not look at the duke, but trusted he would take the excuse she provided.

"How fortunate you returned from your rambles in time to come searching for Lady Hester," the duke said, and Hester was careful not to look pleased that he had taken the out.

"I spent a very lovely afternoon in the company of the charming Miss Sackville-Cooper," Lord Elliot revealed with a smile.

Hester risked a glance at the duke, just in time to see an angry scowl cross his face. She thought of the warm feelings he had inspired within her only moments ago. What was she to make of his annoyance that Lord Elliot had spent time with Damaris?

Surely this was a timely reminder that she must remember the Dark Duke was a master of seduction, and that she could put no credence in his apparent sincere liking for her. What he had said was merely flattery, and probably second nature to him. Perhaps she should doubt his revelation that he had gone to Sally Newcombe's only to visit an old friend, too.

Which did not explain why she took his warning about Lord Elliot so seriously.

"Hatley, put up the roof before it rains," the duke ordered the coachman. "I suggest you get in, Lady Hester."

There being no excuse to linger, she obeyed quickly, Hatley handing her in. Lord Elliot sat opposite her in the carriage and gave a swift, sharp order. The carriage began to move, turning back toward Barroughby Hall.

Hester wished the roof was not up, for she did not enjoy feeling enclosed in such intimacy with Lord Elliot.

Then she realized the duke was riding beside the barouche, on her side, and a sense of relief filled her, which, she realized, was quite the opposite of what most people would feel. Still, it was quite true. If Lord Elliot tried anything improper, the duke was within easy call.

Despite the spirited nature of the duke's horse, he controlled it easily with his strong, long legs, and she was hard-pressed not to stare at the muscular limb displayed so near.

"It was kind of you to make my mother's task a little easier," Lord Elliot said, drawing her attention.

"I was happy to go out," she replied honestly.

"You enjoy walking?"

"Yes, my lord."

"You have such lovely, long fingers, Lady Hester," he said, reaching out to take one in his gloved hand. "Tell me, Lady Hester, what instrument do you play?"

Lord Elliot should not be touching her in any way, and she most certainly did not want him to. Not here and, she realized with absolute certainty, not ever.

"None, my lord," she said, gently but firmly extricating her hand. "I fear I have not a musical mind."

"A great pity," he replied, apparently not offended by her action. "Is painting your forte? Or netting purses? Perhaps decoupage?"

"Sadly, I am not clever with my hands, my lord," Hester admitted,

"My dear Lady Hester," he said, leaning toward her with a smile that did nothing to dispel the sense of entrapment that had descended upon her, "must we be so formal?"

Hester frowned slightly, wondering if it was a family trait to despise formality—which was, if nothing else, a useful means of keeping one's distance from someone one would rather not know well.

"I would be delighted if you would call me Elliot."

She had been pleased when the duke had made a similar request, and now she realized that one reason she found his proposal so much less offensive than the one currently being made to her was that he was simply exchanging one title for another, both equally proper, whereas Lord Elliot's proposal was completely *im*proper. "I could not, Lord Elliot."

"Not when we are in company, perhaps," he said persuasively. "But when we are alone..."

"I could not," she reiterated firmly.

"Of course, you are quite right." He leaned back against his seat and stared out the window.

The only sounds to disturb the silence were the wheels upon the road, the heavy tread of the carriage's team and the lighter step of the duke's stallion.

"I fear I have made a terrible blunder, Lady Hester," Lord Elliot said, regarding her contritely a few minutes later. "My suggestion was very gauche."

She did not answer.

"I hope you won't ignore me completely, for there is something I must speak to you about," Lord Elliot said softly, gazing at her with something of the intensity of his brother, but with some indefinable quality missing. "I want you to beware of the duke."

"Why, my lord?" she asked warily.

The young man sat forward eagerly. "You know his reputation. Surely that is reason enough." He glanced toward their mounted companion furtively.

It was then that Hester realized what was different in the way the two men looked at her as they delivered their warnings. The duke had looked sincere and as if his concern was for her alone; his sibling's expression bore more malice than any thought for her. "I thank you for your interest, my lord," she replied, "and I promise you, I shall be very careful indeed."

He gave her a shrewd look, which quickly changed

to one of wounded sensibility. "Oh, please, Lady Hester," he said softly, "surely you know you have nothing to fear from *me*."

Hester berated herself for not being more circumspect. "I am sure you are a gentleman," she replied, hoping rather than believing this was true.

Lord Elliot smiled warmly. "I am glad of that."

"And I am quite aware of the duke's reputation," she continued, careful to keep her tone one of calm modulation, for an extraordinary reaction might give rise to suspicions of...what?

That she was certainly no longer wary of the duke. That she was intrigued by him, and even sympathized with him. Perhaps that she was beginning to feel something akin to love for the unloved man.

Whatever she was feeling, anything other than dispassionate regard would be a mistake. She could and must have no hope that he would ever return any deeper feelings. She was plain, unexciting Hester Pimblett, and he was the handsome, roguish Dark Duke of Barroughby.

The carriage drew up to the steps leading into Barroughby Hall. "Here we are," Hester said rather unnecessarily, and with every effort to mask her relief. The barouche door opened and she began to get out, expecting to be aided by Hatley.

Instead, the duke waited to assist her. A swift glance over her shoulder showed that Lord Elliot was scowling in a manner that made her wonder if there was something in the Fitzwalter blood to create such black and angry looks; however, that became much less important when she put her hand into the duke's and glanced at his face.

His expression was impassive, his gesture merely polite, and yet what a tingle of excitement sped along her veins when she touched him! And how erratically her heart seemed to beat when she looked at his dark eyes, for try as he might to look nonchalant, she saw a question there.

A question she must and would answer, somehow.

"Thank you, Your Grace," she said in a normal tone before lowering her voice. "For everything, my lord."

Then she walked into Barroughby Hall without so much as a backward glance at the man she now regarded as her protector, whether he knew it or not, and whether she should or not.

Chapter Thirteen

Adrian preceded Elliot into the house and, after both had given their hats and gloves to a waiting footman, turned on him with a fierce and angry eye. "Come to my study," he commanded.

"Who do you think you are, to order me in such a fashion?" Elliot replied.

"I am the Duke of Barroughby," Adrian growled, and for once, Elliot thought he would do well to ignore Adrian's manner and obey as Adrian turned on his heel and led the way to his study.

"What is it this time?" Elliot asked as he entered. "Upset because I used the barouche without asking?"

Adrian shut the door firmly behind his half brother and glared at him. "Don't you ever speak so in front of a lady again!"

"How so?" Elliot queried, forcing a lightness to his tone that he certainly did not feel, suddenly mindful of Adrian's prowess at dueling. He sat casually in one of the large wing chairs while Adrian paced like a caged bear.

"To speak of whores in front of Lady Hester, you disgusting sybarite!"

"Ah!" Elliot said, ignoring the insult because he was aware that there was something different about Adrian's manner, something that made Elliot feel that he had the upper hand. "Apparently it is quite all right for one to patronize such establishments," he continued, affecting a mockingly studious air, "and to reek of them afterward—no matter what pretty excuse Lady Hester makes for you—but one should never speak of them before a lady."

Adrian realized he had made a terrible mistake by confronting Elliot so quickly. The sly rogue had interpreted his concern as genuine regard for Lady Hester, which placed Hester in great jeopardy, as Adrian well knew from sad experience. He reminded himself that Elliot must believe the beautiful, vacuous Damaris was his target. Yet when he considered how his heart had soared to think Hester had placed her trust in him—with his soiled reputation and fresh from a brothel!—he very much wished he did not have to.

"I hope you don't speak that way to Damaris Sackville-Cooper," Adrian said coldly.

"I didn't this afternoon. She seemed very happy to see me, too," Elliot noted.

"As long as seeing is all you have in mind."

"Jealous, are we?" Elliot inquired slyly.

"I won't have you do to her what you did to Elizabeth Howell."

It was Elliot's turn to scowl.

"Why else do you think I came here? I knew you'd

wash up here eventually. I want to warn you against ever doing such a despicable thing again!''

"Or you'll what?'' Elliot demanded just as angrily. "Send me to prison? On what charge? Elizabeth was a silly girl who fancied herself in love with me. She was not averse to more, shall we say, passionate expressions of her devotion, so who was I to deny her?''

"You left her alone and penniless in London, pregnant and afraid.''

"Not alone,'' Elliot corrected. "Her brother was in town, as I believe you discovered for yourself.'' He nodded at Adrian's injured leg.

"That youngster?'' Adrian replied. "He knew even less about the ways of the world than *she* did. I last saw him blubbering like a baby because he was sure he was going to jail for wounding me.''

"So how do you intend to stop stupid young women from offering themselves to me—you who are apparently such a saint?''

"I want you to stop taking advantage of them.''

"When I merely follow my elder brother's example?''

"I *never* seduced and abandoned gullible girls!''

"Oh, that's right,'' Elliot said scornfully. "You are the virtuous one in the family.''

"And you're a devil!'' Adrian retorted. "I won't have you going near Damaris!''

"It's Damaris now, is it, dear brother?'' Elliot said, knowing full well how Adrian hated to be called "brother.'' "I think we should let the beautiful Miss Sackville-Cooper decide with whom she prefers to keep company, don't you, brother? And may the best man win?''

Adrian smiled coldly. ''Very well, Elliot. The best man will.''

Elliot smiled back, his eyes just as cold, and Adrian knew the challenge had been accepted.

''The best man will what?'' the duchess demanded as she entered the room after the briefest of knocks.

''Win,'' Elliot replied calmly.

''Win what?'' his mother asked, her gaze moving from one to the other.

''A competition,'' Adrian answered.

The duchess glared at him. ''Are you trying to make Elliot gamble?'' She faced her son. ''You aren't gambling, are you?''

''No, Mama. This is not about money,'' Elliot said.

The duchess's face showed her relief. ''Thank goodness you are not allowing him to corrupt you. Now, where is Lady Hester, Elliot? I trust she was pleased you went to find her?''

''Indeed she was. Very grateful,'' Elliot said lightly, and Adrian was hard-pressed to keep his face impassive, although it seemed every part of him tingled with curiosity to know what they had been speaking of in the barouche. ''Is she not in the drawing room?''

''No.''

''Then she must have gone upstairs to change her clothes.''

The duchess turned to leave the room.

''We were speaking about winning the heart of Damaris Sackville-Cooper,'' Adrian remarked, his emotions once more under control as he played the devil's advocate.

"I assume you mean that for a joke," his stepmother said with no hint of humor when she slowly wheeled around to regard him with a stony gaze. "She is merely a knight's daughter. Not a fit wife for either of you."

"Nobody mentioned marriage," Adrian noted.

"That's just the sort of lecherous remark I should expect from you," the duchess said testily.

"Perhaps that is why I said it," Adrian replied, sauntering toward the windows so that he wouldn't have to look at the pair of them. "But you must admit, she is very beautiful. And young."

"Damaris will do very well for the wife of a knight or baronet, but certainly never for a duke or a duke's son," the duchess replied. "Not even you."

"Her father is extremely wealthy."

"Money is not more important than rank. She might just as well be a pauper."

"She would not be so for long, if she were to be left penniless. A woman of her beauty would find a 'protector' soon enough," Adrian observed. Even as he spoke, he realized the truth of his words. The loss of her father's wealth would leave Damaris completely helpless.

Hester Pimblett would not be helpless in such a circumstance. She would somehow find a way to survive, not simply with her life, but with her honor and dignity intact. She would become a governess or teacher, or she would be a poorly paid companion to some fortunate soul who would have her company every day, or she would marry a good, deserving man like Reverend McKenna, who would bless her all the days of his life, for she would make his house a place of joyful refuge, a sanctuary against troubles. She would make a fine mother, excellent wife and, remembering her kiss and the gentleness of her touch, a lover without compare—for some other, lucky man who had not destroyed his life by rash and foolish behavior.

"Oh, Mama," Elliot said, "can't you see he's baiting you? Why don't you ask Adrian who *he* was visiting?"

"I fail to see why we are even discussing Damaris Sackville-Cooper at all," the duchess snapped. "She is not to be considered. Why, even Lady Hester would be better than Damaris Sackville-Cooper," the duchess finished in a tone of condescension that was extreme, even for her. "Although her children would be homely creatures if they took after her."

Disgusted, Adrian turned away from the window in time to see the slight nod of agreement Elliot made—and to realize that Hester was standing in the doorway. Judging by the rapid coloring of her cheeks, she had overheard the duchess's last remark.

Adrian had never hated his stepmother more than at that moment.

And he had never admired Hester more, for she continued into the room with astonishing aplomb, only the pink flush to her cheeks giving away anything of her emotional state. Having long practice in keeping his own reactions in check, he could guess the effort it took to achieve such outward calm. "The dressmaker will be here tomorrow afternoon, Your Grace,'' she said softly as the two men bowed to her.

"Excellent," the duchess replied with a slightly guilty expression, and Adrian wondered if that most self-centered of women had finally been made to perceive that she had insulted someone. "Tell me about the fabrics," she ordered, making a gesture toward the chair opposite her.

"If you will excuse me until dinner, Your Grace," Hester replied, "you were quite right about the exertion of the walk, for I find I am quite fatigued after all."

Adrian subdued a smile of satisfaction, knowing, as surely as Hester did, that his stepmother could scarcely argue the fatigue, since she had not dissuaded Elliot from going out in the barouche to fetch her home.

"Very well," the duchess said.

Hester made her curtsy and left the room.

"I don't think she heard you, Mama," Elliot said calmly, and Adrian was pleased to think that Hester had fooled them. "Otherwise, I suppose we should have had to find another companion for you."

"You could always stay here, Elliot," Adrian remarked just as calmly, and was even more pleased to note Elliot's swift and venomous glance.

"Of course nothing would delight me more," he lied outrageously as he smiled at his mother, "but a man of my position must be seen in London."

"Especially if he is to find himself an appropriate wife," Adrian added. "Unless you've already settled upon the beauteous Miss Sackville-Cooper."

His mother darted Elliot a fierce and searching look.

"Of course not," Elliot was forced to confess. "I simply thought it a neighborly duty to pay a call."

"Ah, I see. Duty."

"What would you know about duty?" the duchess demanded sourly of Adrian. "You only live to please yourself."

"Once again I stand condemned," Adrian remarked with a courteous bow. "So, like a condemned man, I shall take myself away from decent, unselfish people."

With that, he gladly left them.

Hester sighed as she closed her bedroom door, seeing little of the room, which was rather too ornately decorated for her taste. The bed was wide, with a tall half canopy, and so high she dreaded breaking a bone if she ever fell out of it. The rest of the furnishings were equally ostentatious, from the heavy damask draperies to the inlaid tables, the slender Regency chairs and the large mahogany armoire.

As she walked farther into the room, she wandered toward the table near the window, which held the list of costs for the ball, the first few drafts of the menu for the supper to be served, the list of flowers and the final acceptances of several guests.

Although she had tried her best to keep expenses within a reasonable limit, the duchess had not been nearly so moderate as Hester had hoped, and she literally waved away any concerns that Hester voiced, claiming that Adrian could well afford whatever was necessary. Hester was not looking forward to his re-action to the final tally.

But that was not what made her sigh and slump dejectedly into the chair in front of her vanity table.

She told herself not to be upset by the duchess's words. The duchess was a vain, stupid woman, and if she thought her companion homely, well, it was the truth. The constant comparison with her sisters had ensured that Hester had learned early and with unmistakable surety that she was not beautiful.

Yet the duke had found her interesting.

Although he seemed very interested in Damaris, too, which was only to be expected.

At this moment Hester wished she had never met the Duke of Barroughby. Better not to have spoken with him, to be with him, to feel such excitement. Better by far to remember that she was most fitted in life for companionship, not love, and that if someone did offer for her hand, it would be because she would make a good wife, not for passion.

At least the duchess had complimented her efficiency in the preparations for the ball. She must have meant it, or she would never have said so to Sir Douglas. Nevertheless, Hester would have preferred to be appreciated for some other quality. The duke—

Hester swallowed hard and told herself to forget the duke. She swallowed again, for her throat was dry and sore, from trying not to cry at the duchess's unexpected pronouncement, no doubt.

With swift, efficient fingers Hester pulled out her hairpins, then shook her hair loose. Not quite as pleasant a release as being free of her corset, of course, but she enjoyed the sensation.

She picked up her brush and started to run it through her thick brown hair. While she did so, she regarded her face in the mirror and wondered how she would look with raven black hair. Or golden blond. Or even red. Anything but this commonplace brown. And what if she had natural curls, thick waves of them to frame her plain face? What if her eyes were green instead of blue? What if her lips were a little thinner? What if her nose...well, mercifully, there was nothing the matter with her nose. If she shared anything at all with Helena and Henrietta, it was the perfect Pimblett nose.

Her figure wasn't bad, either. Not so voluptuous as Helena's, but with the aid of a corset, shapely enough.

Hester set the brush down and considered making the most of her natural assets, such as they were, on the night of the ball. She had planned to wear her blue velvet gown with modest lace bertha, her long white gloves and a few white roses in her hair. More thoughtful yet, she cocked her head and thought about the bertha, which was intended to cover up her exposed chest and the slight swell of her breasts.

The skin of her shoulders and chest was smooth and pale, marred only by one small mole above her left breast. Considering how some women looked in their low-cut gowns, she had no reason to be ashamed of that part of her body.

Why not leave off the bertha? Just this once. Just to see what would happen.

She was being vain and silly. If all a man was

going to be attracted to was a bit of exposed flesh, he really wasn't the type of man she wanted.

And deep down she knew that she could never compete with Damaris Sackville-Cooper's beauty, not even if she went to the ball naked.

A soft knock at the door announced Mabel, the maid the duchess had assigned to Hester the day she had arrived, and Hester swiveled on her chair toward the cheery-faced young woman. She was no beauty, either, Hester reflected.

No other woman in the house was, she suddenly realized. Only the duchess could be considered beautiful, and with an added pang of despair, Hester wondered if that had been one of the reasons the duchess had agreed to have her for a companion. Another, prettier woman might have outshone the older woman.

"Are you quite all right, my lady?" Mabel asked, hesitating on the threshold. "Would you like me to come back later to help you dress?"

"I do have a bit of a sore throat," Hester answered truthfully. "In fact, I believe I shall not go down to dinner. Would you be so good as to pass on my regrets to the duchess?"

"I'll bring some supper upstairs, shall I, my lady?"

Hester nodded her approval. "Also some salt water with which to gargle, please."

"Should we send for the apothecary, my lady?"

Hester smiled and shook her head. "No, it's nothing serious, I'm sure. I simply think it would be better not to be in company tonight. I shall be all right in a short while, if I go to bed at once. Please help me out of my clothes, then take my regrets to the duchess.''

Mabel didn't look quite convinced about the trivial nature of Hester's ailment; nevertheless, she readily obeyed.

When she left, Hester drew on her heavy flannel nightgown with a weary sigh and gratefully climbed into bed. Her throat was indeed sore, but not severely so, and her nose a trifle stuffy. All she needed was a little supper and a good night's sleep in a warm bed to set her right. The fact that she would also be spared having to see the duke and the others was not an unwelcome consequence, either.

Mabel returned with alacrity, bearing a small tray with a light dinner upon it. ''The duchess says she hopes you'll be well enough to finish the menu tomorrow.''

''How kind of her to be concerned for my health,'' Hester remarked, keeping her sarcastic smile to herself.

Mabel stood beside the bed while Hester ate, and after a few moments Hester realized the maid was wringing her hands. ''I'm feeling better already, Mabel,'' she said, her throat soothed by the hot tea.

''It's not that, my lady, although I'm happy to think you're not coming down with something serious.''

''What is it, then?'' Hester asked as she pushed herself back to a more upright position against the pillows.

''Well, my lady, since you ask...'' The pert, dark-haired maid looked around nervously. ''Have you ever heard that Barroughby Hall is haunted?''

Chapter Fourteen

"No, I haven't," Hester remarked, maintaining a serious demeanor, even though she felt the notion of supernatural visitations ridiculous in this day and age.

"No more have I, but I could swear....well, maybe it's nothing, but I get the strangest feelin' sometimes, like I'm being *watched*."

Hester suspected that the young and somewhat giddy young woman was suffering from the effects of ghost stories told in the servants' hall. Nevertheless, she was careful to keep any skepticism from her face, for it was very clear that Mabel was sincerely troubled. "When do you get this feeling, Mabel?"

"When I'm alone in my room, before I sleep."

Hester nodded pensively. "Perhaps it's Jenkins investigating a noise, or locking up for the night."

"It's not him, my lady," Mabel replied. "Haven't you noticed he's nearly as deaf as a post? One of the footmen has to be sent to awaken him in the morning. Oh, no, my lady, he's not prowling about at night, I assure you."

"It couldn't be anyone else, perhaps someone having trouble sleeping?"

"I don't think so, my lady, for the sounds are right outside my door. Once I even got up the gumption to look outside, but I didn't see anybody. Nobody else heard nothing, neither. That's why I thought of ghosts, you see."

"I see," Hester replied pensively. "Would you like to change your sleeping arrangements, Mabel? Perhaps share with one of the other maids? Would that make you feel better?"

"Yes, my lady, it would," the maid replied firmly. "It's getting so I can't hardly get to sleep for ever so long!"

"I'll speak to the duchess in the morning, then."

Mabel smiled broadly and since Hester had finished her meal, reached for the tray. "Thank you very much, my lady. I'm sure I don't want to put anybody to trouble, but, well, it's that worrying."

"I understand. Good night, Mabel."

"Good night, my lady."

Hester tossed and turned fitfully, her throat painful and her body hot. She must have finally dropped off to sleep, she thought drowsily as she slipped one foot out of the confines of the covers.

The cool air made her draw it back in quickly. She swallowed with difficulty and half rose from her bed, determined to get a drink of water, only to have a glass placed in her hand. "Thank you, Mabel," she whispered, conscious now of the presence beside her bed and glad that her maid had taken the liberty of sitting up to watch over her.

The drink lessened the soreness, and she was still convinced she was not seriously ill, but only the victim of a chill and a sore throat. "I'll be quite all right," she said, wondering what hour it was.

It was only when she put the glass on the bedside table that she realized the person standing beside her bed was not a woman, but a man.

"Who is it?" she queried as she drew the coverings up to her chin, frightened to think that any man had access to her bedroom.

"Elliot," his lordship whispered, striking a match and lighting the candle on the table.

She stared at him, aghast, while he smiled as if he had every right to be there. He was most assuredly no gentleman, and she wondered what the duke would do if he found his half brother in her bedroom.

And then, just as suddenly, she knew that Mabel had not been imagining things, and that if anyone was sneaking about the hall spying on the women inhabitants, it was this man.

A chill of fear slithered down her back, despite the slight heat of a fever, and she inched farther back. "What are you doing here?" she demanded.

"I was the last to retire, and when I passed by your room I thought I heard something unusual. I wanted to see if you needed any assistance."

His tone was reasonable, and his explanation was very like her own rationalization for entering the duke's bedroom the night he arrived. Indeed, perhaps she was letting Mabel's fears taint her reason. It could be that his presence here had no ulterior, evil motive, and if Lord Elliot acted improperly, could that not be attributed to the way he had been raised, a spoiled son who seemingly could do no wrong?

"My throat is much better, thank you."

"You don't sound well," he noted, regarding her steadfastly and making no move to leave.

"My nose is a little stuffy," she concurred, and despite her sensible thoughts moments before, wished he would go away at once. "Mabel tells me she's been hearing strange noises at night," she said, carefully observing his reaction.

Which was unconcerned and, she thought, genuinely amused. "I go up on the roof to look at the stars on clear nights," he replied. "I might have been an astronomer, if it did not require so much study."

Hester didn't know whether to believe him or not. He sounded sincere enough, but that did not excuse his presence in her bedroom.

Suddenly she sneezed violently, and was pleased to see him step back at last. As he did, he ran his gaze over her entire body in a way that made her feel completely and ashamedly naked. "Good night, then, Hester," he said quietly, and she was not pleased by his informal address. "I hope you sleep better now."

"Good night, my lord," she replied, and she could not keep censure from her tone.

Mercifully, he said no more, but went to the door and left her.

As Hester grew calmer, she reflected that Lord Elliot's behavior was questionable enough to warn Mabel and the other female servants to take care.

Even when she had no real evidence that Elliot Fitzwalter was up to no good?

The best response might be to tell the duke what she suspected, and leave the matter in his hands.

In his strong, slender-fingered, arousing hands.

She would speak to him first thing tomorrow.

The hand tightened around Elliot's throat with fierce strength, while an arm encircled his waist in an equally strong grip and dragged him into the duke's bedroom. "What the hell were you doing?" Adrian demanded as he shoved his brother against the wall.

"Let...me...go," Elliot gasped, trying vainly to pull Adrian's hand away.

Adrian did, but only long enough to change his hold. He grabbed Elliot by the shoulders. *"What were you doing in Lady Hester's bedroom?"*

"I heard a noise when I was passing by. I wanted to see if she needed help."

Adrian smelled the wine on Elliot's breath. "How solicitous of you," he replied sarcastically. "Do you think I'm stupid, you corrupt little worm? You're lucky she didn't rouse the whole household." Adrian fought to control his rage, for he was severely tempted to hurt Elliot, and that he must not do.

Elliot wrestled out of Adrian's grip and tugged down his disheveled vest. "Well, she didn't," he replied.

"She has a right to privacy," he growled. "Are you drunk?"

"A little. It helps pass the time," Elliot said, apparently convinced he was out of danger. "So what if I have been enjoying some wine? It's from Father's wine cellar. Besides, you're not exactly sober yourself. You've been into the port.'' He nodded toward the open bottle on a table near the bed.

"At least it's *my* port—and I don't go sneaking into young lady's bedrooms.'' Adrian crossed his arms over his chest, very aware of the rapid thudding of his heart, which had not diminished from the time he had heard a small, furtive sound and looked down the corridor to see Elliot coming out of Hester's bedroom.

"You act as if I raped her,'' Elliot protested casually, strolling over to the table and helping himself to the port. "Suddenly gone all chivalrous, have we? For *that* woman? It's probably the closest she'll ever get to *amusing* a man.''

"Shut that filthy mouth of yours, Elliot, and get the hell out of my room.''

"Or what? You'll tell my mother I've been a naughty boy?'' Elliot took a drink of the port. "She won't believe you, especially if I say I saw *you* in Hester's room.''

Adrian scowled, but he didn't respond, because Elliot was absolutely right, as Elliot well knew.

"Not so homely, by the by. Not in her nightgown. Did you know she had the most delightful mole over her left breast? And a fine breast it is, too. Perfect, in fact. Whoever would have guessed?''

"Leave, Elliot. Now.''

"You *invited* me here, dear brother, in your own inimitable way.'' He gave Adrian a coolly measuring stare, not unlike the one that was sometimes on Adrian's face.

"Stay away from the women of this house," Adrian warned. "If you want sport, go to the town and pay for it."

"Why so upset, anyway?" Elliot asked. "You're not thinking of seducing her yourself, are you?"

"I rather thought seducing virgins more your occupation," Adrian observed.

"Are you trying to annoy me?"

"Perhaps. Why not? I think you do many things to annoy *me*."

"And why shouldn't I?" Elliot charged. "You make my life miserable."

Adrian glared at his sibling. "*I* make *your* life miserable?"

"Yes. You always keep me lacking funds, until I have to come begging like a child."

"Oh, that's it, is it? I give you a liberal allowance, and then some."

"A man of my rank has a certain position to maintain."

"And yours seems to be any position, preferably with some naive young thing who doesn't know enough to avoid scoundrels like you."

"While we're talking about money," Elliot replied, not a whit ashamed, "I need more."

"Ask your mother."

"You know I can't," Elliot complained. "Just as you know that I'm right. You can afford it, dearest brother. Why be so miserly?"

"If I wasn't careful enough for all of us," Adrian reminded him, "we would be bankrupt."

"That's nonsense and you know it."

Adrian marched over to his table and poured himself another drink. Elliot was right. He was very rich. However, he also knew that if he gave Elliot more money, he might just as well take the sum and throw it into the sea.

"If I married, would you increase the allowance?"

Adrian downed his drink in one gulp, warmed for a brief instant as he regarded his sibling with a stony gaze. "Which lucky lady do you propose to bless with your hand?" he asked sarcastically. "Damaris Sackville-Cooper? Your mother won't be pleased."

"Of course not. I'm passing the time with her, that's all."

"Who, then? Elizabeth Howell?"

Elliot shook his head swiftly and without hesitation, a response that made Adrian despise him anew. "I assume you have not yet made your choice, then," Adrian said.

Elliot glanced at his half brother, so straight backed and stern and unforgiving. He wanted very much to upset Adrian at that moment, to repay him in some small measure for the way Adrian always made him feel worthless and stupid. Adrian had resented him from the moment of his birth, because their father had loved both his sons, and if he felt neglected, he should have realized that a father had a duty to *all* his children.

Therefore, if he could goad Adrian in even a small way, Elliot vowed, he would, and as he faced his brother's harsh gaze, he began to consider which choice of future wife would most disturb Adrian.

He doubted Adrian had any interest in Damaris

Sackville-Cooper beyond admiring a beautiful face and splendid figure, or he would be pursuing her much more ardently.

Who else could he suggest? Who could he choose that would make Adrian nearly mad with apprehension? Somebody completely unsuitable. Somebody that Adrian would *know* Elliot could never be faithful to, so that self-righteous prig would exist in a torture of dread until Elliot fulfilled his expectations. Somebody Adrian would think far too good for his rake of a sibling.

The perfect answer presented itself and he voiced it at once. "Lady Hester."

He watched Adrian carefully, wondering if this outrageous suggestion would get any reaction.

It didn't, beyond a sardonic grin. "I might have known you couldn't be serious," Adrian remarked.

But then Elliot had one of the great surprises of his life, because however inscrutable Adrian's face, in his eyes was an emotion that looked suspiciously like dismay.

Any emotional reaction at all was so unusual, even the slightest would have been cause for delight, and if Elliot had expected anything, it would have been anger. Not dismay.

For once, Elliot thought triumphantly, he had succeeded in upsetting Adrian! He was so pleased, he pursued his chosen course with relish. "Indeed. Don't you think she will improve me?"

"Nobody could do that."

"So *you* think. I have another opinion."

Adrian tried very hard to maintain his composure,

but inside, his emotions were in an uproar. Could Elliot possibly be serious? Did he truly mean to pursue Hester—and with honorable intentions? In truth, she was far too good for him, yet Adrian couldn't help acknowledging that if any woman existed who could save Elliot from the road to ruin, it might be Hester Pimblett.

If Elliot married, Adrian thought, wouldn't *he* finally be free, too?

What would life be like without having to worry about every female who came into contact with Elliot? Or what would it be like not to have to pay Elliot's gambling debts, or the shopkeepers who let him run up extravagant bills, or for the silence of people Adrian felt soiled to be near?

For so long he had kept hoping Elliot would grow out of his vices, and more than once had even wished him dead—anything to make him free of his promise.

Anything to be free of the fear that one day Elliot would go too far, and he would be unable to take the disgrace of his brother onto himself. That the venerable family name his father had held in such high esteem would be utterly and forever disgraced, rather than the reputation of one black sheep.

Yet even as this vision of freedom revealed itself, Adrian realized, with absolute certainty and conviction, that Hester held *his* chance for happiness, too. If he could have Hester for his wife, his life would be wonderfully different, full of the quiet joys of domesticity instead of the disgusting chaos of his London life.

But could he be *completely* happy, knowing that

his selfish desire for Hester had robbed Elliot of his best chance for redemption?

If he gave up Hester, would this sacrifice not finally free him of his obligation to his dead father?

And what of Hester? He couldn't ask her to take on the burden of the Dark Duke's reputation, real or assumed. She had done nothing to merit the whispers and gossip. She had not sown the seeds of disgrace with its attendant price. He, and he alone, should have to live with his scandalous past.

He, and he alone, had made the promise to his father to do everything he could to keep Elliot's reputation unsullied.

Therefore, he, and he alone, would make this one last sacrifice, no matter what the price, for Elliot's sake, for his father's sake and, most of all, for *her* sake. Because he could never be worthy of her love.

"I grant you, she's not as beautiful as some, but she has a fine figure, and very pretty eyes. Don't you agree, Adrian?"

He couldn't. He simply couldn't offer any encouragement, not now, when the idea of Hester married to someone else, to Elliot, was so new and disturbing.

"I see. You doubt my intentions. I assure you, she will be the perfect wife for me. Look how she manages Mama. Think what she will do for me."

With a final look at his brother's downcast face, Elliot sauntered from the room.

Hester did not get a chance to speak to the duke concerning Lord Elliot, for when she came down for breakfast, her nose runny and her eyes watery, Jenkins informed her that the duke had already departed to visit Miss Sackville-Cooper. He was not expected to return until the evening.

Chapter Fifteen

Adrian was giving a very good imitation of a man fascinated by harp music as he sat in the Sackville-Coopers' drawing room and looked unseeing at the beautiful Damaris. He also took no notice of the examples of Damaris's accomplishments spread about the room: watercolors, embroidery, pastels, netting, crocheted antimacassars, an ornately painted fire screen, the piano and the harp.

He wondered how Hester was feeling, and if she was any better. He had been tempted to send for the doctor before coming here, but his stepmother had informed him that there was no need.

"The Pimbletts all have the constitutions of elephants," she had said dismissively, and for once Adrian accepted her opinion, for however ignorant the duchess was about some things, she had spent so much time with doctors and other medical men, she probably knew as much about illness as any of them.

He had also wanted to remain at home today, but he couldn't, just as he couldn't take the chance of displaying his true feelings for Hester in front of Elliot. If Elliot suspected how much Adrian wanted her, he would pursue Hester with a fierce devotion, just to take away what Adrian desired.

If Adrian hadn't danced so much with Elizabeth Howell, she might yet have her life and reputation intact, instead of being dishonored and abandoned and childless. Elliot would do as much to Hester.

Wouldn't he? Two days ago Adrian would have said the only person Elliot thought of was himself, but that was before Elliot had spoken of marrying Hester. Could it be that her presence touched Elliot, too, and in the same way? Was his selfish half brother that perceptive? Was Hester Elliot's hope for a better life, too?

Adrian silently cursed himself for a fool, because even now he could not completely give up the idea of asking Hester to be his wife. In his mind, he knew he should not propose to her, as much as his heart pleaded, for he loved her too much to punish her by shackling her with his burdens.

No matter how much he loved her. No matter how passionately he thought of her, envisioning her in his bed as his lawful wife.

He had absolutely no doubts that she was a virgin. How wonderful that would be, to be in her arms knowing absolutely that he was the first! There had been no other woman in his life of whom that could be said.

He would be the first to show Hester the several secret places on a woman's body that yielded unspeakable pleasures when a man caressed them. He would be the first to see those shrewd blue eyes widen with delight, shine with passionate intensity, close at the moment of ecstasy. He would teach her all the many variations of a kiss, and other things lips could do. He would neglect no part of her body, not the soles of her feet…the tips of her fingers…the nape of her neck.

No, he told himself. That could not be.

But to give her up to Elliot, who did not deserve her. Who would surely make her miserable. Who would take her to his bed—

Adrian forced the image from his mind, for he simply could not bear it.

He suddenly realized the music had stopped.

"That was marvelous," he said as Damaris regarded him with distaste in her beautiful eyes. She set the harp back and folded her slender white hands gracefully in the lap of her ample silk skirts.

As demure and acquiescent as Damaris seemed, Adrian sensed he was not likely to raise Damaris's hopes for a marriage proposal. If he was any judge of women at all—and given his experience, he must be by this time—Damaris Sackville-Cooper did not want to be in the same room with him, let alone married to him. While this in itself was an interesting novelty, he was in no way intrigued by her, and if he didn't feel that feigning an interest in her was a way to protect Hester, he would never have come near the place.

"I am not much of a judge of harp music, I fear," he said by way of explaining his lack of attention.

"Would you like me to play the pianoforte?" she

asked dully, and he wondered what she would say if he expressed a desire to have her play the bagpipes.

Their awkward conversation was interrupted by the arrival of Sir Douglas, obviously just returned from his business trip to London, judging by his red face and traveling clothes. "Papa!" Damaris cried with an equal measure of relief and joy.

She ran and embraced her father, who smiled down at his daughter and then at their noble visitor. "A pleasure to find you here, Your Grace."

"I trust your trip was enjoyable," Adrian remarked, seeing the happy speculation in the older man's eyes while he disengaged himself from Damaris. It was tempting to imagine Sir Douglas's reaction to the news that the Duke of Barroughby would prefer to marry the plain Hester Pimblett. Too tempting, indeed.

"Very profitable, Your Grace, although I regretted having to miss the pleasure of your company," Sir Douglas said. "Sit down, sit down!"

"No, really, I have no wish to intrude on your return," Adrian protested halfheartedly.

"I must insist you stay," Sir Douglas declared, not noticing or not caring to notice that his daughter was conspicuously silent. "Please, and for dinner, as well."

Adrian nodded his head in acquiescence. He had a role to play, and he resigned himself to playing it. Yet suddenly he felt overwhelmed and helpless, a feeling he had experienced only once before, and had never wished to feel again. He must and would be in control!

"This is wonderful!" Sir Douglas exclaimed, beaming at the young couple. "How is your brother? And the duchess?"

"Lord Elliot and his mother are both quite well," Adrian replied, and he saw that Damaris seemed far more interested in the conversation now that it had focused on the other members of his family.

Adrian began to wonder if he was assuming Damaris was far safer than she was. After all, Elliot could be very charming and very persuasive; there might be other times when Sir Douglas would be absent. The man might even stupidly believe it would be in his daughter's best interest to leave her alone with Lord Elliot, if the duke was not in the running. Surely not even Sir Douglas could continue to be blind to his daughter's dislike of the duke.

"I am sorry to have to tell you, however," Adrian continued, "that Lady Hester is ill."

"Oh, dear, I hope it's nothing serious," Damaris said, genuinely concerned.

"A cold," Adrian replied lightly, "and we hope it disappears quickly."

"Perhaps it's catarrh," Sir Douglas said. "Tell the duchess I recommend a mustard plaster. Does the trick for me every time."

"It would be a pity if she were too ill to attend the ball," Damaris observed quietly.

"She's worked very hard for it," Adrian agreed nonchalantly. "As a secretary, she is indeed a marvel," he continued, with a dismissive and languid wave of his hand that purposely contradicted his words. "My stepmother finds her quite invaluable.

Unfortunately, she's so quiet and unobtrusive, I have the most terrible time remembering she's in the room." He smiled at Damaris in his most charming and seductive manner, making it very clear that he could certainly not forget that *she* was in the room.

Damaris frowned and regarded the duke with a look of scorn that marred her lovely brow. "I think she's very nice," she said with a flash of temper. "And very kind and very sweet."

Sir Douglas cleared his throat so suddenly and so loudly, it was as if a gun had gone off. "Of course, I'm sure the duke meant no criticism," he said, turning red and casting a fierce and condemning look at his daughter. Obviously he did not think a union of the duke and his daughter to be a hopeless thing yet. "She *is* quiet and sweet, of course. Just not a lot of spark to her, eh, Your Grace?"

"She will no doubt make some quiet country gentleman a fine wife," Adrian said, hating the character he had to play and deeply wretched at the truth of his words.

He tried to think of something to turn his thoughts from such disturbing channels, and remembered what Hester had said. If he could not be happy, perhaps he could at least help his tenants, and a truly deserving young man.

"I have been thinking that Reverend Canon Smeech's gifts are quite lost in such a small parish," he said. "I have a friend who's related to the Bishop of Lincoln, and I seem to recall that they need a new dean at the cathedral. It has occurred to me that might be the very place for the canon. Then, of course, the living here will fall vacant, and I believe we have a fine candidate for the position in Reverend McKenna, provided he can pay for it, of course.'' Adrian was sure the Scots clergyman could come up with, oh, say, five pounds.

"Oh, he would be an excellent choice!'' Damaris exclaimed, her eyes shining. "His family is quite well off, so I'm sure the cost of the living will not be beyond his means—'' She paused, suddenly doubtful. "Provided it is a reasonable amount.''

"Oh, I don't think it will be too expensive for a man from a well-to-do family,'' Adrian said. "I believe he will go far in the church,'' he continued, so that Sir Douglas could not doubt that Reverend McKenna stood high in the duke's favor. "He seems a most able pastor.''

"I'm surprised you've noticed,'' Sir Douglas said brusquely. He caught Adrian's questioning glance. "Your Grace,'' he added quickly and deferentially.

"Many people sing Reverend McKenna's praises. I am not deaf to them. Of course, once he is the pastor, he will need a wife.''

Damaris started. "He will?''

"I should think so,'' Adrian said calmly. "I daresay most of the unmarried women in the parish already have their eye on him.''

He let his words hang in the air for a moment.

Damaris frowned and flushed a deep red as she looked away. Her father eyed her warily before turning his attention back to Adrian. "I suppose he would be quite a catch for one of them,'' he admitted grudgingly.

"He would be quite a catch for any woman!" Damaris suddenly declared as she raised her head and glared at them with flashing, defiant eyes.

"He is a *wonderful* man!" Damaris continued passionately. "A most kind, generous, sweet-natured—" She saw her father's expression. He was regarding her with a look somewhere between disbelief and confusion, rather like a man being told his ship was sinking in a foot of water, for it was undeniably clear where his daughter's true affections lay. "He is everything a clergyman should be. I am *proud* of his acquaintance, and I would be more than proud to be his wife!"

Adrian hid a small, self-satisfied smile. He had guessed that while Damaris might be momentarily flattered and overwhelmed by Elliot's attention, when she realized what she stood to lose, she would make the better choice.

And she had.

Hester lay in her bed, her throat still somewhat hoarse and raw, and her head achy, but she knew she was nearly better and would be fine by the next day. As for today, she was quite willing to remain in bed, alone and untroubled by the duchess or any member of her family, even if that meant all she had to do was think about recent events.

Maybe the time had come for her to leave Barroughby Hall. Things were getting too confusing, her emotions too unsettled, the relationships within the family too fraught with conflict. As boring as life with her parents or sisters might be, she was beginning to realize that boredom, with its attendant calm, had a certain attraction.

She couldn't be sure about anything where her own relationships with the Fitzwalter men were concerned. One moment she was certain the duke cared for her; the next, he acted as if she were of less concern to him than his horse. Lord Elliot was inevitably charming, and yet nobody had ever made her feel more uncomfortable.

She could not believe that the duke had any nefarious designs on her, despite her vulnerable position. Indeed, when she considered how he had looked at her that morning in the library, and again yesterday, before Lord Elliot had arrived in the barouche, she thought if anyone was vulnerable, it was the infamous Dark Duke.

It had to mean something that he revealed that side of himself to her. To be sure, that first time in the library, he had been caught unaware. But yesterday, when he had said what he admired about her, when she had been thrilled beyond measure, then there had also been that sense that he was wounded and needed her help, help she would be only too glad to provide.

Why would a man like the duke pay any attention to her at all if he didn't like her, at least a little?

But today, as the afternoon progressed and the duke still did not return, Hester was forced to face the truth.

Which was that she was falling in love with a man who would never marry her. Probably would never even *think* of marrying her, despite his complimentary remarks. His attention had flattered her vanity, and probably meant nothing to him. Unless she wanted to face continual heartache, she should leave.

Hester resolved that she would stay at Barroughby Hall only until the ball. She had worked hard on the preparations, and she had every right to be there, but then she must go.

Forced awake by the commotion in the hall, Hester reluctantly opened her eyes and surveyed her bedroom. By the angle of the moonlight shining in the tall windows, she guessed it to be shortly after midnight, and a glance at the ornate clock on the mantel confirmed her suspicions.

"I said, take your bloody hands off me!" an angry male voice slurred. Unfortunately, since the duke and Lord Fitzwalter sounded very similar, she couldn't be quite certain which of the two it was.

A thump that sounded like a fall followed hard upon the words, and Hester threw back her bedclothes, determined to see what was going on. She quickly put on her robe and cautiously opened the door, peering into the dim hall.

She was not pleased by what she saw, for it was immediately obvious that it was not Lord Elliot who was the worse for drink, but the duke, who faced his brother angrily as he swayed drunkenly. "I said, don't you touch me, you…you…!"

"What?" Lord Elliot asked in a whisper just as fierce, his arms akimbo. "What am I, Adrian?"

"You know bloody well! Leave me alone!"

"All right, then, I shall. And you can fall and break your arrogant neck!"

"You'd like that, wouldn't you?" the duke charged, his voice rising slightly. "Then you would be the duke!"

"At least then I wouldn't have to come begging to you for every ha'penny!" Lord Elliot said, louder still.

"Shhh!" the duke admonished, rocking back on his heels. "Do you want to wake the house?"

"I don't care if I do or not," Lord Elliot replied. "*I'm* not the one who's drunk."

"By some miracle!" the duke jeered, his smile a sneer.

"Elliot!" The duchess's voice pierced the air. "Is that you, Elliot?" Her bedchamber door opened, and the duchess stomped into the hall in outraged majesty, her hair in papers and her robe tightly tied. "Adrian! I might have known! You are drunk! Did you leave the Sackville-Coopers in that disgraceful condition? The whole neighborhood will be full of the tale by tomorrow night!"

"I left Sir Douglas in a worse state," her stepson said with a bow and an imaginary tip of his hat that almost sent him tumbling to the floor. "The poor fellow was quite depressed, since he's finally realized his daughter will never be the Duchess of Barroughby."

Although the duke was well and truly drunk— something Hester was sorry to see, for it seemed to lend credence to some of the stories about him—she was far less dismayed than thrilled by his last words.

The duke was not going to marry Damaris Sackville-Cooper!

"Well, I suppose I should be grateful for small mercies!" the duchess acknowledged angrily. "But can you *never* think of other people, Adrian?" She marched up to him. "You'll awaken everybody, and Lady Hester needs her sleep." She gestured toward Hester's slightly open door, and Hester held her breath, hoping they wouldn't realize she was listening. She would have moved away, but she thought the motion might be noticeable. "If I am able to do without her, you can at least keep quiet."

"Heaven forbid you should have to do something to earn the living I give you," the duke said scornfully.

It seemed his words hung suspended in the air, stretched on the tension between them as the duchess stared at him, outrage in her eyes and a frown deepening. Then she raised her hand and struck her stepson full across his face. "How dare you address me in such an impertinent manner!" she cried.

He didn't even flinch. "No longer concerned about rousing Lady Hester, I see. I thought it was but a momentary lapse into generosity of spirit," he said. "Or that perhaps you had decided Lady Hester would make a suitable wife for Elliot, as he seems to believe."

Hester's hand shot to her mouth to cover her shocked gasp. Elliot Fitzwalter considered her a suitable wife? For himself? It didn't seem possible, and what was more important, the idea didn't please her one bit. The more she saw of him, the less she liked him. Marriage to him—never. She would happily remain an old maid if he were the only one to offer for her.

"What are you babbling about?" the duchess said, turning a disbelieving eye onto Elliot. "He's making this up to annoy me, isn't he?"

Hester leaned a little closer to the door.

"I think we should save this topic of discussion for the morning, when we are *all* well rested, Mama," Lord Elliot answered smoothly.

"But—"

"For once, I agree with Elliot." The duke swayed again, then steadied himself. "Good evening, Your Grace," he said, turning slowly on his heel. "Night, Elliot."

"Elliot," the duchess began, clearly determined to have an answer to the duke's startling announcement at once, "tell me he's making that up. Lady Hester— for you? The notion is preposterous!"

Even though Hester quite agreed with the duchess, she was less than pleased to hear herself so summarily dismissed. She was very tempted to show herself, and in fact had one hand on the latch when she realized she was about to sneeze. Her hand went from the latch to her nose and she hurriedly backed away, even as the sneeze would not be suppressed.

"There! I knew Adrian would waken her," the duchess whispered loudly. Hester heard her approach her room and swiftly climbed into the bed, pulling the covers up to her chin so that her robe was hidden.

"Still asleep, thank goodness," the duchess whispered, her figure visible when she opened the door a crack. "But what nonsense—Elliot? *Elliot?*"

* * *

"Good *night*, Mama!" Elliot muttered as he closed the door to his bedroom while his mother continued to peer through Hester's. He had no patience for her tonight, either her solicitation, her curiosity or her determination to plan his life for him.

God, hadn't she been upset to hear Adrian say her darling boy considered plain, dull Hester Pimblett a suitable wife! It would almost be worth a sincere proposal just to see the look on his mother's face, although he would rather marry one of the statues from the garden. Hester Pimblett would be about as responsive in bed as a figure carved out of marble.

Or maybe she wasn't as prim and proper as she pretended.

Now *that* was an interesting avenue of speculation. Elliot had known a few girls like that—their modesty all for show.

But they'd been pretty and worth the pursuit. Hester was most definitely ordinary.

Well, not her body. That was shapely enough, as he well remembered, feeling a growing tightness in his loins. She could, perhaps, be taught.

When it came to choosing a wife, though, her talents in bed were not that important. He could find his pleasure with other women. Indeed, the more he thought about it, the more he realized Hester Pimblett might be the perfect wife for him—the perfect quiescent wife, who wouldn't argue or protest if he stayed out all night with his "friends." The perfect mother for a lord's children, blameless to a fault. The perfect emblem of a perfect family.

No doubt a woman like her would be just as happy to let him take his lust elsewhere, except for the occasions necessary to produce children.

And if he married, his mother would have to stop treating him as if he was still six years old. She might think Hester not quite good enough for him, but she *was* a lord's daughter, and Hester seemed to be able to handle the duchess in her most fractious moods.

Yes, Hester Pimblett as Lady Elliot Fitzwalter. He could do worse, and she would surely be eager to have such a charming, handsome husband. Wooing her would be almost too easy, and he had plenty of time.

In the end, however, it was for none of those reasons that Elliot decided he would court Hester and ask her to be his wife.

He would marry her because it would vex the arrogantly self-righteous Adrian for the rest of his life.

Chapter Sixteen

"I'm so glad you're better, my lady," Mabel said, putting another pin into Hester's hair as she sat at her toilette the evening of the ball. "It would have been a pity if you'd been too sick to attend, after all you've done."

Hester smiled weakly at the servant's sincere sentiments and surveyed the elaborate hairstyle Mabel had achieved. It was a masterpiece of curls and flowers, accomplished after several minutes of patient maneuvering of curling irons and diligent weaving of stems, leaves and flowers.

At first Hester had declined Mabel's anxious offer to "do" her hair, although the maid promised to show her what she had learned from an older sister who was a ladies' maid in London, but Mabel had looked so crestfallen, Hester had agreed. Nevertheless, she had not felt a hairstyle could make any possible difference in the way she looked. Yet now, she had to admit, it had not been a mistake to agree. Her hair was as stylish as her sister Helena's had ever been. Indeed, with her hair like this, she could actually see a resemblance to her beautiful older sister. The irony of this was, she had never wanted to be homely so much in her life, because the one person who might take notice of a change in her appearance was Lord Elliot.

After that overheard and never-to-be-forgotten episode in the hall, Hester had been incredulous and dismayed, and for a while had hoped that Lord Elliot had not been serious. Unfortunately, it seemed as if he was indeed sincere in his pursuit of her, for he persisted in staying near her. She would have put a stop to his attentions immediately but for two things: she was not supposed to have heard the conversation between the duke, the duchess and Lord Elliot, and she was leaving as soon as possible after the ball. Surely there was no point to creating unnecessary animosity.

Even without Lord Elliot's unwanted attention, she would be happy to be going, because the situation was becoming completely untenable. She could no longer deny that she cared very much for the duke, while he scarcely acknowledged her presence the rare times he was at home.

Nevertheless, she had lain awake every night listening until he returned. Then the steady evenness of his footfalls had told her he had not been drinking to excess. As to what else he might have been doing to occupy his time, she thought perhaps it wiser not to speculate. She wanted to believe that he was worthy of her respect, and if he had deceived her, she would prefer to keep her delusion.

If there was anything good in all of this, it was that

Damaris seemed quite forgotten, or at least forgotten by the Fitzwalter men. Reverend McKenna had accompanied Reverend Canon Smeech to Barroughby Hall one day recently, and a more changed countenance Hester had never seen. Reverend McKenna soon gave Hester to understand that he was most optimistic about Damaris accepting his hand, and with her father's approval, a feat in part accomplished by the unexpected invitation for the canon to become the dean of Lincoln Cathedral. Canon Smeech was to leave in a fortnight, and Hamish McKenna was to take his place as rector of St. Andrew's, Barroughby.

"I hope the duchess appreciates all your work. If you're ready, my lady, I'll tie the laces of your corset now," Mabel said, coming to stand behind Hester.

"I'm sure she does," Hester lied. The duchess had nearly driven her mad by questioning each and every decision—even though she herself refused to make a single one—from the type of punch to the menu for the buffet supper. She had changed her mind regarding the number of musicians in the orchestra, then changed it back. She had fussed over her choice of fabric for the gown so much, Hester had wanted to scream.

It would have helped if she could have had an ally during all the discussions, but the duke was never there, and Lord Elliot seemed determined to take her part in everything against his mother, something that only made his mother more unreasonable.

Hester rose obediently and submitted to the gradual tightening of her laces. "I think that will do," she said before Mabel's strong pull made it impossible to breathe. This evening was going to be difficult enough as it was.

"How are you sleeping these days, Mabel?" Hester asked as Mabel tied the knot. "Better?"

"Oh, aye, my lady, indeed. I must have sounded like a right ninny!"

"As long as you're happy now."

"I am, my lady." Mabel carried the wide hoop crinoline and helped Hester into it, tying it quickly. "Now, then, my lady, you just stand yourself there, and I'll bring your dress."

Mabel had prepared Hester's blue velvet ball gown, and freshened the lace bertha that would be added when the gown was laced. Hester had decided there would be no unseemly, immodest display of bosom.

"I'll hold my hands up to protect your handiwork, shall I?" Hester proposed, visions of a destroyed coiffure and scattered white rose petals filling her head.

"Here we go, my lady." Very slowly and very carefully Mabel lowered the gown. Hester slipped her hands into the narrow sleeves and Mabel helped pull the gown into place, letting the velvet skirt fall to the floor. "This is the most beautiful fabric," the maid said admiringly as she tied it in the back. She stepped away and then turned Hester toward the full-length mirror standing near the armoire. She picked up the bertha, which looked not unlike a limp crocheted doily in Mabel's hands. "Are you sure you want this, my lady?" she asked dubiously. "You look fine without it."

Hester regarded her reflection critically, marveling that a change in hair or the color and cut of a gown could make such a difference. The gown was, of course, a familiar one, and she had seen herself in it before——but with the bertha. Without that covering, the plain bodice seemed to emphasize the pale smoothness of her skin, and the round softness of her breasts. The elaborate hairstyle, a contrast to the usual plain manner she usually chose, did indeed seem to lend her some of her sisters' beauty. She would be no rival for Damaris Sackville-Cooper, but at least she needn't feel like a pauper invited to a banquet by mistake, and if Lord Elliot noticed, so be it, because maybe his brother would, too.

"The bertha, my lady?" Mabel repeated.

"No," Hester said, suddenly resolved. If this was to be her one and only ball at Barroughby Hall, she would dare. "I won't wear it."

Mabel smiled broadly and nodded her approval. "I'm not the only one with cause to be happy, my lady," she said with a sly smile.

"Whatever are you talking about?" Hester demanded, unable to keep the displeasure from her voice, for she could guess what Mabel was referring to.

"We...the servants, my lady. Lord Elliot's been very attentive...."

"He has been assisting in the preparations for the ball. Nothing else," Hester said far too sharply, and she was immediately contrite. "I'm sorry for snapping, Mabel," she apologized. "I'm nervous about the ball, that's all. I want everything to be perfect." She smiled. "And I'm terrified Jenkins will realize that telling him we needed him to serve the special punch and keep track of the crystal glasses was nothing but a ploy to prevent him from confusing the guests' names when they arrive.''

Fortunately, Mabel returned Hester's smile. ''I wondered how you were going to manage that, my lady, but I might have guessed you'd think of something.''

''Now you must swear to keep this a secret, even from the other servants. I wouldn't have Jenkins's feelings hurt for the crown jewels.''

Mabel nodded solemnly. ''I swear, my lady, and no trouble to do so, for a kindlier old gentleman never breathed, I don't think.''

Hester fastened her simple strand of pearls about her throat and drew on her white gloves. Picking up her fan, she gave her reflection one more cursory glance. ''I suppose I'm ready. You'll wait up for me, Mabel?'' she asked, knowing that she would need help removing her gown.

''Of course. I'll be here, or in the duchess's sitting room, in case any of the ladies need any little repairs to their gowns.''

Hester nodded and went to the top of stairs. Below, the duke and his half brother were already waiting, the one dark and brooding and motionless in his formal black evening dress, the other fair and charming and tapping his foot as if impatient for the dancing to begin.

Her gaze was drawn to the duke, leaning his weight on the leg that had not been injured, and she wondered if he would dance tonight. Would he dance with *her*?

Then she took a deep breath and told herself it didn't matter. Tomorrow she would announce her plans to leave to go to her eldest sister, whether Helena and her husband wanted her there or not.

Both men turned to look at her at the same time. "My dear Lady Hester," Elliot said, coming forward quickly and taking her hand in his as soon as she reached the bottom of the stairs. "You look wonderful this evening—and quite well, I'm happy to note." He gave his silent brother a sidelong glance. "Doesn't she, Adrian?"

"Yes."

"I suppose he's saving his manners for our other guests," Elliot remarked snidely, drawing Hester's hand through the crook of his arm and leading her to her place in the receiving line in the large drawing room. The duke was to be first, then the duchess, then Elliot, then Hester. "Mama will be down shortly."

"I should see if Jenkins has everything in hand," Hester said, pulling her hand away. "He might have forgotten—"

"Everything is fine," Elliot assured her as he took her hand again. Indeed, Hester had managed to plan this ball with the precision of a military campaign, as Elliot well knew from having been in boring attendance for the past several days. Nothing had been left to chance, and every servant knew precisely what their duties were.

If there was anything not planned, he now thought, it was the startling change in Hester's appearance. That color suited her perfectly, bringing out the blue in her eyes in a most remarkable fashion. Her hairstyle rivaled anything he had seen in London, and made her look astonishingly sophisticated, almost pretty, even.

As he held her hand firmly on his arm, he considered that perhaps making her his wife wouldn't be much of a sacrifice. Tonight, looking at her downcast eyes, he could even imagine making love with her. "I hope you are going to save some dances for me," he said softly.

She looked at him with surprise, and he smiled even more. Yes, once they were married, she would be so grateful, he could probably persuade her to do almost anything. "We will be second couple for the quadrille, Adrian and my mother being the first, of course."

"Of course," she murmured, and he noticed that she didn't so much as glance at Adrian. Nor did Adrian look at her, after the first glance. "I assume the duke's injury will not prevent him from dancing," she said.

"No," the duke replied nonchalantly. "I intend to do my duty."

Elliot felt some of his pleasure diminish. Adrian seemed quite resigned to the notion of his scapegrace sibling wed to this virtuous maid.

The duchess appeared at the top of the stairs. Her green silk gown was ostentatiously flounced and embellished. She wore a large necklace of emeralds, and long emerald bobs dangled from her ears. About her shoulders was a light shawl of exquisitely fine lace, and her hair was ornately curled.

She started down the staircase, then balked, glaring

at Hester. "Lady Hester!" she cried, her tone one of absolute condemnation. "What is that you are wearing?"

"I believe it is called a ball gown," the duke observed dryly before Hester could open her mouth.

"It's *indecent!*" the duchess declared, marching down the rest of the steps. "I simply cannot permit you to wear such a thing when you are in my household."

Knowing that she would soon be leaving Barroughby Hall, Hester straightened her shoulders, prepared to protest, for the duchess's own gown was cut only slightly higher in the bodice.

The duke took one small step forward, yet that was enough to make the duchess halt. "This is *my* household," he said quietly. "Lady Hester is a guest here, and if this is what she chooses to wear, she will wear it, whether it is appropriate or not."

His tone made it clear that he didn't approve of her gown any more than his stepmother did. Hester blinked rapidly, willing away the tears of dismay. So much for trying to be noticed!

"I think it's lovely, Mama," Lord Elliot said, coming to Hester's defense, albeit somewhat tardily.

Hester did not feel grateful for his compliment. "I am sorry to be such a cause for potential embarrassment," she said with a calmness of manner that took most of what remained of her self-control. "If you like, I will return to my room for a bertha."

"No, never mind," the duchess snapped. "Let us take our places in the drawing room."

"Might I suggest you wrap your shawl more

tightly, Your Grace,'' the duke said, raising one eyebrow. "There is a draft, and you are rather exposed.''

The duchess sniffed dismissively, but Hester noticed that she did as the duke suggested when they took their places in the drawing room.

They were no sooner lined up like soldiers on parade when a voice announced from the door, "Sir Douglas Sackcloth-Cooper and Miss Sackcloth-Cooper.''

Hester turned her head so quickly her neck cracked. Jenkins was at the door. "What is he doing there?'' she said anxiously. "He was to tend to the punch!''

The duke's lips twitched with what looked suspiciously like an attempt to hide a smile—but then, *he* had not worked hours and hours, and put up with the duchess's demands, and worried about a gown only to be criticized. "No doubt Jenkins has forgotten his more important role this evening. I shall endeavor to remind him,'' the duke said before strolling toward the entrance.

"I might have known Sir Douglas would be the first!'' the duchess grumbled as Damaris glided into view.

Her dress was lovely, of pale pink silk trimmed with yards of delicate lace. Her bountiful hair was expertly dressed, and her complexion flawless. She hesitated in the doorway for a brief moment, entering the room shortly before the duke, who quickly resumed his position in the receiving line.

Hester glanced at the two gentlemen near her. The duke's expression was unreadable; Lord Elliot's was not. He approved, and quite highly. Perhaps he was regretting having her for a partner in the quadrille.

Sir Douglas strode in behind his daughter. "Good evening, Your Grace," he said to the duke. "And to you, Your Grace," he continued to the duchess. "You're looking as young as ever."

Hester noticed that the duchess, in spite of her marked dislike for the man, was not impervious to male attention, for there was something in her smile that seemed genuine enough, if only for the briefest of moments. "You are too kind, Sir Douglas," she said. She looked from Sir Douglas to Hester. "I must ask you to make sure Lady Hester has an enjoyable time tonight. I fear she will be so busy, she will not dance."

"Oh, I shall be only too happy to oblige, Your Grace!" Sir Douglas said heartily.

Adrian wanted to break the man's leg. And Elliot's, too. He wanted only one person to dance with Hester tonight, and that was himself.

Which was impossible. It had to be. As official host, albeit against his will, he would have to partner his stepmother for the opening quadrille, and then dance with every young lady who wanted to. He would be lucky if he could get more than one dance with Hester, who had blossomed tonight like a rare and delicate orchid.

How could he ever have thought her plain? He must have been blind. There was nothing plain about her shining blue eyes, nothing homely about those rosebud lips, nothing common about her masses of hair that he longed to bury his hands in. Every particle of his body seemed to remember how it felt to kiss her, and he yearned to do so again. And again. For a very long time.

But he didn't dare to even look at her for more than a moment, because if he did, he would be reminded again of all the reasons he loved her, and it would be too difficult to let her go, quite possibly to Elliot, who didn't deserve to touch the hem of her gown. For that reason, he had spent most of his time in Barroughby of late. He had also been able to comfort himself with the thought that if he was in town, he would soon know if Elliot also came there to sport.

He didn't, so Adrian had been forced to conclude that Hester might indeed be his brother's hope for salvation, especially judging by the approving way Elliot had looked at her tonight.

At least until the lovely Damaris had entered the drawing room. Adrian wondered if Hester had also taken note of Elliot's reaction.

"The Reverend Canon Smeech. Reverend McKenna," a footman intoned.

Adrian kept his dislike for the canon from his face, a far easier matter than ridding his thoughts of Hester and Elliot. "Reverend Canon," he said. "Congratulations on your appointment."

He thought the pompous clergyman would burst his collar. "Ah, thank you, Your Grace. Yes, indeed, a most high honor. Dean of Lincoln Cathedral! I only hope I shall do the office justice."

I only hope you don't make too much trouble there, Adrian thought. He comforted himself with the thought that the canon was likely to do less harm in a large cathedral than he could in a small parish.

Reverend McKenna's eyes strayed toward the lithe form of Damaris, who smiled with such happiness that there could be no doubt where her affection lay. Adrian glanced at Sir Douglas, and while that gentleman did not appear overly delighted, he seemed to have accepted the inevitable. Thank goodness.

"Your Grace, you are looking as lovely as always," Reverend Canon Smeech said to the duchess, moving along the line.

The duchess accepted his praise as her due, rewarding him with a brief smile. She barely seemed to notice Reverend McKenna, despite his bright red hair. The young reverend greeted Elliot, and then Hester, giving her a friendly smile.

"The Duke of Chesterton. Miss Smith."

Adrian turned again toward the entrance. He recognized the Duke of Chesterton, a stiff-backed snob of a man who had disowned his youngest daughter for marrying her dancing master.

Beside Chesterton, whose hair was a most unnatural shade of black and whose cheeks were rouged if Adrian was any judge, was a deathly pale, somewhat pretty young woman wearing a garment that displayed an abundance of bosom above an impossibly narrow waist. If the Duke of Chesterton's latest mistress got through the evening without fainting, Adrian thought, it would be a miracle.

Several more guests arrived at once, and Adrian was kept busy greeting them until it was time for him to lead the opening quadrille. He tried to subdue his dismay that Hester was not his partner, but Elliot's.

Before he could ask Hester for the second dance, which was to be a waltz, Sir Douglas claimed her. Since Adrian was the host, he could not sit out the dance, as he would have preferred; instead, he asked one of the duchess's friends.

He never seemed to get close to Hester after that. She was either dancing, or seeing that other young ladies had partners, or helping elderly guests to chairs, or pointing older gentlemen in the direction of the rooms set aside for cards and smoking.

As he was scanning the room for sight of Hester after a particularly exhausting polka with an energetic young woman who batted her eyes continuously, he noticed Elliot talking to Miss Smith in a rather intimate tête-à-tête. Chesterton had recently left the room, probably to smoke, but Adrian didn't think Miss Smith missed him one iota.

Then Adrian watched as Miss Smith, with a coy and seductive smile, wandered out onto the terrace, leaving Elliot alone. After another moment, Elliot walked the length of the room, pausing to speak briefly to some of the guests, but when he reached the far end, he, too, exited onto the terrace in the direction of the shrubbery.

The meaning of these actions was all too plain to Adrian. Obviously Elliot had not been sufficiently entertained while at Barroughby Hall. Here was a chance to relieve his...boredom.

"Your Grace?"

Startled, Adrian turned to find Hester at his elbow.

She was giving him a shrewd look that he found rather unnerving. "Yes?"

"It's nearly time for the supper. Have you seen Lord Elliot?"

Chapter Seventeen

Adrian considered his options. He could say he didn't know where Elliot was, but they were to lead the way into the dining room and the supper that Hester had planned with such care might be ruined by the delay while footmen looked for Elliot.

He could offer to search for his errant sibling, and in doing so, fetch him and Miss Smith.

Or he could send Hester to search the shrubbery. Let her find Elliot with another man's mistress. Surely then any hope of a marriage between Hester and Elliot would be impossible.

Thereby destroying Elliot's best chance for redemption.

"My lord?" Hester repeated more urgently. "Do you know where Lord Elliot is?"

Adrian raised his eyes to look at her questioning face. Now was the moment of decision. Now he had to decide whether to attempt to ruin any chance of a marriage between his half brother and Hester, even if he could never marry her himself.

As she looked at him, so calm and yet with the

excitement of the ball in her eyes and the flush of exertion on her satiny cheeks, he made his decision, and when he did, he was not considering his own happiness, or Elliot's reformation.

He was thinking only of Hester. Elliot would surely make her life miserable if he married her.

"I believe I saw Lord Elliot wandering into the shrubbery," he said.

"Thank you, my lord," Hester replied before hurrying away.

She went as quickly as she could to the shrubbery, wondering in which direction Lord Elliot might have gone, and angry that he had chosen this particular time to take the evening air. He must have known it was almost time for the supper to be served.

Sighing, Hester entered the dark, scented garden and had gone but a few paces when she heard a noise that made her halt.

It was two voices whispering, a man's and a woman's. Upset, Hester took a few paces forward, then remembered that she had just left the duke and it would be impossible for him to have passed her and be inside the shrubbery. Therefore, the deep voice she could hear had to be Lord Elliot's, and he had somehow found a willing companion for his jaunt in the garden.

Which would, perhaps, explain how he had come to forget the supper.

Determined to remind him, she went on and turned a corner—coming to an abrupt stop when she saw that Lord Elliot and his female companion were not simply talking, although she could discern the incredibly lewd words of direction whispered in Miss Smith's high voice.

And right in the shrubbery, too! With all the guests in the hall!

Hester spun on her heel and marched back to the hall, to find the duke still standing where she had left him. She regarded him steadily, her face blazing with a blush as if she had been the one in Lord Elliot's arms, while she tried to read the duke's expression. Had he known what she would find? Had he sent her there on purpose?

Or was this just another attempt to amuse himself at her expense?

"Supper will be somewhat delayed," she muttered as she passed him.

She did not hear Adrian sigh.

The upper hall was quiet and still. The guests had departed, the duchess retired, and Lord Elliot had gone to his room. Mabel had helped Hester out of her clothes, put the gown away, taken down her hair and then been dismissed, after offering the valuable information that the duke had told his valet he would not be needed later. Below stairs, the hushed voices of the servants indicated that they were still clearing away the remains of the supper, guided by the duke's deeply voiced instructions.

Hester sat at her vanity and stared unseeing at her mirror.

Why had the duke sent her to the shrubbery? She

had been trying to answer that question ever since she had seen Lord Elliot.

Was it because he wanted her to know what kind of man Lord Elliot was? He had already warned her; did he think she would not take his word for it, and so had given her proof?

Did he deem her that blind? Or that easily flattered by a gentleman's attention that she would not realize how bored Lord Elliot was in her presence, try as he might to act otherwise? That she did not see that however suave and charming he was, Lord Elliot was no true gentleman? That his half brother was vain and arrogant in a way the duke could never be?

There was one other explanation: that the duke cared deeply for her and didn't want her to be taken in by Elliot's apparent charm. But she must not dare to think it....

But she *would* dare! she thought with sudden determination. Tonight she would dare to think herself worthy of the duke's love. She would remember how it had felt when he had kissed her, the look in his eyes when they stood together on the road and he told her what he saw when he looked at her. She would remember how his presence alone excited her, and his touch thrilled her. She would dare to believe that what she saw in his eyes was regard, respect, even love. She would even dare to voice her feelings aloud. "I love you, Adrian Fitzwalter," she whispered to her reflection. "I *love* you!"

She rose and began to pace. She was leaving here, if not tomorrow, then as soon afterward as could be arranged. The duke would probably go into town tomorrow. After tonight, she might never see him again.

She paused and looked at her reflection again. "How *much* do you dare?" she whispered intently.

Before she had time to think of a response, she heard the duke's familiar footsteps pass her bedroom door.

She had been good and modest and dutiful all her life, and to what end? Ignored, forgotten, treated like a servant or a secretary when she was remembered at all.

For once, just this once...

Taking a deep breath and gathering her courage, she went to the door, tiptoed into the hall and moved toward the duke's bedroom, which she entered without knocking before she lost her resolve, then closed the door softly behind her.

The duke, who had not heard her enter, stood by the window, looking out at the clear, crisp night illuminated by a full moon. She almost weakened, until she realized how lonely he looked, as if he was looking outside hoping to see...what? A companion? A lover? A wife?

"My lord?" she whispered.

He whirled around and stared at her. "What are you doing here?" he demanded in a hushed voice.

"I must speak with you," she replied, going closer.

"This is neither the time nor the place for any kind of discussion," he said sternly.

"Yes, it is, because tomorrow I intend to inform the duchess that I am going to my sister's home as soon as possible. There may never be another time."

"You are leaving?" He seemed about to take a step toward her, but he hesitated.

"Yes, my lord."

"Why?"

"Because I cannot be happy here."

"I see." She thought he stifled a sigh as he went toward a lamp and struck a match. The flame flared briefly, the sudden illumination catching the planes of his cheeks, creating dark, mysterious shadows around his hidden eyes. "Perhaps that is just as well."

When the lamp was lit, he gestured for her to sit on a chair in the far corner, away from the light and the bed, but she did not. "What is it that you must speak to me about so urgently, Lady Hester?"

"I want to know why you sent me to the shrubbery," she said. "I do not believe you were quite unaware of where your brother had gone, or with whom."

"My God, am I that transparent to you?" he asked, turning away.

"You told me where to go, and I think there is little that takes place here that escapes you. Tell me, were you hoping to shock me?"

He faced her, but he did not meet her steadfast gaze. "Not exactly," he replied.

"Then what? Why send me to spy on them?"

The duke did not respond.

"Is it that you thought I needed to *see* what kind of man Lord Elliot is?"

"Yes," he muttered, and still he would not look at her.

"Why?" she demanded, her heart thudding rapidly.

"Because I thought you should."

"I trusted you when you asked me to. And I am not so naive as you seem to think. It has been evident to me for some time that he is *not* a gentleman."

"Neither am I, and yet you trusted me."

"Why do you say you are not a gentleman? I have seen no evidence of impropriety on your part."

"Except for that day in the library."

"I surprised you. My lord, I believe you to be an honorable man, despite what others say, and I will continue to believe you are not the scoundrel people say you are until you give me evidence to the contrary."

He finally raised his eyes and looked at her, his expression at once defeated and stern. "You do *not* know me. You do not know what I have done. Besides, why should it matter to you if the Dark Duke is a scoundrel or not?"

Hester twisted the tie of her robe around her hand. "Because I care about you," she whispered, wishing she could see his face better. "And I think you care about me."

"Are you telling me you can care about a man who has been with whores?" he asked with a trace of defiance. "Who has been drunk several times, in several public places? Who gambles when the mood suits?"

"Thus far, you sound like many young men of your station."

"Oh, but I am worse, Hester, I am worse."

"I don't believe it. I can't."

His mouth twisted into a mocking, sardonic smile. "Then, my dear young woman, your judgment leaves much to be desired. Have you heard how I began my illustrious career at Oxford?"

"I know a little of your history," she confessed.

He went to a small table and poured himself a drink, then picked up his glass and swirled the contents, glancing at her. "To enable you to make a proper judgment, I see I shall have to give you all the evidence. Please, sit. This may take some time."

Hester obediently sat in the chair he had indicated, while the duke downed his drink in a gulp. He started to pace restlessly, and ran his hand through his thick, dark hair. "I had a good friend, an earl from Wales, named Griffin Branwynne," he began without so much as a glance at her, "who got himself involved with a young lady of somewhat dubious repute, although neither of us knew that at the time. However, certain others amongst our acquaintance did, and one night, at a tavern, they enlightened us. Griffin, despite what you might have heard of the Welsh temperament, possessed a cooler head than I, and was all for letting the matter rest until he could speak to the lady.

"I, however," the duke said, his voice growing bitterly sarcastic, "I, the noble Duke of Barroughby, thought that we had to champion the lady's honor. I called the informant a blackguard and a scoundrel. He reciprocated in kind. Both of us were quite drunk, I might add, and prepared to resort to fisticuffs. Griffin tried to stop us, but we wouldn't listen.

"We didn't even have the decency or intelligence to take our quarrel outside." For the first time since he began to speak, pain flashed across the duke's stern face. "I knocked over a lamp. I heard it fall, but I paid no attention. I was far too intent on beating my opponent to a bloody pulp. By the time I realized the place was on fire, it was too late. Nothing could be done to put it out. I staggered outside, leaving my opponent behind. I was so drunk, I thought it would serve the knave right to die in the flames."

Adrian's voice lowered, and his words came more slowly. "When I heard somebody shouting that the other gentleman was still inside, I was actually quite pleased with myself, until the notion that the other gentleman might be Griffin finally penetrated my sodden brain. Then I became frantic and even more useless." He took a deep breath, but he regarded her steadily. "In fact, by this time, I was hysterical. Nobody would let me near the building. I was too drunk and too upset. I would have gotten myself killed. I offered extravagant rewards to anybody who would go in after him. Nobody was foolish enough to take me up on it.

"And then part of the roof caved in." Hester could hear the sense of helplessness and hopeless anguish in the duke's voice. He took a deep, shuddering breath. "I was sure my friend was dead." He paused, then resumed, his voice growing stronger. "Thank God for the tavern keeper. He heard about Griffin and before I knew what was happening, he threw a wet burlap sack over his head and plunged into the building. He found Griffin and dragged him out. A tavern keeper saved his life, not me."

"Is that why you never visit him?" Hester asked softly. "Because you are ashamed?"

The duke gave her a tortured look. "Have you ever seen anybody badly burned, Lady Hester?"

She shook her head wordlessly.

"It is very painful, and the scars…" He had no need to finish, for the torment in his eyes told her how terrible it must have been. "When he finally awoke, Griffin wouldn't speak to me. He wouldn't let me in his room. He still won't see me. I've tried. He went to his estate in Wales and lets nobody come near him."

"Surely that is his decision," Hester said, feeling helpless, but trying to say something of comfort.

The duke ground his fists into his palm. "You didn't know him, or the promise in him. He was going to be a great man, Hester. A great leader. I took that away from him. I might just as well have killed him."

"It was an accident."

"Oh, but you don't yet know all, my angel," he continued bitterly, looking at her coldly. "I didn't kill Griffin, and I didn't hurt myself. But my stupidity killed my father just as surely as if I had shot him with my pistol."

"How…?"

"He had high hopes for me, my father, and although it is vain of me to say it, not without some justification. I was an excellent scholar, personable, well liked. I was a bit wild, but nothing terrible. Nothing that age and wisdom wouldn't have cured, or so he believed.

"Then the news of my foolishness reached him,

and it was a bitter blow. My rash act caused his fatal attack. By the time I reached him, he was dying.

"I was a great disappointment to him, and that disappointment killed him."

Tears welled again in Hester's eyes to see his sorrow, to know that he was living that terrible time again by telling her.

"Now I think you had better leave my room," he said softly. "You might be discovered here, and while another scandal would be nothing new to me, it would mean trouble for you."

He was quite right, of course, but she was not yet ready to leave. "What you did was foolish, but that was long ago, and you have been sorry for it ever since. Even now I cannot believe that you are guilty of all the things you are rumored to be." A sudden moment of illumination came to her as she recalled the struggle in his eyes before he sent her to find Elliot. "It's *Elliot*, isn't it? He's the one who does the terrible things—and you take the blame! Because you feel guilty about the fire?"

"You do not understand the relationship between my brother and myself," the duke said, cold and distant once more.

"Yes, I do. Because you think it doesn't matter what people say about you, you take all the blame for Elliot's immorality!"

"What does it matter if I do?" the duke asked through clenched teeth as he returned to stare out the window. "I made a promise to my father on his deathbed. I promised that I would ensure that Elliot's name was never tainted by disgrace." His shoulders slumped wearily and his voice dropped until it was barely audible. "Like mine."

There! At last! The key to that troubled relationship. And the flaw in the Duke of Barroughby. "You think that by protecting Lord Elliot from the consequences of his misdeeds, you are protecting him?"

"Of course," he replied. "My name was already tarnished. It didn't matter much to me if a little more scandal attached to it." He faced her and tried to resume his sardonic manner. "Although I must say I didn't know how low he would sink."

"But don't you see, my lord?" she demanded, standing. "By taking all the repercussions onto yourself, you are allowing him to *be* immoral! To continue on his wayward path! You are not *truly* helping him."

The duke stared at her. "How certain you sound! Yet you've been here less than six months, you've known me only a few weeks, and Elliot even less."

"I have eyes. I can see. I have a mind. I can understand."

"No, you can't!" He came close and glared at her. "You can't know the guilt I've felt ever since that night at Oxford. You weren't there to see how ashamed and upset my father was. All he had left to console him was the thought that Elliot was young and unblemished. My promise was the only thing I could give him to try to make it right. I've been *trying* to make it right ever since."

"Why did you stay away from the hall all these days?" Hester asked quietly.

"What?"

"Didn't you stay away because you believed Elliot

was going to ask me to marry him? Didn't you stay away because you didn't want to interfere, even though you cared for me?"

"Hester, I—"

"Did you never stop to consider *my* feelings in all your plans and sacrifices?"

Adrian stared at Hester, aghast. "Yes, I did. That's why I sent you outside tonight. I was so fearful Elliot would make you miserable—"

"And you did not credit me with enough intelligence or discernment to realize that *for myself?*"

He said nothing, too shocked to respond.

"How arrogant! How presumptuous! You do not offer protection—you give it whether it is wanted or not! I am not a child. I am capable of seeing beyond empty flattery. *It is not for you to decide what is right for me.*"

"I was only doing what I thought best," he responded defensively.

"What *you* thought best!" She drew a deep breath, and her anger dissipated at the sight of his dismay. "You cannot control everyone, my lord," she said in a quieter voice. "You cannot be responsible for everyone, nor can you continue to protect Lord Elliot. It isn't good for him, or you, or the other women he may seduce. He has to be held accountable. He has to be stopped. Your father didn't know what he was going to become, or he would never have asked for such a promise."

"It's too late," Adrian murmured. "I can't change what's happened. The world considers me a rogue and a scoundrel and always will, so why not use those prejudices?''

''Because they harm you, as well as your brother. Besides, the world can forget. Do you remember the scandals from five years ago?''

''Yes,'' he replied scornfully. ''I was involved in most of them.''

''You, or Lord Elliot?''

''Oh, what does it matter which one of us was truly involved?'' he demanded angrily, stalking toward the window.

''It matters very much to me, my lord,'' she replied softly.

''But it should not!'' he charged, whirling around to face her again. ''It must not! There can be no future for you with a man like me, no matter how much I want you!''

Neither of them moved. They scarcely breathed.

Happiness—pure, blinding in its completeness—filled Hester. He wanted her! He had said it! He meant it!

All her life she had dreamed of hearing those words from a man like him, a man who did not want her because of her family connection or who was, worse, a ''suitable husband.'' A man who desperately needed what she had to offer. A man who could have his choice of women, and who had chosen *her.*

She went toward him, drawn to the flame of his love and passion, seeking his warmth, his love.

Chapter Eighteen

Adrian stepped back abruptly. "Don't touch me," he snapped.

"But I only—"

He saw the love shining in her blue eyes, and realized she wanted to hold him close in a loving embrace, which added immeasurably to his pain, for he was not worthy of her respect, or her help, or her love. "Listen to me, Hester. I do not need your concern or your comfort. I am what I have made of myself, and have learned to live with it. I will not ask any woman to share it as my wife. I chose my path, and will walk it—alone."

"You do not have to be alone."

He knew what she was offering, and the value of it, just as he knew he could never accept. "Yes, I do," he said firmly, telling himself he was forever locking his heart against her. "I want to be."

"No, you don't," she said, and it was not a question, but a statement of incontrovertible fact.

War raged between his heart and his mind, his hopes and his past, his desire and his fear. Between the damnation of his present and the salvation of the future Hester offered. Between the forgiving, healing love she was offering him and his own unworthiness.

She, alone of all the women he had ever met, she alone could give him peace and true happiness.

Who was proof against such an offer? He, world-weary, bitter, alone, convinced that he must reap what he had sown?

Yes, until now. This moment. This woman. This love that would make him whole again, and fill the emptiness in his life, as his love for her was filling the void in his lonely heart.

So he yielded.

He reached out for her, his deliverer, and drew her to him. With a sigh she came into his embrace, and when their bodies touched, their love became more. The flames of rapture spread through them both, and for Adrian they burned away the dross of years and made him pure again, like metal newly forged. "I love you," he said softly, his need blatant in his desire-darkened eyes.

Hester responded to the wonder and heat of his yearning, giving herself up to the burning need that filled her, knowing he would make her complete.

He kissed her deeply, his touch melting away the last of her reserve. Being alone with him here was right; his embrace was necessary; his body against hers was perfect.

As he held her tightly, she was achingly aware that she wanted him to love her completely, as a man loves a woman. As a husband loves his wife, and whether they were husband and wife was not a consideration.

He broke the kiss, and while she caught her breath, a warm smile crossed his usually sardonic face. "You must go, Hester," he said wistfully, "because if you don't, I am going to pick you up and take you to my bed, and then all your notions of my goodness will be utterly shattered."

Hester knew he was right. She should leave before she was tempted to forget all the dictates of society that forbade making love outside of marriage. Nevertheless, she could not leave his arms at once. "I think I shall discover heaven in your arms, my lord," she whispered, leaning against his heaving chest.

He groaned softly, then gently pushed her away. "I mean what I say, Hester," he warned huskily. "You are far too tempting, and I am not nearly so praiseworthy as you seem to believe."

"Neither am I," she said with a smile.

"What's this?" he cried softly, in mock dismay. "The saintly Lady Hester is really a wanton wench, after all?"

"Only with you, my lord."

"Then there is but one way to ensure that this remains our secret."

She gazed at him questioningly.

"You must be my wife."

She opened her mouth to respond, when he suddenly frowned and put his finger upon her lips. "Let me say that in a less arrogant, presumptuous way— to prove that I am capable of changing." He knelt on one knee and took her hand in his. "Please, Lady

Hester, would you do me the very great honor of becoming my wife?''

Too delighted to speak, she could only nod.

Adrian rose and pressed another kiss to her cheek. "I don't deserve you, and I don't deserve such happiness—"

This time Hester put her finger on his lips. "Such happiness as I can give shall be yours. But you are right. I must go," she murmured. She glanced around the room. "For now."

He chuckled softly. "I shall say adieu, then."

She slowly went to the door, then turned on the threshold, her face bright with a smile. "I wonder what the duchess will say?" she said mischievously.

"Perhaps we should reveal nothing of our engagement for the present. Let me think of a way to persuade her to move to the Dower House first. I wouldn't want her to blame you for 'turning her out,' as she is sure to put it."

"If you feel that best," Hester said. "Now that I know you love me, nothing else seems at all important." She slipped out as quietly as she had entered.

For several delightful minutes after she left, Adrian stood in his room and simply enjoyed the sensation of complete joy.

Until he began to really consider what the duchess, and other people, might say.

Elliot stepped out of the shadowed alcove where he had been hiding, and his bitter, malevolent glare moved from Hester's bedroom door to Adrian's. So, Adrian had had her. *His* Hester.

How else to account for Hester's presence in Adrian's room, the way her clothes were disheveled, the glow in her face as she left him? Truly, there wasn't a virtuous woman in the whole country if Hester Pimblett was willing to bed a man before marriage.

And as for Adrian—he might have known better than to believe that Adrian was ignoring her because he didn't consider her attractive enough. *She lived in his house.* That alone should have told him what would happen.

He should have guessed that Adrian was playing a very subtle game of seduction. No doubt he had gone to town so often only to inflame Hester's desire. Or maybe when he came back, late at night, he had not gone directly to his bedroom.

And he dares to chastise me! Elliot thought angrily.

Probably Adrian had done it to spite him, too, because he knew Elliot wanted to marry her. Typical Adrian! Couldn't let him enjoy anything. Couldn't even let him have a virgin bride. A homely virgin bride.

Then another idea entered Elliot's mind. If Adrian could have Hester without benefit of marriage, then so could *he*.

As he rode into town early in the morning after a sleepless night, the Duke of Barroughby had never been more hopelessly confused and uncertain and thrilled in his entire life.

One moment he was filled with triumphant hope to think that a woman of Hester's intelligent discernment cared for him; the next he was filled with doubts,

convinced he was completely unworthy of her. That
she had no true idea of what he had done, or the mess
he had made of his life. That she saw only his handsome face and vast wealth, and was blind to his despicable history. That he did not dare to tie such an honorable woman to a man like himself with the bonds
of holy matrimony. That he should leave here and
never see her again, and that perhaps the pain that
would surely attend such an action would finally pay
him back for the tremendous suffering he had caused.

Yet even now he knew he lacked the strength of
purpose to make that sacrifice. Weak scoundrel that
he was, he simply couldn't bear the thought of living
without her.

Then he remembered that she said she loved him
and seemed to want him as much as he needed and
wanted and loved her. Could their marriage be wrong
under those circumstances? If marriage was what *she*
wanted, was he being selfish by proposing it?

He also wondered what Elliot would make of this
turn of events. Would he accept it, or would he go
off in a rage, with possibly disastrous results?

Or was Hester right? Was it time to let Elliot bear
the full weight of the consequences of his actions?

Desperate to have another opinion, Adrian had finally decided to do something else he had never done
before: he was going to talk about his worries with a
friend, John Mapleton, who already knew something
of the history of the duke's family.

Adrian kept Drake at a gallop nearly the whole way
into Barroughby, and only when he saw the pink tinge

of the sky behind the surgeon's house did it occur to him that it might be rather early in the day for him to be paying a call.

On the other hand, this way he might stand the best chance of finding Mapleton at home. Therefore, he tossed Drake's reins over the bush nearest the surgery door and knocked briskly.

The door was opened by an unshaven Mapleton. "Adrian!" he said, obviously surprised at the early arrival of the noble visitor. "Are you hurt?"

"I am quite well. I think," Adrian replied with a rueful grin.

Mapleton's good manners asserted themselves, and he invited Adrian inside to his office, a small room cluttered with papers, instruments and books.

A maid came at a trot and stared at the Duke of Barroughby with frank curiosity. "May I take your hat and coat, Your Grace?" she asked softly, blushing furiously.

"No, I don't intend to stay long," he replied.

"You may go, Nancy." The surgeon waited until the maid had left the room.

"Won't you sit down, Adrian?"

"Yes, thank you, John." Adrian removed his hat and ran his hand over his hair as he sat. He placed his hat on his knees. "I need to talk to you."

Mapleton regarded him with a curiosity as frank as Nancy's. "I'm happy to listen."

Now that the time had come to speak, Adrian's usual reticence on personal matters came to the fore. As he hesitated, Mapleton appeared to be the personification of patience, and so gave the duke no assistance or reason to leave. "I'm sorry. I've made a mistake," Adrian said brusquely, rising.

For a man past the midpoint of his life, the surgeon could move with great alacrity. He was at the door before Adrian had opened it, and he leaned back against it, staring into the duke's face. "Sit down and talk to me," he ordered.

Adrian thought about pushing Mapleton out of the way, but he desperately needed another opinion, so he obeyed. "Something has happened, John," he said gravely.

"Indeed?" The surgeon sat opposite Adrian, behind his desk.

"I've asked Lady Hester to be my wife."

Mapleton's eyes widened. "You wouldn't joke about something like this, would you, my lord?"

"No. I'm perfectly serious."

"Then I am delighted for you! *Delighted!*" His smile turned to a worried frown not unlike Adrian's. "Is there a problem I'm not aware of?"

"No."

"Then why be so downcast? I think she would be a most excellent wife for you."

"There is a problem, one of which you *are* aware, John," Adrian said. "My reputation."

"Which you don't deserve."

"Be that as it may, I have it. Isn't it selfish of me to ask a woman of her spotless character to attach herself to me?"

"My lord, what did she say to this 'problem'?"

"She says people will forget."

"I told you she was an intelligent woman. I quite agree with her."

Adrian was not convinced, as the surgeon immediately realized. "The young lady has a great deal of sense, my lord, and if she feels no compunction about marrying you, I think you should accept it." Mapleton chuckled gleefully. "My God, man, don't you *want* to marry her?"

"With all my heart," Adrian answered sincerely. "I just never believed…"

"That anyone would care to see beyond the mask of the Dark Duke?" Mapleton inquired.

"Something like that," Adrian admitted ruefully.

"Well, she has." He regarded Adrian pensively. "She's not very pretty, though."

This time it was Adrian's turn to chuckle. "I have had my fill of so-called pretty women, and believe me when I say I would far rather have Hester's loving face beside me on my pillow than any other."

"Now I *know* you are in love!" Mapleton declared.

"Your diagnosis is quite correct, my friend."

"Is that all that was bothering you?" Mapleton asked after a moment of companionable silence in which Adrian once again felt nothing but joy.

"I must confess, it isn't. There's the matter of Elliot."

Mapleton's expression became grim. "What's the matter with him now?"

"He claims to want to marry Lady Hester."

Mapleton's reaction was a scoffing "Hah! Now *that* is truly an impossible notion."

"He claims to be sincere."

"And after all his deceptions and subterfuges, you believe him?"

"I don't know whether to believe him or not. That is not the trouble, for Hester would never have considered him."

Mapleton looked confused. "So, what is the trouble?"

"You know Elliot. Do you think he will tolerate what has happened?"

"If he cared about her, he might do something stupid. I can't see him being heartbroken about Lady Hester, though," the surgeon said, shaking his head. "In the first place, she's not beautiful enough for his taste."

"That's what I thought. But he was the one who made the suggestion, not me, and as you yourself have said, she will make a good wife."

"Not for him. He'd break her heart in a month. He couldn't be faithful if a thousand pounds depended on it. Don't you think it's time you stopped worrying about Elliot? He is of legal age, you know."

"That's what Hester says. I fear it is an old habit."

"One that should be broken."

Adrian smiled sardonically. "She thinks I've actually *allowed* him to indulge his whims."

"I told you, she's a sensible woman."

"Obviously, I am outvoted." He sighed. "I was only trying to help."

"I'm sure Lady Hester knows that as well as I."

"But to abandon him—"

"How many women has he abandoned?"

"Too many, I know. Perhaps if I give him an allowance..." Adrian mused.

"He will say it is never enough," Mapleton warned.

"You're right." Adrian made a decision. "I shall give him £10,000 and his horses. Then if he runs out of money he will know it is only because of his profligate ways."

"And when he does, and comes begging for more, what will you do?"

"I honestly don't know," Adrian replied softly. "I cannot let him die in the gutter, can I?"

"Well, let us not borrow trouble," the surgeon said, rising. "Let us hope for the best. And now, what about breakfast?"

Adrian smiled at his friend. "I was in such a hurry to talk to you, I couldn't wait for any at home. I'm famished, and it will be good for Drake to have a rest, but then I must hurry back."

"Fine, fine," Mapleton said. "I hope you like oatmeal."

"Have you been talking with Jenkins?" Adrian asked, his brows furrowed with suspicion as he stood.

"I always have oatmeal," the surgeon said, patting his rotund belly. "Very filling."

"Since you've eased my mind, I'll allow you to feed me whatever you like."

Chapter Nineteen

Hester hurried downstairs as soon as she thought breakfast might be ready. She had not slept at all, but felt bright and happy nonetheless, because Adrian Fitzwalter loved her, and she was going to be his wife.

Perhaps, she hoped, he would be in the small dining room, as eager to see her as she was to meet him.

Maybe they would even be alone a little while.

Not alone, she amended with genuine regret, for the servants would be going in and out of the room.

That was a disappointing thought, but not nearly so disappointing and dismaying as the realization that Lord Elliot was already in the dining room, and the duke was nowhere to be seen. "Good morning, Lord Elliot," she said coolly.

Lord Elliot, who looked as if he hadn't slept in days or had imbibed too much wine, gave her such a slyly speculative look that Hester feared he knew she had seen him with Miss Smith in the garden. "Good morning, my dear," he said, strolling toward her and taking her hand. His thumb stroked her palm as he raised it to his lips and pressed a kiss far too long there. "I see late hours don't diminish your beauty, Lady Hester."

Nonplussed by his expression and his attention, she drew her hand back sharply.

"A little cranky, are we?" he noted, smiling sarcastically. "That's to be expected, after all your hard work."

"I am very tired, my lord," Hester lied, deciding the best thing to do would be to pretend that nothing at all was different this morning. If she could.

She went to the sideboard and helped herself to some scrambled eggs, toast and kippers, and didn't see Elliot lock the door and pocket the key. He strolled toward the sideboard and poured himself some coffee, and when she was busy setting down her plate on the table, he leaned over and locked the servants' entrance to the room, taking that key, too.

"Have you eaten, my lord?" Hester asked, realizing that he was still standing.

"I am very hungry," he said. He set down his coffee and looked at her. "Very hungry."

Hester didn't like his innuendo. "Eat, then, my lord," she replied frostily.

"Oh, I intend to." He sauntered around the table, coming to stand behind her. "Eventually."

Hester twisted her head to gaze up at him. "The kippers are excellent."

"Kippers are not quite what I had in mind."

"Oh." Hester turned her attention to her own plate, and tried not to think of him hovering behind.

She jumped when he put his hand on her shoulder.

"I like you, Hester," he murmured, bending toward her so that his words sounded low and intimate in her ear.

She swallowed hard and set her fork down with a trembling hand. "I'm flattered," she murmured.

He put his other hand on her shoulder and suddenly she felt his lips on the nape of her neck. "My lord!" she cried, pushing back her chair and rising swiftly, then turning to face him. "What are you doing?"

He smiled. "Kissing the object of my desire."

"That is most improper," she said firmly, hoping she didn't sound as frightened as she felt.

"I found it rather pleasurable."

"My lord!" Hester said, glaring at him. "You forget yourself."

"I never do that," he replied calmly, taking a step toward her.

"Your mother will be here—"

"My mother rarely comes here, and certainly not the morning after a ball. She will sleep till noon, at least."

"The duke—"

"Has gone into town." Hester gasped at this unexpected revelation. "Surprised?"

Hester quickly regained control of herself. Lord Elliot could very well be lying. "Why should I be surprised?"

"No particular reason, I suppose. I daresay he's gone to visit Sally Newcombe."

Hester had had quite enough of Lord Elliot's lies and disrespectful conduct. She marched to the door, turned the knob—and it didn't open. "It's stuck," she said out loud.

"It's locked," Lord Elliot said close behind her. Suddenly he grabbed her arm, turned her around and pulled her hard against him. "I didn't want to be disturbed."

"Let me go!" she said, panic in her voice and in her heart as she stared up at his face, seeing the lust in his eyes and something more. Anger. Bitter, burning anger that was truly frightening. *"Let me go!"*

"What's this? Going all indignant, are we, Lady Hester? That's a bit hypocritical, isn't it?"

"You should know all about hypocrisy, my lord."

"Such fire! Such a temper! And to think I thought you plain and dowdy. Obviously I was quite mistaken." He forced his hot, moist lips over her mouth, robbing her of breath and filling her with disgust.

"Stop it!" she cried when he finally drew back. "I shall call the servants!"

Lord Elliot smiled and shook his head as he loosened his grip slightly. "That would not be wise, my dear. Not after last night."

"What...what about last night?" she gasped.

"I saw you sneaking out of Adrian's room. Fine companion for my mother you are, I must say. I wonder what she'll say when I tell her about your nocturnal rambles?"

Hester stared at him, unable to speak. Horrified to discover that he had seen her. Very aware of how he would make last night sound to the duchess, who would tell her parents, her friends, even the most minor acquaintances.

His grip tightened. "Of course, there's no need for me to do that."

"No, there isn't," Hester confirmed desperately. "Just as there is no need for me to tell your mother about Miss Smith."

Lord Elliot chuckled. "Go ahead. Tell her. My mother knows what Miss Smith is. She'll be sure the woman enticed me."

"You are *evil*, my lord!"

"Yes, I suppose so," he replied lightly. "Selfish, too, but why not? I can afford to be, since my dear brother takes his responsibilities so much to heart." His expression grew hard and bitter. "You, however, are in no such comfortable position."

"What do you want?" Hester asked, her fear growing with every moment.

"Just what you gave Adrian. A night's pleasure. Or possibly two."

"We didn't—"

"Oh, please, Lady Hester, there's no need to play the virgin for me. It won't help you."

"Adrian and I are going to be married!"

Lord Elliot's frown deepened and a strange expression flickered in his blue eyes. "He told you that, did he? That old ploy!"

"It *isn't* a ploy!" she retorted. "He loves me! And I love him."

"It's a lie," he said sternly. "He won't. He won't want to sully your purity with his debauched reputation."

Desperate to get away, she struggled as he put his arms around her. If the whole household had to learn what had happened last night, she would have to bear that. Anything was better than being trapped in this man's terrible embrace.

"I know all about you," she charged. "I know he hasn't done half of what he's accused of. He's been taking the blame for *your* misdeeds."

"My, my, my, he has been talkative. He must care for you more than I thought. I had assumed he took you just to annoy me."

"He didn't *take* me!"

"More fool him. Still, that means he'll be even more determined to keep last night's visit a secret, wouldn't you say?" Lord Elliot continued to glare at her with hatred in his eyes. "If you don't come to me tonight, I will spread the most vile rumors I can think of about him, and believe me, my dear, I can think of some that are totally disgusting. I have several acquaintances who will be only too happy to support whatever tales I choose to tell, provided I pay a little. Lots of other people won't question the source, not when the Dark Duke's the subject.

"It's up to you, Hester. One night with me to save what's left of Adrian's reputation, or I destroy him."

"You would do that, after all he's done for you?"

Lord Elliot shoved his face close to hers. "You, Lady Hester, are in no position to criticize me, crawling out of my brother's bed like a whore! All I'm asking you is to whore once more, for his sake."

She reddened, but met his gaze squarely. "I am not a whore!"

"A mere academic distinction." He let her go and she ran to the door, rattling the handle and banging on it. "I wouldn't trouble myself, my dear," Lord Elliot said calmly. "The door is thick, and Jenkins is deaf."

"Others are not!" Her hands ached, so she stopped banging and faced Elliot once more. "I know why you are so spiteful," she said. "He presumes too much. He decides for others, whether they wish him to or not. I told him so last night, when he was even going to sacrifice his happiness for *your* sake. He would never have said a word of his feelings for me if I had not assured him that I could never love you. *That* was why I was in his bedroom, to find out once and for all if he cared for me."

Lord Elliot's gaze faltered for the briefest of moments. "Well, you certainly know how to prick a man's pride," he muttered. "However, it matters not to me if you despise me. I will have you, or Adrian will pay the price."

"Don't come near me again!" Hester warned as Lord Elliot looked at her.

"Not for the moment," he replied coolly. "But remember what I said. My mother will learn all about you and Adrian if you don't come to my bedroom tonight after the household is retired, and then I'll show you both just how thoroughly a reputation can be ruined."

"I'll tell the duke what you've proposed."

Lord Elliot looked completely unconcerned as he sat in a chair and crossed his arms. "Go ahead. I shall not suffer for it. The decision is yours, my dear. Tonight with me, or I shall totally destroy the Dark Duke."

Hester regarded him as she would a loathsome insect, and then her brow furrowed as if concentrating. "If I come to you tonight, will you mend your ways?"

"Will you convince your lover to leave me alone?"

"Will you take responsibility for your actions? Will Adrian be free of his obligation toward you?"

"If you come to me tonight, and if you marry Adrian, and if you then convince your husband to raise the paltry allowance he gives me, I will try to be a good boy."

"Elliot? Is that you?" the duchess demanded querulously from behind the locked door. "What is the meaning of all this noise?"

"It's nothing serious, Mama!" Lord Elliot called out. "Jenkins has inadvertently locked Lady Hester and I in here."

"Jenkins!" the duchess shouted imperiously. "Jenkins!"

"Oh, how can I believe you?" Hester moaned softly, paying scant attention to the interruption.

"Because I say it," Lord Elliot said quietly, his face hard and cold as ice on metal. "Despite what you may think, I am not completely and utterly devoid of honor."

"You most certainly are."

"Not yet, my dear, not yet."

"Why do you want me, knowing that I shall despise you all the while?"

Lord Elliot's lips jerked into a sarcastic smile. "Because Adrian does, and you cannot deny he is a man of exquisite taste.''

The door suddenly burst open, to reveal an annoyed duchess and a contrite Jenkins. "I can't think how I did it, and then lost the key," he mumbled, surveying the damaged lock.

"Excuse me, Your Grace," Hester said, pushing past the startled woman.

"Well, really!" the duchess huffed.

"I suppose she's fatigued," Elliot said by way of explanation as he smiled to himself, certain that tonight, she would be his.

She would do everything she could to save what remained of Adrian's reputation.

Because she loved him.

Adrian tipped his hat and strode from Mapleton's house toward his waiting horse, determined to get home at once and see Hester as soon as possible. Perhaps she was still sleeping, he thought with a small smile. It had been a very late night.

His smile changed to a frown. After he saw Hester he would confront Elliot, and tell him he was on his own from this time forward.

Hester was right. He had coddled Elliot far too long.

Then Adrian stopped in his tracks, for as a hired carriage rolled by, he thought he recognized the passenger sitting inside.

Surely it couldn't be. What would Elizabeth Howell be doing here?

Chapter Twenty

Adrian would far rather have left for home at once, but he felt that this mysterious arrival of Elizabeth Howell had better be investigated first. She was supposed to be in Manchester with her brother.

He walked as quickly as he could to the yard of the inn where the carriage had stopped and waited until the woman he thought was Elizabeth had disembarked. Then he sauntered into the public rooms and looked about casually, as if he were merely contemplating a drink instead of searching for somebody.

Around him, people fell silent, for it was not often the duke patronized the Bull and Calf. Most of its customers were the local farmers or travelers passing through.

His eyes came to rest upon a lone woman, seated in a far corner as if she was trying to make herself disappear.

It *was* Elizabeth. What was she doing here? What *could* she be doing here? Coming to confront Elliot? While he could understand that reason, it would do her no good. It would have been better for her to make a fresh start, and if Elliot were to be cast adrift, it might be better if he could start completely afresh, too.

Adrian strolled to her, pensively noting that for once, his reputation came to his aid, for he knew no one would question the Dark Duke's interest in a woman, especially a young and pretty one.

Or, he realized as he sat on the bench, a young woman who had been pretty once. The strain of childbirth and her grief was still evident in her too-pale skin, the dark circles beneath her too-bright eyes, and the trembling of her filthy hand as it reached out for the mug of ale before her.

Worse, he was sure she was not well, for there was a feverish blush high on her cheeks.

"Hello, Elizabeth," he said softly. She looked as if a normal tone of voice would shatter her delicate equilibrium.

Startled, she reared back and stared at him.

"It is I, the Duke of Barroughby," he continued, still in little more than a whisper.

"Have you come to help me again?"

He tried to act as if nothing were amiss, although everything was wrong, from the way she looked, to her traveling alone, to the fervent, feverish brightness in her eyes. "Yes."

"Is he with you?" she asked, looking past him into the room. Those customers who had been surreptitiously watching the duke suddenly turned their attention back to their drinks and conversation. "Has he escaped?"

"Who?"

"Elliot, of course! Is he with you? Has he escaped from the dungeon?"

Adrian frowned. "I don't quite understand," he murmured, yet fearing that he did, all too well.

"His mother has locked him up. I know it. I've come to rescue him." Then Elizabeth gasped and her eyes widened with sudden panic. "You can't stop me! I will free him!"

She half rose, until he put his hand on her arm. "I have come to help you," he said.

"Truly?"

"Yes. Absolutely." He had never seen anyone more in need of help than this pathetic creature. "I am simply surprised that you are here. Didn't you go to Manchester, Elizabeth? Your journey was paid for."

"I couldn't go, not while he was locked away. That's why he hasn't come to find me. He can't. I know it."

Elliot's actions had had serious consequences before, but never anything like this.

Adrian desperately wondered what he was going to do. He couldn't leave her here. "He loves me," Elizabeth continued in a lullaby-soft singsong voice. "He'll always love me. And when he's free, we'll find our baby."

Sweet Jesus, she is mad! Adrian had seen the dead baby, had touched its cold, lifeless little fingers. "Oh, Elizabeth," he murmured, reaching out to stroke her hand. "Elizabeth, let me help you!"

"Can we go now? To Elliot?" She stood, suddenly eager.

"Yes, but not right away," Adrian said, grasping her hand. The extreme warmth he felt told him she was burning with fever. He must get her to help.

Not the doctor. Dr. Woadly was too often employed by the duchess to be impartial. He would probably want to send the poor woman to a madhouse, too. Adrian had seen such a place once, when certain acquaintances of his had suggested a tour of Bedlam as a pleasant afternoon's diversion. He had been the worse for drink, or he never would have agreed. And then he had wished he had been drunker, for the horrendous scenes he had witnessed had been with him vividly ever since. He could not subject Elizabeth Howell to such treatment.

He would take her to John Mapleton. "Come with me, Elizabeth."

Her eyes narrowed as he hesitated and she wrenched her hand from his grasp. "I must help him now!" she cried, drawing the other patrons' attention.

"Elizabeth," he said quietly, "Elliot isn't locked up—he's trying to convince my stepmother that she should meet you. I'm sure he told you what she is like." Adrian could just hear Elliot denouncing the duchess, making himself the misunderstood son of a domineering mother, and so in need of the poor girl's pity and love. He had used the tactic before, as Adrian well knew.

Elizabeth nodded slowly.

"My stepmother has only to see you to love you," Adrian persisted. "But wouldn't you like to be better prepared to meet her? I will take you to another inn, one with rooms more suitable to a lady. There you can wash and change your clothes. Do your hair. And then we will go together to Barroughby Hall."

"I want to see him *now!*"

"In your traveling dress, Elizabeth?"

"I didn't bring anything else," she said helplessly.

"Of course. I should have guessed that. You were thinking of rescue, not meeting the duchess. Shall we surprise her with your beauty? I will buy you a new dress today. At once. And then you can wear it to Barroughby Hall. Wouldn't that be nice?"

She hesitated and he pressed on. "Perhaps some ribbons for your hair. Elliot has told the duchess about your hair." It was a monstrous lie, but his words seemed to be having the necessary effect. "And some shoes. Perhaps a bouquet of flowers to carry? You'll look like a bride."

She twisted a loosened strand of her hair in her grimy fingers, a horrible reminder of one of her formerly common and coy gestures. "I would, wouldn't I?"

"Yes! We'll have a bite of lunch first, shall we? I'm famished, and I'm sure you must be hungry after your long journey. To think you came all by yourself, too. Elliot will be so proud of you."

She smiled, a pathetic creature with hope burning in her feverish eyes, and Adrian despised himself for lying to her. But it had to be done. He had to get her to Mapleton.

To his relief, she looked at him expectantly. "Shall we go, Your Grace?"

"Yes, Elizabeth."

Adrian stood majestically, willing the witnesses to

be awed and thus silent. Then he gallantly took her arm and escorted her from the tavern with great dignity, ignoring the surprised stares of the onlookers.

It seemed the very least he could do.

The duchess entered the drawing room and sat upon the sofa with an unusually languid air, failing completely to notice how tense Hester was as she sewed upon something that was intended to be a reticule but which would be too ruined by uneven stitches ever to be used. She had pricked her finger when the door opened, and now, when she realized it was not Adrian, she turned away to see if she was bleeding.

After she had escaped the dining room, she had risked asking Mabel to find out where the duke was. Mercifully, the maid didn't seem to find her request unusual, and soon returned with the dismaying news that the duke had ridden into town to see the surgeon. Jenkins was sure the dancing at the ball had inflamed the duke's injury, and Hester could believe that, even if Adrian had not spoken of it last night. Probably, she thought with both frustration and acceptance, he had not wanted to worry her.

But why had he not returned? She had been sitting in the drawing room, which had the best view of the drive, for what seemed an age, expecting to see him returning at any moment.

Was his injury so affected that Mr. Mapleton wouldn't allow him to ride home? If that were so, why didn't Adrian hire a coach?

"The ball was a great success, was it not?" the

duchess observed with a congratulatory smile. "Such hard work, but so delightful. Everyone was completely charming."

Hester nodded, reached for her handkerchief to wipe the droplet of blood and remained silent.

"Elliot was very much admired," she continued. "Such high spirits! The fatigues of dancing are nothing to him. He is so like myself when I was young."

Hester realized she was very glad she had not known the duchess in her youth.

"Nevertheless, such entertainments should be done sparingly. It upsets the servants. Look how Jenkins locked that door this morning!"

"Yes, Your Grace," Hester murmured, wishing she dared to say something to the duchess about her son's behavior.

But she didn't, because she doubted the duchess would believe her, and this conflict would be better resolved without her interference.

At least, Hester *thought* that was the best thing to do, once more anxious to speak with Adrian about Elliot's ultimatum. What was she going to do if Adrian did not return home tonight?

"Ah, here is the dear boy now!" the duchess declared as Elliot entered the room. "You were much admired last night!" she repeated.

Elliot smiled at his mother, and Hester fought to keep her face expressionless as she sewed, but she felt his gaze as if it were a poisonous cloud descending upon her. "Not everyone admires me, Mama," he said, sitting beside his mother.

"Well, if they don't, they are simpletons!" the duchess cried in his defense.

"I don't believe Lady Hester would concur," he noted.

Before the duchess could speak, Hester raised her eyes and addressed the older woman with a slight smile. "Your son is a very fine-looking man, and dances very well."

"There, Elliot!" the duchess said triumphantly. "Even Lady Hester admires you."

"Oh, Mama," Lord Elliot said with a light laugh, "I fear that remains to be seen."

Hester suddenly rose. She simply could not bear to be in the same room as this man. "If you will pardon me, Your Grace," she said. "I fear I am not used to such late hours. I believe I should rest in my room."

"Very well, Hester," the duchess said, gracious in her good humor.

Elliot stood as Hester gathered her sewing. "Yes, indeed," he agreed with a sly smile she wished she did not see. "We wouldn't want dear Lady Hester to be too tired."

Hester knew then that she had better decide upon a course of action that did not depend upon Adrian's return.

"Why are we going here?" Elizabeth asked in a puzzled whisper as Adrian led her up the front walk to John Mapleton's house.

Patients usually used the door nearest the surgeon's office; however, there was a sign for the surgery there, and Adrian didn't want Elizabeth to see it. Besides, the people in the tavern would already be gossiping about the duke and the unknown woman, so he might as well use the main entrance.

"You said you were going to buy me a new dress," Elizabeth said.

She looked even worse now, despite the meal Adrian had bought her, which she had consumed with much cajoling on his part. He hoped that Mapleton would tell him that rest and food would set her right, yet he could not help feeling that death had already set its mark on Elizabeth. "I will. I thought we should come here first. This is the home of a very dear friend of Elliot's. I'm sure he would be offended if he didn't get to meet you right away. You can wash and freshen up a bit before we go to the shops. Wouldn't you like that?"

"I want to go to Elliot," Elizabeth said, halting abruptly. "I'm so close to him. I can *feel* him. I know he needs me."

"Don't you want to look beautiful for him? You can wash, and fix your hair, and while you're doing that, I'll fetch a carriage to take us to the shops and then out to Barroughby Hall."

She still didn't look quite convinced, but she let him lead her to Mapleton's door.

When Nancy answered Adrian's knock, she gave him a puzzled look. "Mr. Mapleton is with a patient, Your Grace," the young woman said, running a disapproving eye over Elizabeth's gaunt cheeks, muddy skirts and disheveled bonnet. Another person with an interesting tale of the Dark Duke to tell, Adrian thought with some dismay.

Did Hester really understand the nature of gossip? He had to hope she did, or stories of today's events might come as a forceful lesson.

"What are you talking about?" Elizabeth demanded agitatedly. "I am not sick."

"We are here to see John Mapleton as a *friend*, not as a medical man," Adrian lied. "He is a very old acquaintance of Elliot's, and mine."

He faced Nancy again. "Tell Mr. Mapleton the Duke of Barroughby is here. My companion and I will wait in his study."

The maid dipped a curtsy, and hurried off toward the back of the building where Mapleton's office was located.

"Come, Elizabeth," Adrian said, leading her into the mahogany-paneled room. He hoped Mapleton wouldn't be long; he begrudged every minute that kept him from Hester now, and yet he couldn't abandon Elizabeth. Not like Elliot.

After a few moments which seemed considerably longer, Mapleton bustled into the room. "Your Grace, I didn't expect to see you again so soon, I must say," he remarked, acknowledging Adrian with a brief nod while his attention focused on Elizabeth. Apparently Nancy had forewarned him about the duke's companion.

"John Mapleton, may I present Miss Howell, who is a good friend of Elliot's," Adrian said. "I thought you would like to meet her."

"Oh, indeed, I do. How are you, Miss Howell?" The surgeon bowed and took her hand, and an expression of concern crossed his friendly face.

"I am very well, thank you," Elizabeth replied. "But the duke is mistaken. I am not Miss Howell. I am Lady Elliot."

"You are Elliot's *wife?*" Adrian asked, trying not to sound skeptical.

"Oh, yes. We had to keep it a secret, because his mama might not approve. She will change her mind when she meets me, I'm sure."

Mapleton gave Adrian a significant look, to which Adrian could only surreptitiously shrug his shoulders. Elizabeth had said no word of this before, but she had been in labor by the time Adrian had found her and in no condition to give details of her relationship with Elliot. That she was not legally his wife, Adrian didn't doubt, yet it would not be out of character for Elliot to stage a fraudulent marriage, if that was the only way he could seduce a reluctant young woman.

"That's why you're helping me again, isn't it, Your Grace? Because you know she'll like me. Elliot is so anxious to see me again, too. He wrote me that he was."

"He wrote to you?" Adrian inquired gently.

"Oh, yes. I have the letters in my reticule." She smiled brightly. "You may look at them if you wish. Show them to your friend, because I can see he doesn't believe me."

Mapleton flushed guiltily as Adrian picked up Elizabeth's reticule and wondered what new game Elliot was playing at. Inside, he found several pieces of paper.

Some were bills and the rest were promissory notes to Elizabeth Howell for small sums of money, each one signed with Elliot's flowing hand. "You see how much he loves me?"

"Yes, I see," Adrian said wearily.

"Perhaps this young lady would care for some rest and refreshment before she continues to Barroughby Hall?" Mapleton asked. He gave Adrian another meaningful look.

"We are about to get Elizabeth a more suitable dress," Adrian said. "However, a little wine would be delightful."

"To toast the bride and groom," Mapleton said. "I'll have the maid fetch it." He pulled the bell rope to summon Nancy, at the same time subtly motioning Adrian to move closer to him and away from Elizabeth. "Make sure she drinks what I send in," he whispered. "I must see to another patient, but I'll return as soon as I can."

He went out of the room as Elizabeth began to replace all the papers into her reticule with loving and horrible care. "He loves me," she whispered as each and every piece was folded, until Adrian thought he might go mad, too.

Nancy came as Elizabeth finished her task. She carried a tray with a glass of what looked like red wine. "Oh, dear, I've forgotten a glass for you, Your Grace," she said with a suitably concerned demeanor. Then she winked at him so obviously, Adrian was afraid Elizabeth might notice. Fortunately, she was still fussing with her reticule.

"Here you are, Elizabeth," Adrian said, handing the glass to her after she had closed her bag. "You have a drink while the maid fetches mine. To keep your strength up.''

"The toast—''

"We shall all have a toast when Mr. Mapleton returns.''

Apparently persuaded, Elizabeth took the glass and drank, then uttered a horrified cry and dashed the glass to the ground, shattering the bowl. "It doesn't taste right!'' she cried, leaping to her feet and swiping at her lips. "It's a trick!'' she shouted. She picked up the broken base of the wineglass and pointed the jagged edge of the stem at Adrian. "You're not helping me! You're helping *her!*''

Nancy gasped from the doorway and the glass she held in her hand slipped to the floor. "Fetch John!'' Adrian ordered.

Nancy disappeared just as Elizabeth screamed and lunged at Adrian, the broken glass still clutched in her hand like a dagger.

Chapter Twenty-One

Adrian grabbed Elizabeth's arm. The sharp edge of the glass passed by his neck with a fraction of an inch to spare.

"Elizabeth, stop!" he said firmly as she stumbled. He grabbed her arm again, but she twisted fiercely in his grasp. "No! I'll kill you! I'll kill you!" she cried, blinking and swaying as she crouched like a cat ready to pounce.

Then she launched herself at him, and they fell on the floor. She had knocked the wind out of him and he felt a sharp stab of pain in his injured leg, but Adrian was able to get hold of the wrist of the hand holding the broken glass. He squeezed with all his strength until Elizabeth cried out, and the improvised weapon dropped.

Then, with a sigh, she swooned and would have fallen, had he not already held her. He picked her up and carried her to the couch, laying her down gently.

"My God, what happened?" Mapleton asked anxiously as he hurried into the room. "I gave her a sedative."

"It took a while to work, obviously," Adrian replied, quite calm now that it was all over. He bent to retrieve the broken wineglass, then gasped at the sharp pain in his groin. He muttered a curse when he saw the torn fabric of his trousers and the growing stain of blood. "She cut me," he murmured, hard put to believe that he had felt so little. He straightened and staggered, suddenly dizzy.

Mapleton rushed to his aid. "Sit down, my lord. Here, on this chair," the surgeon ordered. "Nancy, fetch my bag, then clean up all this glass." He swiftly and deftly examined the wound through the gaping tear. "Not deep, thank God," he muttered. He took out his handkerchief and pressed it over the wound. "Close to the other wound, too. A few more inches and it could have been much more serious."

"Then I'm glad it wasn't. What are we going to do about her?" He nodded at Elizabeth.

"Hold this here, tight, until Nancy brings my bag," Mapleton said before going to the couch and regarding Elizabeth thoughtfully. "She's not in her right mind, but I cannot say for certain whether it is merely a temporary state, or a more permanent condition."

"That's not all that's the matter with her, is it?"

"Sadly, no. She may be consumptive. Whatever her condition is, it is serious."

"Is there some place she could go to be cared for? I will pay the necessary expenses."

Mapleton looked at Adrian gravely. "Do you know what her relationship to Elliot is? Could they be married?"

"I doubt that very much."

"She said you had helped her before?"

He nodded slowly. "She was supposed to be staying with her brother, in Manchester."

"Away from Elliot?"

"Yes."

Nancy came into the room with the surgeon's bag and a bowl of clean, hot water. She gave Adrian a dismissive glance, then regarded Elizabeth more sympathetically before she left the room.

"Your maid seems singularly immune to my charms," Adrian noted dryly.

"This does look rather odd," Mapleton observed. "Off with your trousers. I'll clean the wound and bandage it. I recommend you stay the night in town."

"That is impossible," Adrian replied. He had spent far too much time in Barroughby today as it was. He had to get home to Hester.

"This wound could bleed quite profusely if you ride. You lost a lot of blood before. It would be risky for you to lose more now."

"What if I ride slowly?"

"You would do better to stay in town. I have a room here—"

"Thank you, John, for your offer, but it is quite impossible. However, I would be very grateful if you would keep Elizabeth here, at least until I can make other arrangements for her."

"I do not keep an asylum, my lord," the surgeon said with a frown. "I'm not equipped to handle such a patient."

"I don't want her to be in an asylum," Adrian replied. "I will write to her family in Manchester. It could be that she's run away, and they don't know where she's gone."

"That sounds like a good idea, but it may take some time to hear from them."

"Is there no place close by she could stay temporarily?" Adrian asked, a note of desperation creeping into his voice.

"Here is what I will do, my lord," Mapleton said slowly. "She looked completely exhausted, and that attack probably took what was left of her strength, so she may sleep for some time. She may stay here until her fever decreases, provided she exhibits no return to hostility."

"I'm grateful to you, John," Adrian replied. "In the meantime, I'll find someone to take her to her family in Manchester in my private coach. There I shall pay for whatever nursing care is judged necessary."

"I know a doctor in Manchester, a good man whose opinion you can trust, both for diagnosis and the cost of her care," Mapleton offered. "I shall write his address out for you."

"Good. Now all that remains is to find someone to travel with her."

"I could let Nancy and her husband go with her, if they're willing. She's an excellent nurse, and he would be very helpful to carry Miss Howell in and out of the carriage." The surgeon thought a moment. "She could be sedated for most of the way, I should think."

"Then I shall leave Elizabeth in your capable

care." Adrian reached out to take Mapleton's hand. "I owe you a debt of gratitude."

"Think nothing of it, my lord. Now that we've taken care of Miss Howell, off with your trousers."

Adrian complied, trying to keep the bloody handkerchief in place as much as possible.

"There is one way you could repay me," Mapleton said, dipping the cloth into the bowl of water as he prepared to wash the wound.

"Whatever you like," Adrian said, removing the handkerchief and sucking in his breath as Mapleton wiped away the blood with the damp cloth.

The surgeon hesitated and gave Adrian a stern look. "Don't let Elliot get away with this. And don't look at me like that. You and I both know that he's responsible for this poor girl's state." Mapleton put the soiled cloth into the water and picked up a clean white bandage. He began to wrap it around Adrian's leg.

"I was thinking it might be better for Elliot to be completely unencumbered when I cut him loose."

Mapleton frowned. "I'm not completely in favor of that, my lord, but you know him better than I."

"Then let me take care of Elizabeth while I force Elliot to fend for himself. She's better off having nothing whatever to do with him, anyway."

"As you wish," Mapleton agreed as he knotted the bandage.

"I see I shall have two scars," Adrian noted. "It's a pity she didn't cut the other leg. Then I would have a matched set."

"This has been a truly astonishing day," Mapleton

remarked. "I will loan you a pair of trousers. No need to cause idle speculation among the townsfolk."

Adrian grinned ruefully, thinking he would be a fine spectacle in the surgeon's trousers. He hoped John would also provide a belt. "There's probably a lot of idle gossip going on already. Now, if you are finished, I will accept the loan of trousers and leave you to your patients."

"I'm finished. But let me warn you again, ride slowly. I have no wish to be summoned to Barroughby Hall in the middle of the night, nor do I wish *my* trousers stained. Unlike some people, I have only a few pairs."

"I'll go at a most dignified pace," Adrian replied, although he would have preferred a breakneck gallop and damn the consequences. A slow ride meant he wouldn't get home until nearly midnight. "Thank you again for helping with Elizabeth."

"I hope everything will work out for the best," Mapleton said sincerely.

"Since I am going to marry Hester, I think it will."

Hester laid her hand on the knob of Elliot's bed-chamber door.

She would have preferred to confront Elliot with Adrian by her side, but Adrian had not yet returned, although it was nearly midnight. Therefore, she had no recourse but to confront Elliot alone, and to make an ultimatum of her own, one that would ensure that Elliot would not trouble them again.

The only weapon Elliot had was a threat of scandal, which he had used to manipulate Adrian for years.

The duke was a proud man bearing the weight of a promise made to a dying father.

She had no such baggage, and if Elliot thought he could use a taint of scandal to compel her to dishonor herself when she was more than willing to accept the duke's alleged history as the price for marrying him, he was about to discover the magnitude of his mistake.

With a determined expression, she opened the door and slipped inside. A single candle on a table near the window illuminated the vast, luxurious room. She noticed few of the details, for all her attention focused on the man standing at the window, who slowly turned and looked at her with a strange and unforeseen expression.

She had expected Elliot to look triumphant, at least at first. Instead, he looked surprised and even disappointed. Because she had come?

But that lasted only for the briefest of moments. Then he smiled and made a mocking bow. "Why, I am honored, Lady Hester," he said.

"I am not," she replied softly, coming farther inside the room and closing the door.

"Come, now! You should be flattered. Surely it isn't every day a man of my attributes wants you."

"I do not take it as a compliment that a man of your 'attributes,' as you call them, wants me now."

Elliot's eyes narrowed. "You don't have to stay if I repel you so."

"If I don't, you say you will ruin your brother."

Elliot's only response was a slow nod as he came closer.

Hester crossed her arms as she regarded him steadily. "Tell me, my lord, do you honestly believe that because I am homely, I am stupid and friendless, too?"

"It is not your intelligence or your society that I seek."

"Nor I, yours. However, I thought this would be the best, most private opportunity I might have to speak with you, to give *you* an ultimatum, my lord."

Elliot halted and stared at her. "You?" he scoffed. "You will give *me* an ultimatum?"

"Indeed."

"This should prove interesting."

Hester raised her chin defiantly. "You are not the only one who can ruin a reputation with a few well-chosen rumors, my lord. I, too, have friends—influential people who move in the highest circles." Elliot looked about to protest, but she held up her hand to silence him. "For instance, the wife of Lord Paris Mulholland is a very dear friend of mine. Perhaps you know them?"

She watched as Elliot's expression became a scowl, for Lord Paris Mulholland was extremely well-known in London. Then Elliot smiled sarcastically. "He *was* quite popular, until he married that little nobody."

"Perhaps he will not have the influence of the past, but there are many people who will listen to what he has to say. I am also fairly well acquainted with the family of the Chancellor of the Exchequer, the Radcliffe-Bellings of the East India Company, and one of my mother's oldest friends is a lady-in-waiting to the queen. Oh, and of course, my sister, Helena, has several friends who dearly love to talk. So, you see, Lord Elliot, you are not the only one with the power of gossip at your command. I have simply never chosen to exert my influence.'' Hester's expression grew stern and firm. ''But I shall, if I must, and I fear I have not the patience of your brother. I shall begin writing letters the moment I leave here. If necessary.''

''You stupid—''

''I am *not* stupid.''

''*I* have friends, and so does my mother, if it is a battle of words you want.''

''What type of friends do you possess, my lord? Ones whose opinions are valued? I think not. As for your mother, she has been quite on the fringe of society for the past ten years, as you should realize. Any influence she might have wielded has been diminishing steadily.

''And how is she known?'' Hester pressed. ''As a doting mother who spoils her son. I have heard her described so more than once, by my mother and others.'' Hester drew herself up and smiled. ''How am *I* known? As a sweet, retiring, *honest* young woman. As your mother has been so kind to note, I am homely, my lord, so no one would believe I could have any personal motive for discrediting you.''

''They will if I say you came into my room at night with the intention of—''

''What?'' Hester demanded scornfully. ''Seducing Lord Elliot Fitzwalter? Timid, shy, reserved Hester Pimblett intending to seduce the bold and dashing Lord Elliot Fitzwalter? The idea will be considered

completely ridiculous. Or will you say that *you* seduced *me?* That would hardly be a credit to you."

"You must care for Adrian a great deal," Elliot
replied sarcastically, "if you are willing to put your
word against mine."

"I love him."

He reached out, grabbed her by the arms and said,
"Maybe I can't ruin Adrian, but I can ruin *you.*"

Hester did not move. "No, you will not."

"Oh, yes, I will. I will take your honor. I will make
you unfit to be any man's wife."

"What would that get you?" she asked quietly.

"Satisfaction, although no other soul need ever
know. You will know, and I will know, and with your
sweet honesty, you will not wish to go to any husband
when you are no longer a virgin." He yanked her
against him. "I will destroy Adrian's life as he has
ruined mine!"

"You won't," she said firmly. "You are not that
evil."

His grip loosened slightly and a look of surprise
and sudden understanding flickered across his face,
followed again by malice. "I can see why Adrian fell
in love with you," he growled. "So much forgiveness, so much faith—it is a heady mix!" Then his
hands tightened upon her again, his strong fingers
bruising her flesh. "But I cannot have your love, so
I will take what I can, if my only satisfaction can be
to pay Adrian back for some of the pain he has caused
me."

"After all he's done for you—"

"After all the guilt he made me feel," Elliot demanded fiercely, "when I did no more than my friends? Tell me, Hester, do you know what it's like to have a martyr for a brother? Waiting for him to rush in to save you, whether you wanted him to or not? Seeing that condescending look on his face? Wanting to wipe it out forever, to do something so awful that for once, he would lose that damn self-control and react like a man and not a saint? Well, maybe this time I will finally succeed."

Chapter Twenty-Two

"*Let her go, or by God, I'll kill you!*"

Adrian's words rang out in the night. Elliot and Hester both turned toward the door, to see Adrian standing there, his fists clenched and on his face an expression of absolute fury.

Elliot pushed Hester away so hard she fell on the floor. "Did you hear me, Adrian, you self-righteous prig?" he demanded, glaring at his half brother. "I am sick to death of your interference in my life!"

Adrian ignored Elliot and hurried to help Hester to her feet. "Are you all right?" he asked.

"Yes," she whispered, taking hold of his hand and never wanting to let go.

"Oh, yes, she's fine. She's well and happy. She loves you. You two can marry and raise a brood of sanctimonious brats!"

"Shut up, Elliot. You'll wake the house."

"What do I care? Let them come! Then you can poison them against me, as you did *her*."

"Poisoned me against you?" Hester asked incredulously. "You did that yourself."

"I was going to ask you to be my wife."

"I would have refused, absolutely and unequivocally, whether I loved your brother or not. Lord Elliot, I could never care for you."

For one very short moment, Elliot resembled his brother as pain flashed in his eyes. Yet it was but a short moment, the fleeting emotion replaced by one of malignant hatred.

"For your sake, I'm glad you didn't hurt her," Adrian said very slowly and very deliberately.

"What would you have done if I had?" his half brother said scornfully. "Told me to go stand in the corner? Treated me like a child, as you always do?"

"As you deserve!" Adrian said sternly.

"You should be grateful that he cared enough to take your sins for his own," Hester said, rubbing her arms where Elliot had grabbed her.

"Grateful?" Elliot cried. "Are *you* grateful for the offer I made you?"

Hester turned to Adrian, regarding him with love, and yet aware that he was not blameless, either. "He resents you for being too protective."

"Did you never stop to think that I might not appreciate your watching me like a nanny all the time?" Elliot charged.

"If you had acted like a man, I would have treated you like one."

"Listen to him!" he jeered. "This man who has spent many pleasant hours in whorehouses, or taverns, or gambling dens. Who nearly killed his best friend in a drunken brawl. Where were you all day today, Saint Adrian? Sally Newcombe's? Such a paragon!''

"I went to see Mr. Mapleton and met a...mutual acquaintance. Elliot, I have never claimed to be perfect. I know full well my own sins.''

"Well, to think I should live to hear you say so,'' Elliot replied sarcastically.

"Nevertheless, he has taken the blame for many of yours,'' Hester pointed out.

"Did I ever once *ask* him to?'' Elliot demanded. "Did I?''

"No. But I promised Father—''

"Did *I* ask you to?''

"Is that what you would have preferred, to suffer for your many misdeeds?'' Adrian demanded coldly. "You dare to criticize me for protecting you?''

"Yes, I do, if what you have done could always be called protection.''

"What are you talking about?'' Adrian asked scornfully.

"That little whore, Daphne—you think I threatened her for no good reason, don't you? Just because I'm a vicious brute.

"Well, I'm *not*, and she was not so innocent. She was going through my pockets, and when I saw her, she started to shout and cry and accuse me of attacking her.

"Did you ever think to ask *me* what had happened? No. You only listened to those whores. Would you even have believed me if you had? No! You would have taken the word of a *whore* over mine!''

Adrian looked stunned. "But you always—" he began in a whisper.

"You have never given me a chance to explain!" Elliot continued forcefully. "I assure you, Adrian, I *can* change if I want to, and if you'll let me."

As the two men, who were alike in some ways and so very different in others, regarded each other, Hester softly asked, "Do you truly want to, Elliot?"

"Of course I want to," Elliot said. "But I cannot do it alone. If I had a wife to help me..."

"Not Hester," Adrian said sternly.

"Please, Hester," Elliot pleaded. "I...I've behaved badly, I know, especially today. It's just that I'm so unused to doing things properly, in the right way. I saw you come out of Adrian's room, and I have been mad with jealousy ever since. You must believe me." He went down on his knees and clasped his hands together in a gesture of supplication. "I want you to be my wife, and help me to reform!"

Hester could scarcely believe what was happening as she looked from the pleading Lord Elliot to the duke, who had lowered his head and was gazing thoughtfully at the floor. When she was a young girl she had often imagined having two suitors asking for her hand. It had been a delightful and quite impossible fantasy, she had thought.

This was no delightful fantasy. This was terrible.

Because she knew that she might hold the key to the redemption of one and the happiness of the other. She, plain Hester Pimblett!

"Adrian, you know I'm right," Elliot pleaded.

"I'll just ask this one thing and I'll never trouble you again. Let me have her."

The duke raised his head. "No. You can have money and horses, but I will not let you have the woman I love. I could never let her go. I need her too much. I love her too deeply. This is one sacrifice I cannot make, not to save your life, or my family's honor, or even to fulfill my promise to our father."

As Elliot got to his feet, Hester stared at them both, incredulous. "Have you forgotten that it is for me to decide whom I marry, if anyone at all?" she demanded. "You both are the most selfish men it has ever been my misfortune to meet. Maybe I should not marry at all!"

Adrian stared at her, aghast. Elliot reddened, and genuine disappointment appeared on his face.

Then Adrian sighed and looked away. "I think you may be right, Hester," he admitted quietly. "Perhaps you would be better off without me, no matter how much I want you. Or need you. Or love you..." His voice trailed away into a hopeless sigh.

"Oh, Adrian!" Hester cried, running around him and taking his shoulders in her hands, forcing him to look at her. "I would be a fool to leave you. You may be noble enough to sacrifice yourself for love, but I am not. I love you, and I need you as much as you need me!"

Hope kindled in his dark eyes and a self-deprecating smile played about his lips. "You're crying," he whispered.

"It's not from soot, either," she replied, sniffling

and smiling at the same time as she embraced him. "I'm crying because I'm so happy."

"Well, isn't this a charming little love scene," Elliot said mockingly, rage burning in his hard blue eyes. "Down curtain, applause, end of show."

As Hester and Adrian moved apart, the duchess marched into the room, her robe askew and her hair in curlpapers. "What is going on here? Have you all gone mad? Hester, what are you doing in my son's bedroom? Explain yourself."

"Lord Elliot invited me here," Hester said staunchly, unmoved by the duchess's condemning eye.

The duchess looked at her son, who smiled winningly, all trace of anger apparently dissipated like mist on a sunny day. "I didn't think she'd really come, Mama," he said, spreading his hands in a gesture of wonderment. "I was simply teasing her. Apparently she took me seriously. The poor girl is under the impression that I am in love with her. I must say she was extremely eager to find out just how I might express this love. I confess I was as shocked as you are to find her here."

Hester stepped forward, prepared to upbraid him to his face, but Adrian held her back. "You had better be careful what you imply, Elliot," he said quite calmly.

"This is ridiculous," the duchess answered with her usual charm. "I've never heard anything so silly in my life. Hester Pimblett and you?"

"Perhaps you would prefer it if I were to accept your son's proposal?" Hester asked.

The duchess snorted as she turned to Elliot. "This girl is mad."

"No, she isn't," Adrian said, "but I know another who may very well be. Elliot knows her better than I, however. You recall I mentioned meeting a mutual acquaintance in Barroughby today? Her name is Elizabeth Howell."

"*I* have never heard of her," the duchess declared with outraged majesty.

"I never said you did," Adrian responded.

Elliot's gaze darted from Adrian to his mother as if he was a cornered rat. "I don't know who you're talking about!"

"Allow me to refresh your memory. You saw me dance with her at the Pump Room in Bath, when she was just out. A pretty, pale young woman you then deemed worthy of pursuit, as you have pursued and seduced so many others. What was it that attracted you, Elliot? Her delicate features, or the fact that I danced with her?"

"*You're* the one who's gone mad," Elliot declared.

"No." Adrian shook his head. "You seduced her, and when you found out she was with child, you abandoned her. She bore your child a few weeks ago."

"So this woman says her child is mine. Anyone could make such claims."

"I found her in the filthy back room of a work-house, half-starved and feverish."

"All the more reason to believe that she was mad when you found her. I won't be held responsible for the claims of an insane woman."

Adrian regarded his half brother with a mixture of condemnation and pity. "Aren't you curious about your child, Elliot?"

For a brief moment a keen and questioning look flashed across Elliot's face, but then it was gone. He looked at his mother and frowned. "I told you, she's lying."

"He looked very like you, Elliot."

"Looked?" the duchess demanded warily.

"He is dead."

"Elliot!" the duchess cried sharply. "Can it be true, what Adrian is saying?"

"You know he's simply trying to discredit me," Elliot snapped. "He's never liked me. He's always been jealous of me."

His mother nodded, and turned to Adrian with cold loathing. "I will not listen to your falsehoods."

"Don't you want to know how I am aware of Elizabeth's current condition, or do you intend to blot out all memory of the poor creature you abandoned?" Adrian demanded, ignoring the duchess.

Elliot straightened. "I don't have to listen to these wild tales."

"You'll both listen to what I have to say tonight," Adrian said warmly, "or you'll never get another penny!"

"This is blackmail," Elliot replied.

"Something with which I take it you are not totally unfamiliar," Adrian noted, glancing at Hester. "Elizabeth Howell is in the village right now. She came here believing that your mother was holding you prisoner. The poor woman wants to set you free."

"Come, Mama, let us leave this place at once!"

"If you go now, not a farthing more!" Adrian warned.

"Elliot, he can do it," the duchess protested. "He can cut us off without a cent!"

"Mama, either leave this house with me, or I shall go without you and never see you again!"

The duchess held out her hands submissively, suddenly nothing more than a pathetic old woman. "Elliot, don't ask me to do such a thing. I won't believe him, but I cannot be penniless!"

"You will choose his money over me?"

"Elliot!"

"Very well," Elliot growled, his glare traveling over all of them. "I don't need you. I don't need—" he jabbed his finger at Hester "—*her*. And I don't need—" he jabbed his finger at Adrian "—*you* or your money! I don't need your help or your condemnation or your bloody interference. I am leaving this house, and I hope to God I never set eyes on any of you again!" He ran from the room, slamming the door behind him.

"Elliot!" the duchess cried, taking a step after him, then sinking to her knees. "Adrian, go after him," she begged pitiably. "Please!"

Adrian shook his head, his mouth firm, his hands bunched into fists, although his eyes were full of pity. "Not this time, Your Grace. Not this time."

Hester went to the sobbing woman. Kneeling beside her, she cradled her gently in her arms and looked beseechingly at Adrian. "He is still your brother," she said softly.

Adrian sighed wearily. "Because you ask it of me, Hester, I will go."

It was only when he was limping from the room that Hester realized there was something odd about his trousers, and blood was on the floor.

Hester had barely managed to assist the weeping duchess to a chair when she heard feet pounding on the stairs.

"Elliot!" the duchess cried hopefully.

Hester didn't know what to think as the door to the bedroom burst open. She half rose at the sight of a frantic Jenkins in his nightshirt and cap, standing on the threshold. "It's the duke, Lady Hester. He went to mount his horse and fell down in a dead faint!"

Chapter Twenty-Three

"Where is he now?" Hester demanded, gently trying to extricate herself from the duchess's clutching fingers.

"We laid him on the sofa in the study," Jenkins replied anxiously. "I've sent one of the footmen for Mr. Mapleton."

"Good," Hester replied, finally succeeding in loosening the duchess's hold. "Fetch Maria to tend to the duchess. I will go to the study."

Jenkins nodded and disappeared.

"Hester, don't leave me!" the duchess pleaded as Hester rushed to the door.

Hester turned to the woman with sincere pity and said softly, "I must see to the duke. I'll send one of the footmen to the stable to see if your son is still there. If not, the groom can ride to the village. Surely Elliot can't have gotten far."

"Yes, yes, you're right," the duchess said hopefully. "And as for all this business of an illegitimate child, it *can't* be true."

"If the duke says it is so, I think you would be

wise to believe him. There are other things, Your Grace, other...activities...of your son's that the duke has long kept from you, for the sake of a promise made to his late father.''

''My son has no secrets from me,'' the duchess feebly protested, but Hester could see the doubt in her eyes. ''He is a spirited, bold fellow, perhaps easily led astray by unworthy friends. Yes,'' she said, sitting straighter, her indomitable will and blind faith in her son reasserting itself. ''He may have made some mistakes. That is to be expected of a young man of his humor. I daresay the young women...'' The duchess faltered.

''Elizabeth Howell is surely deserving of our help and pity,'' Hester said softly, realizing that the duchess, try as she might, was not able to completely ignore this last evil deed of her beloved son.

Dressed in their nightclothes and looking completely befuddled, both Mabel and Maria hurried into the room, halting in puzzlement. ''Jenkins said one of us was to come here at once,'' Mabel announced, ''but he wasn't sure which.''

''Maria, take Her Grace to her room and stay with her,'' Hester ordered. ''I am going to the study.''

Hester found an anxious Jenkins waiting at the foot of the stairs. ''He's come to, my lady,'' the butler said immediately. ''He says it's his leg. It seems he hurt it again in town. He's been bleeding. Nothing serious, he says.''

Hester sighed with relief as they hurried along the

corridor as fast as Jenkins could move. "How long before the surgeon arrives?"

"Knives? Oh, he wasn't stabbed with knives, my lady. Glass, he said."

"Glass!" Hester whispered as she broke into a most undignified run. "Fetch water and bandages!" she called back to the butler.

She entered the study to see a very pale Adrian lying with his leg elevated and his eyes closed. "My lord!"

"Was that addressed to me, or the deity?" the duke asked as he opened his eyes and smiled. Hester knelt beside him on the sofa and took hold of his hand. "I believe I understand why young women swoon so much," Adrian continued wryly. "The attention is truly gratifying."

"Are you much hurt?"

"It's merely my leg again."

Hester stared at the red stain on his trousers. "Jenkins said you were stabbed!"

"The unfortunate Elizabeth. She thought I was in league against her, poor woman."

"Is your wound painful?"

"Not so much as my heart when I had no hope of you."

She smiled back at him, then realized the stain was growing larger. "I must fetch some bandages—" She went to stand, but he held on to her hand and tugged her back.

"If I bleed to death for it, I will not let you go until you promise to marry me as soon as possible."

She gave him an indulgent and happy smile. "Of

course—but I won't if you don't release my hand immediately!''

He dropped it at once and smiled broadly. "Very well. I release it for now, until I can claim it officially in the village church.''

She returned his smile and turned, nearly colliding with Mabel, who was carrying a basin of water with several white cloths over her arm. "Is he dying?" she whispered loudly while she stared at the duke with wide, astonished eyes.

"He's opened his wound, I think. I believe we'll need more water.'' She looked at Adrian and frowned worriedly. His eyes were closed again. Perhaps he was more seriously wounded than he was letting on.

"Oh, aye, my lady," the maid said, backing toward the door.

Adrian suddenly moaned loudly, which sent Mabel scurrying from the room like a terrified mouse and made Hester hurry to the sofa. "My lord!''

Adrian opened one eye and gave her a roguish grin. "Is she gone?"

"Yes." Hester was tempted to scold him for scaring them, except that she happily realized if he was in a mood for humor, he must not be terribly hurt. "We've sent for Mr. Mapleton.''

"He's not going to make me feel any better." He reached out and pulled her toward him. "This will.''

He kissed her with breathtaking passion, all the more astonishing because he had looked so pale and weak moments before.

He reluctantly released her and caressed her cheek. "That is all the physic I need.''

"As much as I appreciate your evaluation, my lord, I will be more relieved when I hear Mr. Mapleton tell me not to be worried."

"This will never do," Adrian said with a frown.

"He's a surgeon," Hester began to protest, until Adrian put his finger on her lips.

"You simply must stop referring to me by these exalted titles. 'Your Grace.' 'My lord.' I want to be your love."

"My love," she whispered, pressing another kiss to his warm, inviting lips.

"Let's tell Jenkins to send John home," Adrian muttered even as they continued kissing. "He'll just tell me he told me so, and that I should rest."

Hester moved back. "He knows about your wound?"

"Happened at his house."

"Then he knows about Elliot and Miss Howell?"

"He knows all about Elliot. Has for some time, and it seems he's in complete agreement with you. He says I should have left Elliot on his own years ago." Adrian grinned ruefully. "I went to see him this morning. Quite frankly, despite your most charming and impassioned words, I couldn't believe you would wish to marry a reprobate like myself. John convinced me that you knew what you were doing."

"Then I will tell him how grateful I am, although I must say, it is a little disconcerting to think you took his word over mine."

Adrian frowned. "That does sound rather bad, doesn't it? I knew that I was hopelessly in love with you and I wanted very much to believe that you meant what you said. I just had to make certain.''

"Get another opinion, as if you had a disease?"

"That's one way to put it, I suppose."

Hester embraced him lightly. "I shall forgive you, provided you don't doubt me ever again."

"I didn't when I got home and saw your bedroom door open. I thought something was amiss, and heard your voice in Elliot's room."

Hester's eyes widened. "What exactly *did* you think?"

"That Elliot was up to no good."

"I'm glad you trusted me."

"*You* trusted *me*. How could I do less?"

She gave him a warm smile, then grew serious again. "How did you meet Miss Howell?"

"I saw her arrive in Barroughby. Fearing some trouble, I went to speak with her."

"Poor woman! And to lose her child..."

"I've told Mapleton to do all he can for her. I will assume all the costs. It seems the least I can do."

Hester caressed his pale cheek. "What of Elliot, supposing we can find him?"

"I don't know," Adrian answered truthfully, hugging her to him. "I honestly don't know."

Jenkins hobbled into the room. "My lady!" he wheezed, seeing Hester on the sofa with the duke's arms around her.

"It's perfectly all right, Jenkins," the duke said calmly. "Lady Hester and I are engaged to be married."

"I beg your pardon, Your Grace?"

Adrian raised his voice. "Lady Hester and I are going to be married."

Hester thought Jenkins still had not heard properly, for his expression barely altered. Then he said with a courteous bow, "My felicitations, Your Grace. Mapleton has arrived."

"I knew something like this would happen if you didn't follow my advice," the surgeon chastised as he bustled into the room. He gave Hester a broad smile as she rose to greet him. "Best wishes on the forthcoming nuptials, my lady."

"Thank you," she said, blushing like a bride.

"As much as I would enjoy hearing you two lovebirds sing each other's praises," Mr. Mapleton continued, "I see that I have work to do." The surgeon set his bag on the table and opened it up, glancing at the duke's bloody trousers. "You'll have to remove those yet again, my lord, so I must ask Lady Hester to take her leave."

Adrian nodded, giving Hester's hand a farewell kiss. "I'm sorry about your trousers, John. Have your tailor send me a bill."

"Oh, I will. Now, off with them, my lord."

"Although this is getting terribly monotonous, I am only too happy to comply."

The surgeon sucked in his breath when he saw the opened wound. "This will never do, my lord. You cannot keep opening old injuries and bleeding. You've been very lucky escaping infection so far, but you can't trust to luck forever, you know."

Adrian winced as Mr. Mapleton started to clean the gash again. "I know. I'll do as you advise. After all,

I shall have a very charming young lady to keep me company in my convalescence.''

Mr. Mapleton chuckled. ''If I had known that was what it took, I would have hired a nurse before.''

''Surely not, given my reputation.''

''Which I never gave much credence to.''

''You should be pleased to know, John, that Elliot's gone from this house, quite possibly for good.''

Mr. Mapleton glanced up at his patient's serious face. ''Really? When?''

''Tonight.''

''Oh. I heard a horse galloping over the fields and thought I caught a glimpse of a rider. It might have been Elliot.'' Mr. Mapleton returned to his task. ''About time you cut that young fool loose. He was like infected tissue, poisoning your life as well as his own.''

''Amputations are never easy, John. You, of all people, should know that.''

''Yes, my lord.'' Mr. Mapleton rose. He went to his bag and seemed to be looking for a specific instrument, which he apparently located. ''Have you got any brandy about?''

Adrian pointed to his cabinet. ''Forgive me for not offering you a drink sooner.''

''It's not for me. It's for you.'' Mapleton went to the cabinet and poured a large tumbler of brandy, which Adrian eyed suspiciously. ''First we'll get you up to your bedroom. Then I'm going to have to cauterize the wound.''

Much later that night and after enduring an agony of waiting outside Adrian's bedchamber, Hester was assured by the surgeon that the duke would do very well since the wound was cauterized. Now, she rose from the straight-backed chair in the hallway where she had kept her vigil. She did not go her to own bedroom, however, although she had never felt more exhausted in her life.

She crept softly to Adrian's bedroom door as she had that first night, which seemed so long ago, and very gently opened it, determined to see for herself how he rested. He looked much as he had that other night, lying in his bed.

This time, however, she looked at the slumbering duke not with curiosity and a dreadful fascination, but with the tender eyes of a lover. She allowed herself the luxury of gazing at him as he slept, knowing that one day she would be sharing this bed, too.

Not content to be even this far from him, she ventured closer, a shudder of dismay at the lingering odor of burnt flesh running through her.

Suddenly Adrian's hand shot out from beneath the covers and he grabbed her wrist. She gasped as he tugged her down to him. "I'm not going to let you go without a kiss this time," he said, smiling.

"Mr. Mapleton says you should rest."

"My lips aren't sore. Just my confounded leg." He kissed her tenderly.

She pulled back. "If somebody finds me here—"

He covered his eyes with his hand in mock shame. "Oh, woe is me! A scandal! The Dark Duke has sinned again!" He took his hand down and pouted like a recalcitrant boy. "You said you didn't mind my reputation."

"I don't, but I see no need to promote it," she said, pouting nearly as well, yet her merry eyes betrayed her true state of mind. "People will say you're marrying me because you *have* to."

"I don't care why people say you're marrying me, as long as you do it, and soon."

"Well, my lord—"

"*Adrian.*"

"Well, Adrian, I have *our* reputation to consider, and that of our..." She hesitated, flushing with both the heat of embarrassment as well as desire.

"Children?" Adrian ventured in a low, seductive tone. "I want to have lots of children. *Your* children."

"*Our* children," she whispered.

"Therefore," he continued, his voice even lower and huskier, "I shall endeavor to lead an exemplary life. Which should not be too difficult, considering I shall never be tempted to leave my house."

They kissed again, this time with such unbridled passion that Hester felt absolutely wanton, a sensation she very much enjoyed, until she accidentally pressed on Adrian's sore leg, causing him to start so suddenly, their teeth bumped.

"I'm sorry!" Hester cried softly, just as she realized that they were not yet married and if she was not more careful she would be behaving in a most unseemly manner. "Adrian," she whispered, "what about Elliot? Do you think he'll ever reform?"

Adrian shrugged his shoulders. "I don't know."

"If he comes home, what will you do?"

"Hester, don't say anything to the duchess, but I don't believe he will ever come back here again. I've seen him angry before, but nothing like today. He meant what he said."

"What do you suppose will happen to him?"

Adrian smiled ruefully. "Do you know, I think he'll manage. I believe you were right, and I was wrong. I shouldn't have been so protective of him. And I think he can change. He showed himself not completely beyond hope by wanting to marry you, my own redeeming angel."

"You will be making me vain," Hester chided. "You have always been good and honorable. I had nothing to do with that."

"You gave me hope, when I had none." He stroked her cheek. "Perhaps Elliot will find a woman to give him hope, too."

"I wish that with all my heart, Adrian, for your sake as much as his."

"For my father's, too," he whispered, looking at her lovingly.

"You're going to have me weeping in a moment," she warned, reluctantly getting to her feet and seeing that she was not the only one whose emotions threatened to reveal themselves in tears. "You should rest."

"This damn leg!" He clasped both of her hands in his. "I'll let you go only if you promise to wed me as soon as possible."

"As soon as your leg heals."

"It's much better already."

"Liar," she teased. "I shall have to write my parents in Europe. And my sisters."

A very real frown appeared on Adrian's face. "I suppose I'll have to ask your father for his permission to marry you. I shudder to think what he'll make of the notion of his cherished daughter marrying a rascal like me."

This time it was Hester's turn to smile roguishly. "I think if you invite them to stay with us, giving them the opportunity to select either your estate or your London town house, whichever they prefer..."

"Thereby demonstrating my vast wealth?"

Hester nodded. "I confess my father is rather keen on money," she said ruefully. "I think he would excuse your past...excesses...under such circumstances, and provided I reveal your undying devotion to me."

"You have it, Hester, forever," Adrian said with utter sincerity and heartfelt joy.

Hester took a step back from the bed before she was tempted to forget everything she had ever learned about ladylike behavior and join him there. "I will write to them tonight."

Shortly after the duchess moved into the Dower House of her own volition, the Pimblett family descended on Barroughby Hall in a flutter of happy pride, although none was so happy or so proud as Hester, who became, for the first time in her life, the center of her parents' attention. Lady Pimblett declared that she knew Hester would make a marvelous match; her sisters, after an understandable pang of jealousy when they saw the opulence of Barroughby

Hall, wished her as happy as they were. The rather opinionated Lord Pimblett was completely speechless with delight, and he stayed that way for several days, an effect that was considered something of a blessing by his wife and daughters.

When Clara Mulholland, the wife of Lord Paris Mulholland, received a letter from Hester telling her of her engagement, Clara hurried to tell her husband as fast as her advanced pregnancy would permit.

Paris Mulholland commented that marriage seemed to be catching these days and he hoped Hester Pimblett wouldn't regret the infection. "As you know, my darling, love has felled stronger constitutions than hers," he declared with a charming wink.

Clara retorted that Hester Pimblett would never marry foolishly. The scandalous tales told about the Duke of Barroughby must be false, if Hester thought Adrian Fitzwalter worthy of her hand.

And all their friends agreed.

* * * * *

Author Note

Poor Elliot! So bitter, so angry, so misunderstood.

Actually, in the first version of *The Dark Duke*, Elliot died. You see, he was a completely irredeemable cad.

To be absolutely honest, he was also a completely one-dimensional character.

Since I don't enjoy writing about one-dimensional characters, even when they're villains, I began to find ways to make Elliot more complicated.

Then, when I gave him a reason for doing the things he did, he began to change. Soon I knew I wouldn't be satisfied until he got a second chance.

What happens to Elliot after he storms out of Barroughby Hall? Does he ever see his family again? Does he find love? What kind of woman could care for a man like him?

Or does he try to keep his sordid past a secret...

Look for *The Rogue's Return* in the summer of 1997.

And the Winner Is...
You!

...when you pick up these great titles
from our new promotion at your
favorite retail outlet this June!

Diana Palmer
The Case of the Mesmerizing Boss

Betty Neels
The Convenient Wife

Annette Broadrick
Irresistible

Emma Darcy
A Wedding to Remember

Rachel Lee
Lost Warriors

Marie Ferrarella
Father Goose

Look us up on-line at: http://www.romance.net

ATWI397-R

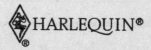

HE SAID

♥

SHE SAID

Explore the mystery of male/female communication in this extraordinary new book from two of your favorite Harlequin authors.

Jasmine Cresswell and Margaret St. George bring you the exciting story of two romantic adversaries—each from their own point of view!

DEV'S STORY. CATHY'S STORY.
As he sees it. As she sees it.
Both sides of the story!

The heat is definitely on, and these two can't stay out of the kitchen!

Don't miss **HE SAID, SHE SAID.**
Available in July wherever Harlequin books are sold.

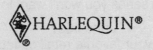

HARLEQUIN®

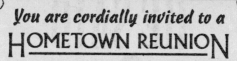
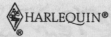

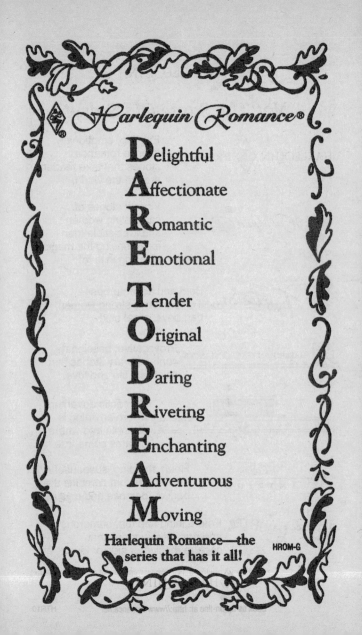

Harlequin Romance®

Delightful

Affectionate

Romantic

Emotional

Tender

Original

Daring

Riveting

Enchanting

Adventurous

Moving

Harlequin Romance—the
series that has it all!

HROM-G

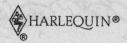
HARLEQUIN®

Not The Same Old Story!

HARLEQUIN  PRESENTS® Exciting, emotionally intense romance stories that take readers around the world.

 *Harlequin Romance®* Vibrant stories of captivating women and irresistible men experiencing the magic of falling in love!

HARLEQUIN®  *Temptation* Bold and adventurous—Temptation is strong women, bad boys, great sex!

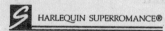 HARLEQUIN SUPERROMANCE® Provocative, passionate, contemporary stories that celebrate life and love.

 AMERICAN ♦ ROMANCE® Romantic adventure where anything is possible and where dreams come true.

HARLEQUIN®  INTRIGUE® Heart-stopping, suspenseful adventures that combine the best of romance and mystery.

LOVE & LAUGHTER™ Entertaining and fun, humorous and romantic—stories that capture the lighter side of love.